# GLIMMER IN THE DARKNESS

## COVENTRY SAGA BOOK 1

### ROBIN PATCHEN

JDO PUBLISHING

*For Jennifer Courtney.*
*Your stories make me laugh.*
*Your insights make me think.*
*Your phone calls keep me sane.*
*Your friendship means the world to me.*

# ACKNOWLEDGMENTS

This book originally appeared in the Dangerous Deceptions boxset, and I'm so thankful for the other authors in that set for all the work they put in to make the book a success.

Thank you to Misty Beller, Christy Johnson, Laura McClellan ,and Erin Taylor Young for your help brainstorming this story.

Thank you to my critique partners, Kara Hunt, Candice Sue Patterson, Susan Crawford, Jericha Kingston, Sharon Srock, and Terri Weldon for helping me pull this story together. Special thank-you to Pegg Thomas and my editor, Ray Rhamey, for showing me the holes and helping me plug them up.

Thank you, readers, for diving into a new series with me. I can't wait to see where it goes.

Finally, thank you to my family for putting up with my wild moods, which often reflect where I am in a story. Mostly, thank you to my Lord and Savior, who has given me everything I need to accomplish all He's given me to do.

## CHAPTER ONE

*My name is Ella, and I am precious.*

No matter what anybody said, Ella Cote knew who she was. Daddy had said so.

She lay curled on the thin pad, thumb in her mouth like when she was a baby. She closed her eyes because, even though it was dark then, it was less scary than when they were open and everything was still dark.

The howling outside the cave sounded like those wild dogs she saw in movies, the kinds that snatched away pets and little kids and ate them up.

*The wind. It's only the wind.*

Owls had been hoot-hooting. Now, other birds were tweeting to each other, probably saying to go back to sleep 'cause it was still dark.

Inside the cave, crickets had chirped all night long. They sang to her after the sun went down. They kept her company when she was alone. The crickets were her friends. Like Jiminy Cricket, only they didn't dance.

Being alone with the crickets was better.

Her forehead and knee were pressed against the cold stone wall beside her. She'd scooted as close as she could, but the man had only scooted with her, his heavy arm wrapped over her middle. His hand on her tummy. His front against her back. He was hot and sweaty and smelled like Daddy after a workout, except not good and comfortable. This man smelled like something yucky, like onions and green beans and old fish.

She wanted Daddy.

The man's breath blew against the back of her head.

She wanted her soft bed and her stuffed animals and her daddy to kiss her and tell her she was precious. Tell her she was worth more than all the diamonds and all the rubies and all the emeralds in all the world. Tell her he wouldn't trade her for ten bazillion dollars.

Tears fell into her hair and onto the skinny blanket beneath her, but Ella didn't wipe them. She didn't dare move.

Finally, light glowed beyond her closed eyelids. Morning again. Maybe today, Daddy would come for her.

*Please, God. I wanna go home.*

# CHAPTER TWO

Cassidy Leblanc kept her head down as she drove through downtown Coventry. This was the third day in a row she'd made this drive, but today, instead of normal traffic near the municipal building, a crowd had gathered in front. Traffic slowed to a stop as drivers and passengers gaped at the spectacle—Reid Cote and four older people, probably the missing little girl's grandparents. Together, they were a display of grief and terror.

Men and women, some uniformed, others in suits, crowded around the family on the stairs of the old brick building. While a few seemed eager and sure of themselves, most looked worn and haggard, having lived long enough that hope felt as elusive as vapor.

Or maybe Cassidy was projecting.

Reid stepped up to the microphones.

Cassidy couldn't hear her former friend's words, but she could imagine them—pleas for the return of his five-year-old daughter, Ella. His and Denise's daughter. Cassidy had learned that much from the newspaper articles, but Denise was nowhere to be seen. There must be a story there, one Cassidy didn't know and probably never would.

Watching the scene were mothers with hands over their

mouths, eyes wide. Fathers with clenched fists, looking ready to take on the world to protect their own. As if they could prevent danger and violence by sheer will.

That protectiveness had always hummed beneath the surface of this little New Hampshire town. Cassidy had felt it keenly, especially when people learned where her mother was and why. Many of the residents had looked at Cassidy as if she *were* her mother, not one of Mom's victims. It was unfair, and they'd probably all admit that if pressed. But when it came to safeguarding their families, fairness was irrelevant.

Finally, traffic moved. Lifting a prayer—one of the many she'd uttered since she'd learned of the girl's disappearance—Cassidy left downtown behind. This would be her third attempt at finding that hidden cave on the mountain. Third attempt, but unless she was successful today, not the last. She'd keep looking until she located it. That was the only way she could save that missing child.

By the time she parked in a small gravel parking lot on the outskirts of town, it was almost nine-thirty, and the sun was warming the mid-July morning. With the humidity, it would be a scorcher. She climbed from the car and grabbed her backpack. Inside were water bottles, sunscreen, bug spray, granola bars, a rope, a first-aid kit, a lighter, a flashlight, and extra ammo—everything she thought she might need.

The only thing she carried that wasn't in the backpack was her Glock 19. The guy at the gun shop had talked her into it. Knowing next to nothing about guns, she'd trusted his judgment, and he hadn't steered her wrong. The Glock felt manageable in her hand, and she'd hit the target on her first try. Granted, the target had only been about ten feet away. With more training, she'd gotten better, more comfortable. She could shoot a man if she had to. She would, if she had to.

After she got the backpack settled, she checked the Glock. It was loaded and ready.

So was she.

Or as ready as she could be for mountain-climbing. She slipped the gun into its holster on her side, dreading the day ahead. More than once, she'd described herself as *indoorsy*. Hiking, backpacking, camping... Those weren't her scene. She should've known she'd be back here. She should've prepared. Truth was, she avoided anything that reminded her of that day ten years prior. She'd stayed happily surrounded by high-rises and concrete instead of trees and mountains. Any love she'd once had for the wilderness had died that night ten years before on Mt. Ayasha. When she ran away, she swore she would never return—not to Coventry, not to the forest, certainly not to this mountain.

She started on the trail that had become familiar. If she could start higher up, this would be so much simpler. If she could camp overnight on the mountain, she'd surely have found the cave by now. But the ghosts were too close.

What she needed was help. As with everything she'd ever done, Cassidy would have to do this alone.

She hiked through the forest until she caught sight of the campground on the edge of the lake. Pulling the bill of her cap low and pushing her sunglasses higher on the bridge of her nose, she made her way along the narrow path that led past the tents and RVs. James's old familiar house was on the other side, but the forest was too thick to see it, the trail that led there overgrown. It was probably a good thing she couldn't see the property, but who could blame her for wanting a glimpse at the one place she'd ever felt loved?

She kept her shoulders back, pretending to belong.

The story of her life. Though, to be fair, Cassidy had found a place to belong. She'd built a life for herself in Seattle, far from the memories and accusations. She'd graduated from high school, earned a bachelor's degree in counseling, and gotten a job helping at-risk youth, girls like the one she'd been. Young women who'd run away or been discarded by their families, who had nothing and nobody. Ever since little Hallie's death, Cassidy's life had been about finding and saving lost girls.

A few children played on the playground while four preteens

smacked a volleyball on the sand court. Adults occupied benches and picnic tables, some sipping from mugs or picking at muffins. Beyond the little building that housed the communal bathrooms, a few kids already splashed in the lake. The sandy beach was busy with walkers, joggers, and early sunbathers. Laughter, chatter, and a faraway motorboat created the perfect soundtrack for the vacation day. One would never know a child had been snatched from a home just a few miles down the road.

Cassidy left the vacationers behind and hiked the trail she'd climbed the previous two days, trying to focus on the here and now and not the fears that haunted.

Thirty minutes into the hike, she left the marked trail, relying on old memories she'd worked so hard to bury. All she had to do was steer clear of anybody who might recognize her and keep hiking, keep searching. Little Ella was out here somewhere. Maybe today would be the day Cassidy would find her.

# CHAPTER THREE

James Sullivan stayed at the edge of the crowd, watching the press conference and battling memories best left buried. Memories of his parents standing on those same steps while James hovered off to the side, trying to be invisible. Dad saying the same things then that Reid was saying now.

James hoped that, this time, the outcome would be different.

When Reid finished talking and the police chief stepped up and fielded questions from reporters, a lot of the onlookers wandered away.

People James had known most of his life were interspersed with newcomers and curious tourists.

A few faces jumped out at him, mostly because, though they were trying not to be obvious about it, they were watching him. The high school principal, Mr. Flores, who'd been the vice principal back then, averted his gaze the instant James noticed him.

Tip Dion, the manager at the restaurant James owned but rarely visited, lifted a hand in greeting but wore no smile. Tip should be behind the coffee counter at The Patriot, not standing on the sidewalk out front.

James had gone to school with others in the crowd, and there were parents of old friends, people who'd known his family for years. Some waved, some just nodded. What did they expect of him? To dissolve into tears? To raise his fist in anger?

The urge to turn and walk away was strong, but he tamped it down. This wasn't about him, despite all the looks. This was about Reid and his missing daughter.

Sweet little Ella, who kissed James's cheek and made him play with dolls whenever he went to Reid's house. Ella, who loved to be swung around in the yard like a monkey. Ella, who trusted James and Reid and her grandparents to protect her. Who'd learned too young that the world was a very dangerous place.

*Please, let her still be alive.*

The prayer slipped from his heart before he could stop it. He'd been doing that a lot lately—accidentally praying, forgetting that God didn't answer his prayers.

On the far side of the crowd, Wilson Cage hung on the police chief's words. Both Wilson and his son Eugene had been suspects in James's sister's disappearance ten years earlier, mostly because their campground abutted James's land and the trails. But there'd never been any real evidence linking them to the crime. At least none that James knew of. Of course, he hadn't known everything. His parents had tried to shield him, as if more pain would have pushed him over the edge.

James didn't flinch when a hand clamped on his shoulder. Lots of people had touched him that morning, spoken words of encouragement and solidarity. It should have helped.

Beside him, Vince Pollack dropped his hand. "How's Reid holding up?"

"How do you think?"

Vince said nothing, his gaze scanning the crowd around them. Something snagged his attention, and James turned to see a little girl, about four years old, holding her mother's hand.

So vulnerable. So innocent. Would she, or a child just like her, be the killer's next victim?

A look of anguish crossed Vince's features.

The police chief stepped away from the mic, and the mayor took center stage with a prepared speech.

"Why aren't you up there?" James asked.

"You don't think there are enough spotlight-loving windbags already?"

"What's one more?"

Vince chuckled. "Been studying the crowd. Sick people who do stuff like this, they like to see the results of their evil, you know?"

James tore his gaze away from the press conference, though the scene was magnetic, like all great tragedies are.

On TV, police detectives wore suits, but Vince had on khakis and a golf shirt. Blending in. "See anything interesting?"

"Just locals. Some families on vacation who couldn't get away fast enough. Nobody noteworthy."

"How's the investigation going?" James asked. "Anything new?"

"Nothing. Kid was playing in her grandparents' backyard one minute, gone the next. Just like the girl last month."

"But you think she's still close?"

He shrugged. "Normally we wouldn't, but last time, if the kidnapper'd taken her away, why come back to dump the body? She's gotta be nearby."

James wondered if by "she," Vince referred to the child or the kidnapper. He wondered, but he didn't ask.

Dylan O'Donnell approached, his red hair bright in the morning sunshine. He shook both men's hands. "What can I do to help?"

O'Donnell was a private investigator who specialized in finding lost people. But not kidnapped people, as far as James knew. Runaways and homeless loved ones. Addicts, alcoholics, the mentally ill.

Vince said, "Nothing at the moment."

"Chelsea thought she might offer a reward for the kid's safe return." Dylan's wife was the president and CEO of Hamilton

Clothiers, the town's largest industry and the state's largest single employer.

A reward seemed like a good idea to James, but Vince said, "Take it up with the chief, but I don't think that's the way to go. This person's a serial kidnapper and murderer. We gotta catch her"—Vince's gaze flicked to James—"or him. Not fund the operation."

*Her.*

Everyone thought it was her.

Even though he was a newcomer to town, Dylan knew the story, and he glanced at James too. "Let me know. Money, time, expertise. We're happy to help however we can."

"Will do." Vince waited until Dylan was a good distance away before he spoke again. "I'd take him more seriously if his hair weren't the color of a firetruck."

"I hear he's good, though."

"I wish I could put him to work. Truth is, we got nothing. The kid just vanished."

They listened to the mayor drone on for a few minutes. There wasn't much to say, but he managed to use a lot of words to say it.

James asked, "How's Lorelai doing?"

The hard lines in his friend's face softened. "Good. Real good. I don't know what she sees in a guy like me."

"I always figured she's slow-witted."

Vince liked that.

"You gonna make it official?"

"I hope. She thinks it's too soon, but I'm ready."

Vince's mother had died a few months before. As far back as anybody could remember, it had only been Vince and his mom. Vince had taken the death hard.

"You doing okay?" James asked. "Anything I can—?"

"I'm good. Thanks."

James didn't press. He knew better than to think there was anything he could do to help.

Vince had hardly aged since James first met him. Or, more

likely, James had always thought of him as older than he really was. Put a uniform on a guy, give him a sidearm, it makes him look mature. James had been about fifteen the first time he'd seen Officer Pollack. He realized now that the badge had been freshly minted, the uniform starched to sharp edges. Vince had stood front and center at the school assembly once a year to tell the kids not to do drugs.

Like his classmates, James had snickered at the straightlaced cop. Other than that, he never thought about Vince or anybody else in law enforcement. James wasn't one to get involved in drugs or underage drinking. Only time he ever broke the law was when he and his friends would sneak past the *No Trespassing* sign and prowl the campground on summer evenings to play volleyball and swim at the beach. As they'd slipped from childhood into teens, they went not to play but to prowl for pretty girls.

Officer Vince had been an hour-a-year distraction almost all the way through high school.

Until James's sister went missing.

Vince had been the first on the scene when Hallie's body was found.

The chief had been around back then, the lead detective, lots of other cops, but it was Vince whom James remembered most from those days. An arm slung around his shoulders when James was too overwhelmed by grief to speak. A kind word for his mother. A shoulder-clasp for his father. Vince had been there.

What James had learned back then, the truth that had gotten him into town this morning, was that even if you could do nothing else, even if you had no idea what to say, you could be there.

He was trying to be there for Reid now. God knew Denise wouldn't be. She'd filed for divorce and taken off just months after Ella's birth.

James had caught Reid's eye before the press conference, but Reid had hardly acknowledged him. Too much terror in there for much else. Would Reid ever be the same?

If Ella didn't return, James knew the answer already. His own life was marked by one glaring before-and-after moment.

Before Hallie'd been kidnapped, James had been one of the popular kids. He'd played sports well enough that colleges had been talking scholarships. James'd had a lot of friends, good friends, or so he'd thought. He'd made good grades and goofed off. He'd been happy.

The kid he was before, that dumb arrogant jock, died the night his sister disappeared.

Most of the friendships he'd have sworn were strong fell apart. It wasn't that his classmates and teammates didn't care. But ever since Cassidy had started at Coventry High, rumors had swirled around her. With her mother in prison for beating her little sister to death, Cassidy had borne more tragedy than anybody else at the sheltered little school, and their classmates loved to speculate about the events surrounding the little girl's death. Because Cassidy had been the one to call 911. She'd claimed their mother was abusive, and her testimony had sent the woman to prison.

Such juicy details for a bunch of teenagers with no real drama in their lives.

They hadn't known the Cassidy he knew, the girl who was tender and gentle. Once Hallie died, the rumors had been too meaty, too nasty, to ignore.

High school was a time for hyperbole and melodrama. Everything seemed so big and so important, but James—and his friends, he thought—had believed, deep down, that the worries they dealt with were just kids' stuff. Despite the vicious stories about Cassidy's mother, nobody'd ever really believed Cassidy capable of violence. Their lives were too insulated for that.

James and those he'd gone to school with for twelve years had been fortunate. No suicides, no drug overdoses, no major crime. Sure, there were drugs, but no serious addictions, no runaways. There were a handful of teenage pregnancies and rumors of more. But, for the most part, life was simple.

Which was why Cassidy had been so intriguing.

When Hallie disappeared in the spring of his senior year, the fantasy of safety was snatched away.

The other kids hadn't known how to deal with it. What was there to say to a guy whose girlfriend kidnapped and killed his little sister?

There were no pithy lines for that.

Only Reid had stuck around.

Every evening after baseball practice, Reid would come and knock on the door. James would tell him to go away, but Mom would welcome him in, offer him a Coke. No matter how painstakingly James ignored him, Reid would stay. Plop down on the couch beside him, tell him what he'd missed at practice, give him a rundown of every game James no longer cared to play. Tell him all the latest gossip—all that hadn't been related to Cassidy, anyway.

They'd play video games, mostly in silence, for hours.

No matter how rude James was, Reid kept coming. Kept coming until, one day, James said, "Wanna go hit some balls?" And just like that, things started toward a new normal.

That was the thing about life's befores and afters. There was an after. No matter how impossible it seemed, life went on.

Most of his *before* friendships had fallen away. But the *after* friendships were stronger. The old life was gone, but, no matter how little James wanted it to, a new life was formed.

A new James had emerged. Not better, necessarily, but wiser and more compassionate.

He never played another baseball game. Instead, he attended Plymouth State, right down the road, where he could be close to his parents. Reid went with him, and Vince had checked up on him often over the years.

James didn't know if he'd have survived without Vince and Reid, especially after his parents passed.

Vince slapped him on the shoulder and squeezed. "This has gotta be killing you."

The memories were all too close today. James feared that if he turned around too fast he might catch a glimpse of one.

"It's the same guy," Vince said. "Least we think it is."

"You mean girl?"

After a long silence, Vince said, "I know you always thought it was an accident."

"Cassidy wouldn't have hurt my sister."

"You're the most loyal person I know. One of your best qualities. But in this case... If you hear from her, if she shows up—"

"Cassidy's long gone. She's not coming back."

The press conference broke up, and James left Vince and made his way toward his friend, waiting until most of the others who'd come to offer their prayers and support had walked away before approaching. "Anything I can do?"

"Just keep praying."

He tamped down the guilt. James had done enough of that. Prayer always made his hopes climb like a helium balloon. The higher it soared, the farther the pieces fell when it burst.

Reid's eyes were red-rimmed when he turned them on James. "Why would she do this to us?"

*She.* Even Reid believed it, though he'd been friends with Cassidy in school.

"If I ever get my hands on her..." His voice cracked.

He seemed to be waiting for a response. James didn't know what to say, but more guilt pressed in. As if Cassidy's actions were somehow his responsibility. As if he should have known.

As if he should agree.

He didn't, though. He couldn't.

Detective Cote, Reid's uncle, approached, and James stepped away to let them talk, thankful for the reprieve. Because he wanted to be there for his friend, but he wasn't about to jump on the Cassidy-is-guilty-of-everything train. The girl he'd known, the girl he'd loved, was no kidnapper, no murderer.

No matter what everybody believed.

# CHAPTER FOUR

I
f only Cassidy had the courage to stay overnight on the mountain.

But she didn't, and when she realized the time, she hurried down, back to the trail. The sun was falling behind the trees, the woods dark and deep. She'd encountered lots of folks on the way up, but the trail was deserted now. The campers at the foot of the mountain were done with hiking for the day. Smart. Staying up here after dark...

Fear crawled up her spine like ants on a watermelon rind.

Most folks would argue that this mountain was safe, that no crime could touch this place. She knew better. This mountain offered more than pretty views of Lake Ayasha and Mt. Coventry and, in the distance, the snow-capped peak of Mount Washington. There were places to lurk and hide. Dark places filled with evil.

She had to stop those thoughts. Focus.

But the fear didn't lift.

Something was... following her.

It wasn't so much a sound as a feeling, a whisper that sneaked through her being and gripped her heart. She'd had that sense once before, and she hadn't heeded it, a mistake that had proved fatal.

Now, the feeling pushed her off the trail and into the woods.

Should she hide? She looked around for a place to take cover. A downed tree, a large rock? All she saw were thin trees and overgrown shrubs.

She was too vulnerable.

Picking her way through the underbrush, she tried to gauge where she was. She'd traveled most of the way down, hadn't she? She should be near the base. The campground. Safety.

She crept forward, away from the trail, as quietly as she could.

The feeling that she was being followed only intensified. And... the sound of heavy footsteps on the path. Someone was there. At least she wasn't crazy. Small comfort.

The man—she was sure it was a man—was closing in.

A branch snapped, too close.

Adrenaline coursed through her veins, set her hands trembling and reaching for her Glock. But she didn't pull it out. Better to get away. She felt as if she were in a nightmare, frozen by sleep, trying to scream, trying to wake herself up. Her lungs and vocal cords wouldn't obey.

But her legs weren't paralyzed. She pushed herself faster, ignoring the branches that slapped her in the face and thighs.

Past bushes, around trees, she kept on, trying to keep barriers between her and the path above.

Through the thick underbrush, she saw a flash of white. Was it James's house, the place that had been a sanctuary to her so many times? Without thinking, she broke into a run. But thorns and twigs and branches slowed her progress.

She glanced behind her and saw a flash of red not thirty yards back.

She was making too much noise. He'd find her for sure.

The memories pressed down on her, tried to immobilize her. It had been winter the last time, and the child in her care had been giggling, running ahead. Too far ahead.

This was different. She had only herself to protect now, not a sweet innocent child who'd trusted her.

The going was rough as she forced her way through the underbrush, yanking her clothes from the grip of thorns and the sticky fingers of low bushes, ignoring scrapes and gouges on her legs and arms.

The house had to be close. The trail wrapped around the mountain behind it. Surely, surely she'd reach it soon.

*Hurry, hurry.*

She pushed past a bush, ducking beneath a dead and leafless limb. On the other side, her foot landed in a depression and she stumbled, almost fell. Twisted her ankle, but not badly.

Glanced behind.

Still, a flash of red.

Ahead, there was a brightening, perhaps a break in the forest, or...

The white siding of James's house. Then she saw the roof, the wood deck off the back, the windows reflecting the orange-and-pink sky.

Finally, she left the woods and landed on soft grass. She rushed across the backyard, only realizing then that it probably wasn't James's property anymore at all. His parents had lived here, and he was an adult now. Surely he'd moved on. And anyway, after Hallie's death, they'd likely sold this old place. Who'd want to live with those memories?

She rounded the structure on the far side, away from the man following her. If someone *had* been following her. It was entirely possible she'd gone crazy, that her treks through the woods were messing with her mind.

At least she'd be relatively anonymous to whoever lived in this house now. They'd probably never heard of her, probably had no idea of her history in Coventry. But when she glimpsed the front yard, she froze.

The old red canvas-topped Jeep Wrangler, the one James had driven back in high school, was parked in the driveway, dirt caked along the side as if it had recently been off-roading. A jack held a rear tire off the ground.

She should turn around, except... She felt eyes on her. Whoever'd followed her was watching. He knew she was here. He knew who she was.

No. That couldn't be true. She had to think clearly.

The blinds on the house were open, and she slipped off her sunglasses and glanced inside the dining room window. She'd spent many happy meals there. The same weathered oak table, the same ladder-back chairs, the same sideboard with the same portrait hanging over it. A portrait of the family she'd loved as her own. Mr. Sullivan, Mrs. Sullivan, James, and Hallie.

They'd loved her, too. Once.

The memories hit so strong and hard that she squeezed her eyes to shut them out. The fear that had gripped her moments before vanished, replaced by grief so potent it felt like tentacles pulling her down.

Cassidy was a fool. She should've stayed on the trail and faced the pursuer. That would've been easier than facing this. She swiveled and started toward the road. She'd avoid the trail now, take the long way back to her car. Her pursuer—if she hadn't dreamed him—was on the far side of the house. He wouldn't be able to see where she went.

The door opened, and the screen squeaked on its hinges. She didn't turn back and didn't slow, but a voice called out. "Can I help you?" It was a voice she knew. A voice her dreams still produced.

*No, no, no.* That was the last thing she needed.

Without turning, she called, "Sorry. Just took a wrong turn."

Nearly jogging, she waited for the door to open again and slam, proof the person had gone back inside. Instead, the thud of feet on the patio stairs followed.

He couldn't be chasing her.

Maybe he wouldn't recognize her. Maybe, if she stopped him before he got too close, he wouldn't see her beyond her cap, her new haircut, and her new hair color. Everything about her was new. She turned suddenly, hoping he'd stop where he was. "Didn't mean to interrupt you. I'll just—"

"Cassidy?"

She wanted to laugh it off, give her fake name, pretend. But the words were caught.

Her sunglasses hung uselessly from her hand. She should have slipped them back on. Stupid mistake. Fatal mistake.

He was there, just ten, maybe fifteen feet from her. He looked so different. The clean-cut high school jock now had long hair, a mustache, and a beard. He'd broadened, matured. But the eyes... Those milk chocolate eyes hadn't changed, even if they were filled with malice right now.

"What are—?" He closed the distance between them. When he was inches from her, he froze. "What are you doing here?"

She swallowed all the emotions trying to climb out of her throat. Fear, affection, grief.

Love.

How could she still feel that after all the years, after the way he'd betrayed her? Of course, he thought she'd betrayed him... More than betrayed him.

He thought she was a murderer.

She didn't know what to say. There were no words.

"You just gonna stand there looking at me?" he asked. "I think I deserve to know why you're on my property, especially now."

The accusation in his tone brought her voice back. "What does *that* mean? Especially now? Especially now that another kid is missing? Especially now that everyone suspects I did it?" She hurled the words, praying he'd soften, tell her she was wrong, that he believed in her.

"Yeah, Cassidy, and your being here right now—"

"Proves it? Right? Is that what you're going to say?"

He crossed his arms, shrugged. He didn't speak the words, but the accusation was clear in the hard stare.

"I didn't kill your sister. I would never..." Old tears she'd thought long dried, rose to her throat. She'd always hoped, deep down, that James didn't really believe what everyone said. But her hope had been futile. Of course it had. Hadn't all her hopes proved...

*Stop that. No pity-parties, not even today.*

"If you didn't do it," he asked, "then why did you run?"

"You know why. I would never have gotten a fair shake here. I ran because I didn't want to end up in prison."

"Maybe you and your mother could've shared a cell."

He might as well have struck her. That James, *her* James, could speak to her so cruelly, could have so thoroughly lost his faith in her... "Like mother, like daughter. Is that it?"

"You said it, not me."

"Whatever." She swiveled and started back toward the trail.

He grabbed her upper arm and whipped her around to face him. Though his grip was firm, he didn't squeeze, didn't hurt her. "I'm calling the cops."

That would ruin everything. If he called the police, she wouldn't get to Ella in time. "Please, James. If you ever cared for me, if you ever believed in me, even the tiniest bit, please don't turn me in. I promise you, I didn't hurt your sister, and Denise and Reid's daughter... I would never..." Her emotions were bouncing around like a pinball. "I'm here to see if I can find her. I'm the only one who can."

His flattened lips turned white. He didn't believe her. Of course he didn't. Why would he? Why would anybody put faith in Cassidy Leblanc?

She was innocent, and she'd give anything to prove it, anything to take that accusation out of his expression. But that wasn't why she was here. "You could help me, you know. You could help me find them."

"Who is *them?*"

"Ella and the kidnapper. I know where they are."

"If you know where she is, it's because you put her there."

"I didn't!" How could he even think such a thing? "I wouldn't... I was at work. When Ella went missing, and the other little girl, I was thousands of miles from here. I can prove it. I didn't take them. I wouldn't have—"

"Then tell the police. Prove it."

"I can't. If I did, they'd know I didn't take Ella or Addison, but there's still the warrant because of Hallie. I'm doing all I can without ending up in prison. I'm trying to help."

His dark eyebrows rose. "Do you expect me to believe that, after all these years, you decided to come back and *help?* After another child's already been murdered?" His voice rose, became nearly a shout. "Now? Now, you've decided to tell what you know? Decided you need to play the hero? Why not tell the police every—"

"I tried!" She took a breath, then another. "I told them everything. I called. I called the day I ran away. I told them exactly where the kidnapper took us. I thought they'd find his hideout, maybe DNA evidence or something. I figured, when they caught the real kidnapper, I'd come back. But they didn't care what I had to say. They thought I was guilty. They told me to turn myself in, and then they'd hear me out. As if I'd believe them."

When he finally spoke, his voice was soft. "You called them? Back then?"

He hadn't known? Why had she thought he would?

"Of course. I called again last month, after the other girl was taken. I tried to convince them that I knew where she was. I told the cop everything I know, which, honestly, isn't much. I don't know if they followed my tip. By the time I decided to come here myself, the child's body had been found. When I called back to find out if they'd located the cave, the cop on the phone... He recognized my voice, and he lost it. Screamed at me, told me that he would find me and see me punished for what I did. You asked me why I haven't turned myself in? Because if I go in, they'll declare the case closed. And Denise and Reid's daughter will die."

The last few words hung in the cooling air.

James dropped her arm. "You're saying...?" He rubbed the back of his neck before meeting her gaze again. "You're saying that you think you can rescue Ella?"

"I have to try. I have to."

He said nothing, just watched her.

If only he'd believe her. A new thought occurred to her, an idea that could change everything. "You know this mountain better than I do. I need to find the cave. No matter what they say, I know it exists. I was there. I almost died there."

He stepped back, swallowed hard. "My sister..."

"She did die there." Cassidy couldn't keep the tears from her voice now. The memory was so close—Hallie in her arms, eyes open, lifeless.

"You're saying you're going to the place where you..."

*Where you killed her.*

That's what he'd almost said. That's what floated between them now.

She let it go. He believed what he believed, and there was nothing she could do about that.

He started again. "You're going to the place where my sister died?"

"I believe it's where he's holding—"

"Who is he? Who did this? Why don't you—?"

"I have no idea!" She hadn't meant to shout and tried to calm down. "If I knew who he was, I'd have told the police ten years ago. I can tell you it was a man. I can tell you that he was almost as scared as I was. I can tell you that... I don't think any of it was planned. He wanted to take her. I was extraneous." Hadn't she always been that? "He didn't expect me to be there. I just—"

"I don't want to hear this." His voice was cold. "I can't listen to your story." He seemed as emotionally overwrought as she was. She remembered the way his chest would expand when he was upset. The way his jaw would go from rounded to hard. Even past the cropped beard, she could see the softness had disappeared with age, or grief. James was all hard angles and anger now. Maybe the anger was her fault.

He started again, his tone measured. "I don't want to hear your story. I'm not ready to..." He lifted his hand as if he were going to rub the back of his neck again but dropped it before it got there.

She wanted to press him, to beg him for his help. James would keep her safe at night, and he would know how to cover more ground, cover new ground. He wouldn't go in circles like she had. But she couldn't convince him. He had to decide where to go from here. Go with her, ignore her, or turn her in. There weren't a lot of options, and one of them would be the end of her, the end of little Ella Cote.

"Where are you going?" he finally asked.

"It's up on the mountain somewhere. There's a rock formation that forms caves. I never knew it was there before, and I don't think anyone else does either. It's way off the beaten track. In all the aerial photos I've seen, there's no indication of it. I've studied and studied and studied this mountain—as much as I could on the internet, anyway—and there's no record of the cave I'm talking about."

"Maybe that means it's not there."

"It is. It haunts my dreams. It haunts..." Her voice was too full of emotion. She had to stop that, had to be stoic. James wouldn't believe her tears if she shed them.

"How far away is it?"

"I don't know exactly. I was so afraid... It took hours to climb up. I came down a different way. It was dark, I was terrified. I just... I just don't know. But I know it's up there. And I know that's where Ella is. In my heart"—she pressed her hand to her chest —"she's still there. And she's still alive. For now. If you care at all about Reid, if you care at all about his little girl... If you ever cared about me... I need your help. I can't do this by myself."

# CHAPTER FIVE

J ames stared at this apparition from his past.

That very morning, he'd held close the idea that Cassidy was innocent. Even as Vince and Reid and the rest of the town accused her, he'd believed in her.

But now, looking at the last person to see his sister alive, the only person who could have answered all the questions and given his parents peace... How could he trust a word she said?

If she did do it, if she was responsible for the death of the girl last month, and if she knew where Reid's daughter was now, the best course of action would be to call the police immediately. They could get the truth out of her better than James could.

But what if Cassidy *was* telling the truth?

He tried to read her gaze, but it seemed so unfamiliar, he wasn't sure what to think of what he saw there.

Her hair had been dyed black in high school, and she'd always worn caked-on makeup, along with too much black eyeliner and black lipstick. She'd hidden behind Nirvana T-shirts and torn jeans and black sweatshirts and ugly hiking boots.

Today, she wore no makeup, and her cheeks and nose were dotted with freckles. Her lips were pink, her teeth... she must've invested in braces, because the ones that had been crooked were now straight.

The only thing that hadn't changed were her eyes.

The irises were rimmed in dark green, but inside were flecks of blue and gold and other colors that seemed to change with her mood. Right now, he saw reddish-orange, the color of glowing coals.

Even with all the goth foolishness she'd worn in high school, he'd thought her pretty. Now, she was downright gorgeous.

And, based on the fire in her gaze, furious.

She had a lot of nerve being mad at him.

"Why are you here, Cassidy?"

"I told you, I'm here to find—"

"No." He swept his arm across his yard. "Here. On my property?"

Her gaze flicked behind her, and a flash of something new entered her expression. He couldn't have named it, but his heart pounded. "What?"

"I'm probably being paranoid. I thought..." She flicked a gaze at the mountain.

"Thought what?"

She swallowed. "I thought somebody was following me. It creeped me out."

"It's a hiking trail," he said. "Lots of hikers in the summer."

"I know that." Did he catch defensiveness in her tone? "This felt different. It felt..."

Was anybody there? The trail was a quarter mile up the mountain from the house. Nobody should be there.

"Explain what you saw."

She crossed her arms, then uncrossed them. "I'm sorry. I shouldn't have..." After a long breath, she said, "I'm here now. I'm going to have to trust that God knows what He's doing."

God? Did she mean that, or was she playing him? Back in high school, he'd told her about his faith, taken her to church. But after

Hallie's death, then his parents', God felt about as close as Antarctica, and just as cozy.

"If you need to turn me in," she said, "I understand. I'll tell the cops everything I know. Not that they'll listen to me this time."

"They'd have listened to you last time if you hadn't taken off."

She took the baseball cap from her head, yanked out a ponytail holder, and ran her hand through her hair. Not black as it had been in school. Light brown. After she returned the cap, she sighed. "I panicked. I shouldn't have..."

He was about to demand she finish her sentence when movement caught his eyes. A flash of red in the woods, there and gone too fast to define.

Branches rustled.

Somebody *was* there.

The kidnapper? A cop on her trail?

He grabbed her arm. "Come on."

"What?" She whipped her head around to look at the mountain, but he pulled her toward his house.

"What are you doing?" She tried to yank away.

But she was tiny, and he maneuvered her easily. At the foot of his porch steps, he said, "Go inside, lock the doors, and don't open them for anybody but me."

Before she could argue, he bolted across his yard.

He reached the edge of the forest and stepped in. There was no trail here, and he hadn't trimmed back or yanked out any of the underbrush on purpose, a good way to keep strangers from wandering onto his land. He fought his way through and made it to the place where he thought he'd seen the flash of color. Nobody there, of course, but bent twigs told him somebody had been. Cassidy could have done that. Was paranoia contagious?

Or had somebody recognized her? Was that somebody calling the cops right now to report a Cassidy Leblanc sighting?

If so, would the cops show up to take her into custody?

He turned back toward his property, wondering if Cassidy was still there or if she'd run off again, returning to wherever she'd come from even now. That would make his decision for him. He'd call Vince, report that Cassidy was in town, and be done with it.

That feeling in the pit of his stomach, grief and fury, would fade to a gentle ache. It always did.

The real problem was that the emotions he'd experienced when he'd first seen Cassidy hadn't been grief. And the thought of her disappearing again didn't bring fury. He *missed* her. Everyone else thought she was a murderer, but what James had felt for her in high school lingered.

He took the key he kept hidden beneath the potted plant on his patio and unlocked the door. She was probably gone, but no matter how many times he'd tried to plug it up, hope was a bubbling brook that wouldn't be contained.

He closed the door behind him. The house felt unnaturally quiet.

He glanced in the living room. Empty, of course.

But when he peeked into the dining room, he saw her standing in front of the sideboard, staring at his family's last portrait.

Tears streamed from her eyes.

They looked... authentic.

She must have heard him because she wiped her cheeks. "Being back here. It's..."

Again, she didn't finish the thought. Maddening.

"Was anybody there?" she asked.

"Somebody had been."

"It's weird, right? That somebody would follow me off the trail?"

"Were you recognized?"

She looked out the window that faced the forest. "I didn't get close to anyone, at least not that I saw. Even if I had"—she flipped off her baseball cap and stepped closer to him—"do you think anybody would recognize me?"

He turned on the dining room light and took in her features once more. She looked like a different person. Fresh and young and innocent, though she was a decade older than the last time he'd seen her. "Your eyes are distinctive."

She put the cap back on. "I wore my sunglasses until it got too dark to see."

After a moment, he broke eye contact, walking into the kitchen.

She followed. "What happens now?"

"I don't know." He sat at the old round table that his mother had bought a million years ago. "I didn't think you'd still be here."

She pulled out the chair beside him and sat. "You sorry I am?"

"Why are you?"

"Obviously, I wasn't going to tell you I was in town. I know it puts you in a terrible position." She traced a scratch on the table with her fingernail. Even her nails were different. Back in school, they'd always been short, bitten to the quick, and painted black. These were manicured and pale pink.

Pink. This girl who'd eschewed all color ten years prior wore pink nail polish.

"Even though I hoped you knew I would never hurt your sister, I couldn't count on it."

"If you hadn't run—"

"I wasn't going to tell you I was here, but now that you know, I need help. I've been trying for days to find that cave, but they're far, and... and I pretty much stink at this hiking thing. And..." She focused again on the scratch on the table. "To be honest, I don't even like going up there in the bright daylight. I'm terrified to camp. I want to save Ella, but I fear..."

Fear. He understood that too well.

"Will you help me?"

"No." He tried to think through his options, but there weren't many. "I don't know."

She pushed back from the table and stood. They watched each other for a moment and, as much as he told himself he should, he couldn't seem to tear his eyes away from her.

"Okay, then." Walking through the dining room, she snatched

her backpack from the floor and slid it on. At the front door, she turned. "I'm searching again tomorrow morning. I'll leave at seven."

"Don't do that." A strand of his long hair covered his eyes, and he pushed it back, wishing he'd put it in a ponytail. "Look, I need to think. If we're going to do this, let's not do it blindly. Let's try to figure out where we're going."

"How?"

"There are people who know the mountain better than I do." He needed more information—about Mt. Ayasha, about the investigation, and about Cassidy.

"We don't have time to wait," she said. "Ella doesn't have time—"

"We can't save her if we don't know where she is. You said yourself you have no idea where the cave is. It's a big mountain, Cassidy. There's no sense wandering around aimlessly."

"Then when?"

"Do you have a phone number? I'll do some digging, call you tomorrow night. We'll make a plan then."

"It's a mistake to wait."

"It's a mistake to go without a plan."

Her lips pursed, but she rattled off a New Hampshire number. Did that mean she lived nearby? Or had she bought the phone recently? He snatched his from the table near the door and punched in the numbers.

A phone rang from her backpack.

He ended the call, satisfied he could reach her.

She opened the door and stepped into the dark night.

"Where's your car? I'll walk you—"

"I'm okay."

"I thought somebody was following you. I thought you were afraid."

The slight lift of her shoulders didn't tell him anything. "It's at the lot on the far side of the campground. I should be safe."

He wasn't sure about that. "Do you remember Eugene Cage?"

"That learning disabled kid? Barely. Wasn't he a few years older than us? Always got picked on?"

"Yeah. His dad, Wilson, owns the campground. They were both questioned... back then."

Her eyebrows hiked. "Really? I never met Mr. Cage. I don't think I ever spoke to Eugene, though he seemed like a sweet enough guy."

"It's possible it was one of them. Back then or following you today." He snatched his keys from the table near the doorway. "Whoever it was, you're not walking by yourself."

He'd trekked the trail enough as a kid that he had no trouble getting to the walkway that circled the campground. Voices and laughter carried in the darkness, along with the scents of grilling burgers and steaks. The sand volleyball court was empty. Most folks congregated outside their campers and tents, though a few people splashed in the lake.

Cassidy kept her head down and said nothing.

Finally, they reached the parking area. A black compact sedan was the only one in the lot. She tossed her backpack onto the passenger seat and turned to face him. "You'll call tomorrow?"

"Yeah. And you call me if anything happens. Meanwhile, stay out of sight. Everybody's looking for you. And stay away from the trails. Okay?"

"For one day," she said. "After that, whether you go with me or not, I'm resuming the search."

She seemed determined. Was she innocent, as he hoped? Or guilty, as everybody else believed?

Was he a fool to consider going with her onto the mountain? Probably.

He could always turn her in instead. Either way, he needed more information.

～

LATER THAT EVENING, James threw the new tire into the trunk of his car and backed out of the parking spot at his mechanic's, turning away from his home. He wasn't ready to face the ghosts, not yet.

Five minutes later, he parked in front of Teresa's. The owner, a sixty-something guy named Ernie, had chosen the name because he thought it sounded exotic. The name was common enough to fit the fare he offered—Mexican food. And Italian food. And a bit of American food to round out the menu.

Odd as the place was, it drew a crowd. At nine-thirty on a Monday night, all the booths along the walls were taken, as were the rectangular tables in the center of the large room. Many of the seats at the bar were filled as well. People munched appetizers and sipped drinks and laughed. The mood was subdued, though, the laughter forced. The news that hovered, the recent murder, the current kidnapping—true joy was gone from the tourist town.

A few heads turned when James walked in, some friendly faces, most just curious about the guy whose sister had been the first victim.

Ten years had passed, but in a small town, nobody forgot.

He weaved among the tables and found a seat near the end of the bar.

Ernie wiped the surface in front of him. "Drinking tonight?"

"Just a Sprite and potato skins."

James caught the eye roll as Ernie turned to fill his glass. He'd been known to have a drink or two on occasion, but those occasions were rare. Celebrations. Parties he couldn't get out of. Some said they drank to forget, but for him, drinking only fed the memories and revived the ghosts.

He sipped his soda, ate potato skins, and tried not to think about Cassidy. But she might as well have been seated beside him for all the good that did.

Her presence felt so real that, when someone did sit beside him, he half expected it to be her. Instead, a twenty-something brunette smiled at him. He didn't recognize her, and she was too dressed up for a Monday night at the local bar. Skinny jeans, tank top with skinnier straps. She propped her stilettos on his barstool. "Wanna buy me a drink?"

He nodded to the margarita glass in her hand. "You've already got one."

She giggled and hiccuped. "Another one, silly."

"Not interested."

She leaned closer, not getting the hint. "What are you interested in?"

"Being alone."

Her eyes brightened, and a smile tipped her too-red lips.

"Alone alone," he clarified, "not... with someone else alone."

She got the message and sauntered to a table in the far corner where four other women had watched the scene. When she sat, they all leaned toward her, shooting him furtive glances.

"You know what your problem is?"

James turned to the other side, where Vince had slipped in without him noticing. "Please, enlighten me."

"With that beard, you look like Aragorn from the *Lord of the Rings* movie."

"Whatever," James said.

"Not my words. Lorelai said that. I think you look more like Gimli."

Across the bar, Ernie'd been pretending not to listen, but his laugh gave him away.

"No clue who that is," James said.

"The dwarf. The little one who wasn't a hobbit. You know who I mean."

He did, but he wouldn't give his friend the satisfaction.

Vince sipped his drink, said nothing for a minute. Then, "You work today?"

James worked every day. He owned a restaurant in town, but the manager made most of the day-to-day decisions. He traded rare coins and bullion in his spare time because it had been a hobby of his father's, one he'd come to love. But in the summertime, most of his time was spent in his third business, private back-packing tours.

"I cancelled the tour I had booked for this week when Ella went missing. In case Reid needs me for something."

"You're a good friend."

James shrugged. Wasn't much he could do, but he'd be there for Reid. "Where's your girlfriend tonight?"

"Away on business."

Lorelai worked in sales for Hamilton, the clothing manufacturer that kept Coventry and the surrounding communities afloat. Her work took her out of town often.

"Just as well," Vince said. "It's not as if I could spend much time with her with everything going on."

"Right. And your need to hang out at townie bars and drink."

Vince sipped his beer and lowered his voice. "You'd be amazed at the tidbits I can pick up just by listening. People know more than they realize. They see things, hear things."

"You pick up anything good today?"

"Nothing but a lot of speculation. Guy at the far table's trying to resurrect the theory that Eugene Cage was involved." Vince helped himself to one of James's potato skins. "Everybody wants to pin it on the weird kid."

Eugene's disability had always set him apart. In a small town where everybody knew everybody, sometimes the worst thing was to be set apart. His disability was severe enough that he'd never had a job except maintenance at his father's campground.

Once upon a time, the campground had belonged to James's family, but his father had sold it to Wilson Cage when James was in elementary school. They'd never had any trouble with Wilson as neighbors or as owners of the campground that abutted their property, but both Eugene and Wilson had been questioned in Hallie's disappearance. The news media had reported Eugene was a "prime suspect," but their information was faulty. The only suspect the authorities had ever seriously considered was Cassidy.

"Any reason why they suspect Eugene now?"

Vince finished off the potato skin and reached for another.

James moved the plate away. "Get your own, man."

Vince chuckled and ordered another plate. "Aside from the fact that he's different? No."

"You talk to him?"

Vince leveled James with a look. "Not you, too. The guy's slow. That doesn't make him a killer."

"It doesn't make him *not* a killer, either."

"They had alibis when your sister went missing."

Alibis could be fabricated, couldn't they? Had James's own neighbor killed his sister, run his girlfriend off?

"I know what you're thinking, but don't. Eugene didn't snatch Hallie. And Wilson—"

"He was at the press conference this morning. I saw him. You said it yourself—people like to see the result of their evil."

"Should I suspect everyone who showed up today? You were there. Did you do it?"

At James's glare Vince's hands lifted. "Just saying..." He dropped his hands, sipped his beer.

"What do you make of the killer coming back?" James asked. "Ten years later, and all of a sudden, he's back at it."

"Good question. We're in contact with the FBI, but they can't connect these crimes to any others in the country. They're also coordinating with authorities in Canada, just in case. For whatever reason, it seems this person kidnapped your sister, then took a ten-year break, and then started again."

James ate the last potato skin on his plate, slathering on a good bit of sour cream. It wouldn't be enough food to last until morning.

"Anything else?" James asked. "Any other rumors? Any Cassidy sightings?"

There'd been enough after the disappearance of the little girl, Addison, a month prior. Maybe the mention of it wouldn't raise any red flags.

"Couple." Vince waved hello to someone behind James, but James didn't turn to see who it was. "About as credible as last month. People seem to forget that she'd have aged in the last decade. Why do you ask?"

"What if it wasn't Cassidy back then? What if it's not her now? Everyone's so intent on finding her, but—"

"We're looking at all the options."

"What other options? Have you had any leads?"

Vince stared at the mirror behind the bar, but his gaze flicked here and there. Studying the people around them. He was good at seeing more than everyone else did. James figured it was what made him such a good detective.

"You know I can't talk about the investigation."

"Search party going back tomorrow?"

"For all the good it'll do. Reid insists we keep looking. He's sure she's on Coventry."

Addison had been snatched from a neighborhood in town, but her body had been found on the back porch of a house near the edge of the lake at the base of Mt. Coventry.

Ella had been snatched from Reid's parents' house. They lived in town, also nearer to Mt. Coventry. Not that there was any reason to believe she was on the mountain, but search parties had been sent onto Coventry for days in hopes of catching a scent.

"What if the killer left Addison's body by Coventry to throw everybody off?" James asked. "What if Ella is somewhere else? Like... on Mt. Ayasha."

There was a long pause. James looked at the mirror behind the bar and saw Vince was staring at him now.

"Interesting theory."

Ernie delivered another plate of potato skins, and James snagged one.

Slowly, Vince turned his way. "You come up with that theory all by yourself?"

"Back then"—they both knew when *back then* was—"everyone believed Hallie and Cassidy had been on Ayasha."

"So you figure it's a good place to start?"

He shrugged. "What have you got to lose?"

Vince said nothing.

He was wasting his time trying to get information from Vince. "After... everything, you assured me you knew Cassidy was alive. Nobody suspected that she, too, had been murdered."

"Except you."

"How could you have been so sure?"

Vince lifted his beer, set it back down. When he faced James again, there was a grim set to his lips. "I didn't want you to grieve her."

"I know."

"I can tell you I knew she was alive. Beyond that, I can't talk about it."

"What? It's top secret? It's been a decade, Vince. A decade later, everybody thinks my high school girlfriend murdered my sister. It's time for you to tell me how you were so sure she was alive. And why you were so sure she did it."

Vince finished the beer. Set it on the bar and waved at Ernie. Ernie delivered another, and Vince glared at him until he walked out of earshot. Ernie was known for eavesdropping—and sharing what he heard.

Only after Vince took a swallow did he turn to James.

James held his breath.

"It's still an ongoing investigation. You got a problem with that? Take it up with the chief." Vince leaned in, so close James inhaled the scent of beer on his breath. His gaze was steely. "Why do you want to know now? Tonight?"

James faced forward, going for casual despite Vince's thinly veiled intimidation. "Just trying to piece it together."

Vince had gone from cop to friend somewhere in the last decade, but, studying him in the mirror, James saw only a detective, a detective on the trail of a killer.

This had been a mistake, but he was too deep now to swim his way out.

"You get any closer," James said, "people are going to talk. Wouldn't want Lorelei getting jealous."

Vince backed away, faced forward. "I know what you're thinking." Vince's tone was as relaxed as James's demeanor. Neither of them was fooled. "Should I trust him? I mean, yeah, we're friends. But I'm also a cop, a cop who thinks your ex-girlfriend is a killer. You have information, but you're afraid to tell me because telling me means you'll have to reveal where the information came from. Maybe it's nothing to worry about. Maybe it is. Maybe you don't even know. I can tell you this, James. You don't tell me, and your friend's kid dies..." He lifted his bottle, sipped, and set it down gently. "Trust me. That's the kind of pain you never get over."

James didn't want to consider that.

This was a dangerous game.

The only way forward was to be honest. Or at least, nearly honest. "I talked to Cassidy."

Vince's expression didn't shift, didn't register surprise or any of the thoughts James guessed were going through his head. Maybe that was another thing that made him such a good detective.

James should've kept his mouth shut.

"Talk to her, did you?"

"She said she told the police years ago what happened. Said she and Hallie were taken higher up." He faced Vince again. "On Mt. Ayasha."

Vince cast his glance around the bar.

People were talking, laughing. Nobody was paying them any attention.

"What else?" Vince asked.

"She wanted to know if you were searching the mountain, and I told her I didn't think so. She seemed convinced Ella was on Ayasha."

"She tell you about a cave?"

"She said she and Hallie were kept there for days."

"She tell you how Hallie died?"

"Conversation didn't go that direction."

"Interesting."

Vince ate another potato skin, taking his time with it.

"What?" James asked.

"I've lived on Ayasha all my life. So have you. You ever seen any caves up there?"

"No, but—"

"There are no caves. There's no place like what she described."

"You're sure? So sure, so... arrogant... that you know every nook and cranny of that mountain that you won't even look?"

Vince's glare had James leaning back. "I have looked." His voice was low, almost menacing. He turned forward again, but not before James caught the shift in his expression, from anger to... something else. "I never wanted to get your hopes up. And I never wanted you up there looking. If there was a murderer on that mountain... The last thing your family needed was to bury another kid." Vince ate the last potato skin, then pushed the plate away. "So, after the chief called off the search, I kept at it. I bought rock climbing gear. Bought a satellite phone so I'd be able to go for long stretches and not be out of touch. I've been looking ever since that first call. Ten years, I've searched that mountain. There. Are. No. Caves."

"Why would she say that then?"

"Maybe she was on a different mountain. Maybe she was confused. Maybe she made the whole thing up."

"Why would she do that?"

"There's only one way to get the answers you want. You gotta tell her to come in. Tell her to come in, and we'll listen to everything she says. Maybe, if we could question her, get more information, maybe we could figure out where she really went that night. Maybe we could find Ella."

"Is that what you think will happen? She'll lead you to the kidnapper?"

"It's the only option."

"You still think she *is* the kidnapper."

Vince said nothing, which told him everything he needed to know.

Cassidy was their only suspect. Vince didn't want to say that to

James—nobody did. Because they pitied him or distrusted him or both.

As long as Vince and the rest of the police department were focused on Cassidy, the real kidnapper, the real killer, could operate freely.

James slipped his billfold from his back pocket, dropped a twenty and a five on the bar, and stood. "Cassidy didn't do it."

Vince watched him in the mirror. "What if you're wrong?"

"What if you are?"

"Tell me where she is, James."

"I have no idea." At least that was true. He headed for the door.

James managed to make it all the way to his car without meeting anybody's eyes. Maybe it wasn't a feat, though. Maybe they were avoiding his gaze as much as he was theirs. This town that stuck together, that hated outsiders. This town that never gave Cassidy a chance.

He drove the narrow back roads toward Lake Ayasha and home, wrestling with his choices. When he was surrounded by people who accused her, James was sure she was innocent. But looking into her eyes, he questioned it. Questioned her.

The people of this town, even the police, were all so certain. If it wasn't her, their certainty would keep them from looking for the real killer. Their certainty was jading them.

If James turned her in, they'd treat her like a suspect, question her, try to get the truth out of her. Would she be able to convince them she was innocent soon enough to get them to look where she claimed the kidnapper had taken her and Hallie before?

What if she couldn't? What would become of Ella? What would become of Reid?

He'd watched his mother wither after Hallie's death. Dad had kept their family together, kept Mom alive, by the strength of his will and his faith. Maybe he could have kept it up longer, but, thanks to the cancer, they'd never know.

After Dad died, Mom had been inconsolable. She faded away long before the heart attack claimed her.

James wouldn't let Reid suffer the same fate. He couldn't.

So what were his choices? He already knew he wasn't going to turn Cassidy in, but he could let her search alone.

Except that somebody'd been following her. Somebody who hadn't turned her in. Had it been random, some creepy guy who'd seen a pretty girl?

Or had her pursuer recognized her? Had it been the killer?

James couldn't let her go back on the mountain alone.

If he turned her in, at least she'd be safe.

James hadn't prayed a lot in recent years. Hadn't had much reason to. Everything he'd wanted had been denied him. He no longer cared about anything enough to pray about it.

But he needed wisdom. Direction.

*What should I do?*

*Can I trust her, Lord?*

The answer felt obvious. He would try to figure out where those caves were, then go with Cassidy and learn what he could. If he decided she wasn't telling the truth, he could always turn her in later. And maybe, maybe they'd be able to find the place she was looking for.

Maybe he'd learn the truth about his sister's death. Maybe, finally, he could have some peace.

But this wasn't about him or his losses. It wasn't about Cassidy and her story. This was about Ella.

If James could rescue his best friend's daughter, if he could protect Reid from the pain his parents had endured, it would be worth it.

# CHAPTER SIX

The man was gone. He'd come late the night before, long after the world beyond the cave walls had grown dark. Ella had been listening to the night sounds, which seemed louder and scarier when she was alone with the crickets. She didn't want the man to be there, but she didn't like being alone, either. Especially at night. When he'd come in, she pretended to be asleep, and he curled up against her, slinging his arm over her, and released a sigh as if the world were a happy place.

She didn't remember anything after that.

Ella turned over and peeked at the entrance. It was light outside. Today would be the day. Today, she'd get to go home. *Please, God.*

She didn't see the man, but he probably went to pee.

She scrambled to her bucket and did the same, hurrying and hoping he wouldn't come in. She wanted to be quiet, but the chain connected to the strap around her ankle clattered when she moved. Had he heard her?

When she finished, she dug in the cooler and took out a juice box. It took her two tries to get the skinny straw through the little hole, but she finally did it and sucked some of the strawberry drink.

A shadow fell over her. She didn't have to look to know he'd stepped into the entrance. "You're thirsty this morning, little sister."

"I am not your sister."

He ignored her. "Remember when Mommy used to make us Kool-Aid? Your favorite was red, but I liked orange better. Since Mommy loved you best, we always had red."

Ella didn't know what he was talking about. Her mommy hadn't ever made her Kool-Aid. She lived in a big house in California and starred in movies. When Ella went to visit, the only thing she'd had to drink besides water and juice was yucky stuff called Lacroix, which was bubbly like soda but tasted icky.

"In the summertime," the man continued, "we would put the Kool-Aid in ice trays and make popsicles. We'll do that again when we have a freezer, okay?"

That did sound sort of good, except not with him.

He ruffled her hair, and she scrunched up her shoulders, too afraid to pull away.

She pretended he wasn't there. Maybe if she ignored him, he'd go away. Like Clara at school, who used to stick out her tongue at Ella and call her "Ugly Ella," even though Ella wasn't ugly. She was pretty—everybody said so. Grammy and Gramps and Nana and Papa all thought so. Uncle James said she was so pretty she was gonna be a heartbreaker someday, whatever that meant. And Daddy said she was the prettiest girl in the whole school and that stupid Clara was only jealous. Except Daddy didn't say stupid. And Daddy said that, if Ella ignored Clara, she'd stop being a meanie, and it had worked. Clara left her alone. So maybe if Ella ignored the man, he'd go away too. Or take her to Daddy.

He took a drink from the cooler—a little bottle of orange juice. "I'm glad you slept well. Sleeping beside you again... It reminds me of when we used to hide from Mommy when she got angry. You remember?" He didn't wait for her answer, which was good, 'cause she didn't know what to say. "You were so little then. I'd read you stories. When Mommy would come to the door, we'd both pretend to sleep."

Daddy read her stories. This man had never read her stories before, and she didn't want him to now.

*I wanna go home.*

He tapped her nose. "You used to be such a chatterbox. That guy ruined you, but I'll find the real Maryann in there again. We'll get you back to normal."

*My name is Ella.*

"Look at me."

She gave him her angriest look, even though she probably shouldn't have. "I'm not your sister, and my name isn't Maryann. My name is Ella, and I am precious." She slapped her hand over her mouth. What was wrong with her? But the words were in her mouth, and they had to come out, because this man, this terrible man, had stolen her away. "I want my daddy!" Her scream bounced off the walls of the cave and hurt her head.

She dropped the juice box and covered her ears and closed her eyes. *Please, God. I wanna go home. I want my daddy. Please, please.*

The man lifted her and set her on his lap like Daddy did when she scraped her knee or was sad because stupid Clara was mean to her. But this wasn't her daddy, and she didn't want him. He wrapped his arms around her and hugged her too tight. She squirmed, but he only hugged harder. "I know you're scared, Maryann. And I know you miss the man you thought was your daddy. But he isn't your daddy, and he doesn't want you anymore. He never loved you. You belong with me. I'm your real family."

"Liar, liar, liar, liar, liar." She mumbled the words, afraid for the man to hear. But they felt squishy in her mouth, like cooked zucchini that she had to spit out or she'd get sick. So she said it again, just in case. "Liar."

He pinched her shoulders in his giant hands and pushed her back so he could look in her face. He got real close to her until their noses were almost touching. Almost close enough to kiss. Even though he had that mask on, which covered everything but his pale lips and his ugly brown eyes, she was scared he was gonna try it.

She pressed her mouth closed real tight and shut her eyes and scrunched up her face and prayed he wouldn't.

"I know you're scared. I know this isn't the most comfortable place to be. But things are going to get better for you and me. We're going to live where it's warm and there are palm trees and fresh coconuts, just like I always promised. You love coconut."

She hated coconut.

"We're gonna walk to the beach every single day, and I'll teach you how to swim."

She already knew how to swim. Daddy had taught her. Because he loved her and wanted her to be safe in the water. Because she was more precious than all the jewels in the whole wide world.

"The waves will be big and warm," the man said, "and we'll body surf and build sand castles, just like we read about. It's going to be perfect. And I'm going to take care of you forever and ever. I promise."

He pulled her close again and hugged her. "You'll see, little sis. We're gonna be happy together."

# CHAPTER SEVEN

The keyless entry was Cassidy's favorite amenity in the rented cabin because it meant she hadn't had to see anybody to gain access, cutting down on the chance someone would recognize her. There was no air conditioning, but fortunately it cooled off enough at night that the breeze through the open windows had chased away the heat of the day.

When she woke Tuesday morning, the cabin was downright chilly. After prayer and Bible study and breakfast, she prepared not for a day of mountain climbing but for a day at the lake. She didn't even own a bathing suit and wouldn't have brought one on this trip even if she did. She made do with a halter top, shorts, and flip flops and stuffed her backpack with sunscreen, water bottles, and one of the towels from the rental cabin. She added a sandwich and tossed in the novel she'd bought at the airport bookstore.

She hated to lose a day on the mountain, but she'd given up believing she could find anything on her own. She needed help, and James would give it. She had to believe that.

If events unfolded like they had with the last missing girl, Cassidy should have time. Addison, the girl who'd been snatched a month before, had been alive until just a few hours before her body was found, ten days after she'd gone missing. Ten horrible days, no doubt, but she'd been alive.

Ella had only been gone four.

Cassidy didn't want to think about what the killer was doing to the girl, though she could imagine. A shudder rippled through her. She knew how he'd treated her. The thought had her wanting to head up the mountain immediately.

If only James would hurry up and decide to join her.

It was a thirty-minute drive to Coventry. Cassidy hadn't wanted to stay any closer to the small town she'd once called home. She needed a sanctuary, and the cabin far from town, a place to be herself after a long day of hiking and praying nobody would recognize her, was just the thing.

She parked in the same lot where she had the day before. It was later than it had been the other days she'd come, and cars crowded the lot. Nobody would pay attention to her rented Honda with the local plates.

Sunglasses on, she walked toward the trailhead but veered off at the campground and headed to the beach, where she laid out her towel and made herself comfortable.

If she blended in, if she chatted with other campers and looked like she belonged, nobody would question her being there.

Cassidy had always wondered where their kidnapper had come from. Both the trails and the campground were closed in the winter, the parking lot blocked off.

The two-lane road didn't have much of a shoulder, and a car parked along it would have drawn attention. The campground offered plenty of places to park, but the owners would surely have noticed a strange car in the lot. Not many people lived within walking distance of the trails besides the Sullivan family and the Cages.

She'd never thought about what Wilson and Eugene did all winter long and hadn't considered them as suspects until James had mentioned them the night before. Now, the idea had taken root and blossomed. They both had access to Mt. Ayasha, and what else did they have to do in the wintertime besides maintain the campground and hike the trails?

And kidnap children.

A great theory, except it wasn't winter now. Based on the number of people on the beach, the many tents and campers among the trees in both directions, the campground was busy, which meant Wilson would be, too. And, presumably, Eugene.

How much time would it take to snatch a kid and take her up to his lair?

Lair. Like she was in a graphic novel featuring superheroes and villains. She was no superhero, and this villain had no extraordinary powers. He was just a scared, sick man. At least that had been her impression. Which made her wonder... could it be Eugene? Learning disabled didn't mean evil. She'd met plenty of LD kids in her work with troubled girls, not as severely disabled as Eugene but with reading or other cognitive disabilities. They knew right from wrong. They didn't always choose right, but then, who did?

It wasn't fair to suspect Eugene just because he was different.

And nobody knew as well as Cassidy how unfair it was to be suspected of evil because of things out of your control.

But learning disabled also didn't mean *not* evil. The things weren't mutually exclusive. The question was, could he have pulled it off? Or would he have had help?

Wilson could be the kidnapper. Or he could have protected his son when he'd found out what happened.

Cassidy could be way off but, since she'd promised James she wouldn't go back to the trails today, she had nothing else to do but hang around, see if she could get a glimpse of the father-son duo, try to hear them say something. Maybe their voices would trigger a memory. If not, she'd know that neither of them had been her captor. Either way, she'd learn something.

If only the man hadn't worn a mask. All she'd seen were his

eyes, an ordinary brown. But his voice... that she'd recognize. She had no doubt.

At least it would be better than sitting in that dingy cabin all day long. She had to act. She couldn't do nothing knowing Ella was out there. She'd never met the child, of course, but she felt a kinship with the pretty brown-eyed girl whose face was plastered on every TV screen in the country. She could only imagine what Ella was going through. James was right—they needed more information. There was little she could do to gather it, but she could do this.

A family plopped down a few yards from her on the crowded beach. Mother, father, and three little boys. While the parents got their blanket and towels settled, the two older boys, maybe five and seven, took off for the water. The youngest wore a blue swim diaper and toddled after them.

The father chased the littlest boy down and swung him over his head. "Let's get your floatie on, buddy."

The kid whined while the father wrangled him into a vest and fastened it on. Then, the kid toddled to the shore and plopped down on the sand.

The mother finished setting up their little spot and glanced Cassidy's way.

"Good-looking boys you have there."

The woman shaded her eyes with her hand and watched her sons. "They're a handful."

"I bet."

The woman took in Cassidy's towel and backpack. "You camping alone?"

"I wasn't up for another day of hiking." There. That was true, even if she'd implied things that weren't.

"Don't like hiking?"

"It's fine, but I don't go on vacation so I can tromp through the woods every day." Also true. Not that this was a vacation.

"I understand that." The woman settled in beside her husband.

48

"Family vacations aren't so much vacation as business trips, since I'm bringing work with me."

"I can only imagine." Cassidy had never been on a family vacation. Not with her mother and any of the guys who used to hang around. Not with any of the foster families that'd taken her in.

She faced forward and laid her head back, angling her cap and shielding her face. The last thing she needed was more freckles. She wished she'd brought a chair. It was hard to observe facing the sky.

After thirty minutes, she stood, adjusted her sunglasses, and packed her things.

"Giving up so soon?" the woman asked.

"My skin can't handle much direct sunlight. It's the vampire in me." There was a picnic table beneath the trees near the volleyball court. "I think I'll go sit in the shade."

Cassidy settled at the picnic table and took out her novel, keeping her eyes on the surroundings. Across the dirt road from the restroom, the office was a one-story wood-sided building. It sat in the center of the campground, and dirt roads led in from both directions by the lake. She and James had snuck onto the property enough that she knew that those narrow roads branched off, so some campers were nearer the lake and some higher on the hillside.

Where were Wilson and Eugene Cage? Wilson was probably in the office. Eugene? He had to be around here somewhere.

She ate her sandwich and sipped her water, refilling it once at the fountain between the restrooms.

One thing she'd learned in her decade as a fugitive was how to look like she belonged, like she had nothing to hide. She donned that look now, resting one foot on the bench beside her and propping her elbow on the table, her chin in her hand. She smiled at passersby, always making eye contact. She had little to fear here at the campground, anyway. The lifeguard on the lake was too young to remember her from ten years past, and she'd seen no other employees. The campers were all tourists and likely not paying that much attention to local news.

Wilson and Eugene... She'd never met either of them. Officially. Of course, if one of them had kidnapped her and Hallie, then he might just recognize her. And be a threat.

Which was why, behind the casual smile and novel lifted as though she were reading, she kept her gaze scanning the campground. Where were they? Would they recognize her? And if so, what would they do?

# CHAPTER EIGHT

James pushed into The Patriot just after noon, pleased to see all the tables were full. Between the lunch crowd from HCI and all the tourists in town, the restaurant stayed busy most of the time. He waved to the hostess and the server and headed for the coffee bar, stopping to wait for the chair he wanted.

Tip cashed out the customer, and she left with a bag full of take-out.

James slipped onto the vacated stool.

"In town two days in a row." Tip grabbed a plastic tumbler and filled it with iced tea. "That's gotta be a record."

James sipped the brew. "Went by to see Reid."

"How's he holding up?"

"About as you'd expect." Which was to say, not well.

Reid worked at HCI corporate, which was just a block behind Main Street, but he hadn't returned to work since Ella's disappearance.

James had stopped by the little house a few blocks from here that Reid and Denise had bought right after the wedding. Though Reid could afford better now, he'd kept the place. Easy to keep up, he always said, and close to work and the daycare where he left Ella a few days a week.

Both Reid's parents and Denise's had been at the house that morning, along with a police officer. With no new information, the mood had been somber, to say the least. After James had greeted and hugged the family, he'd found a spot on the couch, and they'd all sat, mostly in silence, for a good half hour.

Based on the fact that nobody had reamed him out when he walked in, Vince hadn't told Reid that James had spoken with Cassidy. He'd need to thank his friend for that mercy.

The only topic of conversation had been Denise.

It seemed Denise had been high on the list of suspects in Ella's kidnapping. Nobody had more motive to take Ella than her mother, who'd lost custody, and what better time to snatch her than right after another kid went missing?

The news of the day was not only that Denise couldn't have done it, as she was in Oklahoma, of all places, shooting a movie, but that she didn't plan to return to Coventry anytime soon.

"It's not like she could help." Denise's mother, Mrs. Masterson, had always been her daughter's biggest—perhaps only—defender in Coventry.

James had expected Reid or one of his parents to reply to that, but it was Mr. Masterson who snapped at his wife, "What kind of mother could stay away? What kind of mother could playact for a camera while her daughter is in the hands of a monster?"

That was when Reid pushed up from his chair and escaped out the back door.

James had followed, but he hadn't had any words of wisdom. Nothing would comfort Reid until Ella was safely in his arms.

He clasped his friend's shoulder and squeezed.

"I can't believe she's not coming home."

Denise, of course.

Denise, who'd claimed to love Reid. Who'd agreed to marry him when she discovered she was pregnant. Who'd fallen into a deep depression after Ella's birth and then, when her child was barely six months old, had disappeared.

Reid hadn't heard from her in months, and only then when he'd been served divorce papers.

They later learned she'd gone to Hollywood to fulfill her life-long dream to be an actress. They'd all scoffed at her choice, right up until she landed a supporting role on a Netflix Original series a couple of years prior.

Now, James had no idea what to say.

When Reid dropped his head into his hands, James slipped an arm around his shoulders and prayed, even though he had no reason to believe it would help. The prayer was not for Denise, who'd made her choices, but for Ella. Only God could bring the child home.

IN THE RESTAURANT that had been his father's and now belonged to him, James turned to the old man on the stool beside him. "How you doing today?"

Bart Bradley studied him through steel gray eyes. "Tolerating the tourists." He gazed around the full restaurant. "They're good for you, though."

"Good for the town, most of the time."

Bart grumbled something about litter and noise, but James wouldn't rise to the bait. He wasn't here to talk about Coventry's booming tourism.

"I heard a rumor about your mountain recently." The man's family had lived on the mountain as far back as anyone could remember.

Bart's raised eyebrow was the only indication he'd heard.

"Someone told me there's a cave up there. You ever seen anyplace like that?"

"There are no caves on Ayasha." Slowly, Bart turned to face him. "Not a single one."

Amazing how many people were so certain of something that wasn't there.

"What about rock formations that could form caves?"

Bart squinted. "There's some big rocks. I never been much of a climber, so I never scaled 'em."

James took out the trail map of Ayasha that he'd grabbed at the tourism center on his way into town that morning and opened it on the bar. "Where abouts?"

He flicked the paper. "They're not gonna be on that map. They're up high, nowhere near the trails."

James folded the map and put it away, then pulled out his phone and, after opening to a satellite view of the mountain, turned it to face Bart. "Can you point them out here?"

"What am I, a cartographer?" But he slipped on a pair of reading glasses and peered at the screen. A moment passed before he pointed to a spot at the southeast slope of the mountain. "Prob'ly over near here."

James narrowed the view of the mountain and turned it to face the old man again. He shrugged. "Can't say for sure."

"How would you reach them?"

"I stumbled on 'em hiking a few years back, but I only saw 'em from below. I wasn't about to break my neck climbing."

"If I were to start at your house—"

"You'd be wasting a lot of time. I live on the north side. And I don't like trespassers."

Never mind that James had known Bart Bradley all his life.

"There's an old logging road"—James adjusted the map—"here. Would that be a good place to start?"

Bart shrugged. "Why you want to find it?"

"Curiosity, I guess."

Again, the gray eyes found his. "This have something to do with your friend's missing kid?"

James lowered his voice. "Just a hunch."

"Seems the cops had the same 'hunch' back when your sister was taken."

Just like that. Unlike the rest of the residents in Coventry, Bart didn't waste any time worrying about people's feelings. "Vince Pollack asked me about them back then. Told him the same thing I'm telling you. I figure it'll do you about as much good."

If Vince had already asked, and already searched, then James was likely wasting his time. But he had to try to help find Ella. And Cassidy might see something that would lead them in the right direction.

Assuming she was recalling the incident correctly. And assuming she wasn't making up the whole story.

~

AN HOUR OR SO LATER, James followed Detective Cote into an interview room at the rear of the small police department and took a seat at a wide table. Cote settled his substantial girth across from him. "I got plenty to do, but since your sister was the first victim, I'm making time for you."

"There's the silver lining."

Cote almost smiled at that. "What do you need?"

The detective's question told James that Vince hadn't reported that Cassidy had contacted him. Otherwise, Cote wouldn't need an excuse to talk to him. Probably, James would have been *invited* to the police station earlier than this.

James had come prepared for this meeting with a copy of the local newspaper, which he set on the desk, facing Cote, where Cassidy's senior picture was displayed alongside a photo of Ella that James knew had been taken right before her fifth birthday, and a photo of Addison, the victim from a month prior. The article, heavily quoted from the man sitting across from him, named Cassidy as the prime suspect.

Cote barely glanced at the article. "What about it?"

"I'm not saying you're wrong," James said. "Just that I'd like to know why you're so sure Cassidy is guilty."

"You read the article?"

He had but, though Cote hadn't been shy about naming the suspect, he hadn't given any evidence linking the crimes. Even though Vince was taking the lead in the current investigations, Cote had been the lead detective in Hallie's disappearance. James needed to confirm what Cassidy had told him—that she'd called the police years before and told them what happened. Cote would be more likely to tell him what he needed to know. In many ways, Vince saw James as a little brother, a victim. Someone who needed to be protected. Cote wouldn't waste a second worrying about James's feelings.

"It's a little thin on details," James said.

"It's not a courtroom, it's media. We have to be careful what we share."

"I've lived through this. I know the drill."

Cote shifted, and the chair beneath him squeaked. "You know how hard it is, this balance between what we share and what we hold close. And now your best friend's going through it. This can't be easy for you."

"Or you." Detective Cote was Reid's uncle, Ella's great-uncle. This kidnapping had hit a little close to home for the Cote family.

"I'm not with the media," James said.

Cote's expression didn't shift. He said nothing.

"I have a few questions."

"I'll answer if I can."

"I worried, back then, that Cassidy had been killed too. But Vince assured me that you guys knew she was alive. I always wondered how you could be so sure."

His eyebrows lifted. "You don't know? We told your parents."

Because of James's relationship with—and loyalty to—Cassidy, the conversations with his parents about what happened had been awkward... tender. Like open wounds nobody wanted to press too hard, wounds one jab away from bleeding. In the interest of protecting their relationships, of protecting his feelings, he supposed, his parents hadn't shared much.

When he didn't respond, Cote said, "She called us on the day

Hallie's body turned up, told us a story about having been kidnapped and held on the mountain for two nights against her will."

Cassidy had told James the truth. About the call, anyway. "Did you follow-up on that?"

"Gee, should we have?" The sarcastic remark sounded off coming from the sixty-something professional.

"Everybody was so sure she was guilty, I just wondered if her claims were dismissed out of hand."

He leaned across the desk. "We don't dismiss anything out of hand. We checked the mountain, asked around. Nobody's ever heard of any rock formations on the mountain a person could climb into. Bart Bradley told us about some big boulders up there, and I had someone check 'em out. They found nothing like the place where Cassidy claimed she'd been kept, and no evidence anybody had been there. Not only that, but it was the dead of winter, and she claimed to have spent that first night out in the open. It was in the thirties that night. Little chilly for a campout."

"Wasn't like they went up for fun."

"Kid your sister's age probably wouldn't have survived, especially considering she'd been sick."

She'd had the flu, had been confined to the house for a week. Hallie was never one to stay inside for long, much less a week, despite how sick she felt. It was probably the reason she and Cassidy had been out that afternoon. Hallie had probably begged Cassidy to take her onto the trails.

"Hallie was better by then. And she was tough, tougher than you'd think."

"Still... little as she was, and your mom said she hadn't been eating. How would she have survived the elements?"

Cassidy would have taken care of her.

"According to your girlfriend, they were on the trails on Ayasha when they just happened upon a man, who just happened to be a kidnapper. But the parking lot was blocked off. Nobody but

57

Wilson and Eugene Cage had been at the campground, and no strange cars were found anywhere at the base of the mountain."

He started to ask about the Cages, but Cote lifted a hand, silencing him. "We looked into Wilson and Eugene. Wasn't them."

"No chance you're wrong."

"I've been doing this a long time. Wilson told us he saw Cassidy and Hallie on the trail, but he and Eugene had an alibi for that night."

"You and Wilson's family go way back, don't you?"

"What are you getting at?" Cote asked.

"Getting at the idea that it's easier to blame the outsider than—"

"A little girl was dead, Sullivan. You think I didn't care about who did it? You think I was more concerned about protecting an old friend?"

"I think it's hard to believe ill of somebody you think you know."

The detective's steely gaze bore into him. "You'd know that better than anybody."

Fair point. "I'm just trying to figure out why you're so sure Cassidy is guilty."

"Aside from the fact that Hallie was with her when they disappeared? That your sister's body was found wrapped in Cassidy's sweatshirt?"

James swallowed. "Yeah. Besides that."

Cote sat back, took a breath. "Lotsa reasons. Cassidy claimed they'd been taken to rock formations way up high on the mountain. Even though she swore she wasn't sure where it was, she claimed she knew it was high because the air was thin." His smirk told James what he thought of that. "But when your sister's body was found, the coroner said she'd only been dead a couple of hours, and based on the schedule of the family who lived in the house, the body would have to have been left more than an hour before they found her. So, if the kidnapper killed Hallie, and if Cassidy escaped the kidnapper with your sister's body, and if they'd been as high on the mountain as she said, how did only an hour pass from when she escaped to when she got all the way to the lake?"

"Did she explain—?"

"Never stayed on the phone long enough to explain squat. But lemme ask you this. Let's say the kidnapper did kill Hallie, and Cassidy escaped. Why take your sister's body? If she's running for her life, wouldn't she leave her? Wouldn't she feel like she had to save herself?"

He could imagine Cassidy wanting to return Hallie to their family. But would she have risked her life for it? Or would fear and survival instinct have kicked in?

"Doesn't add up," Cote said. "Plus, we got a report of a teenager and a little girl matching their descriptions. Came from the rest stop just south of Concord on I-93 the day before their bodies were found. The woman said she thought the teen called the little kid Hannah. Hannah, Hallie. Pretty close, don't you think?"

Had Cassidy kidnapped Hallie and run off with her?

No. He didn't believe it.

Couldn't believe it. "Hallie's body was found here. If Cassidy had been nearly to Manchester, why bring her back?"

"Who knows? Your sister died. Maybe an accident, maybe on purpose. Cassidy came back to Coventry, left the body, then called with her crazy story hoping to throw us off her scent."

"So, do you think...?" James rubbed his temples, tried to put it together. "Do you think Cassidy was trying to kidnap Hallie and then accidentally killed her, or—"

"I always thought that," Cote said. "Still manslaughter, but I never thought she wanted your sister dead. But now, with these recent kidnappings—"

"You're sure they're related? It's not some copycat?"

"The details are too similar," Cote said. "Details nobody outside this department knows."

Cote spoke as if leaks never came from the police department, but that couldn't be true. These were just people, after all, and people talked.

Still, he asked, "Details like?"

"Like details I'm not sharing."

"Then tell me the stuff that's public knowledge. What makes the crimes similar?"

Cote lifted a sausage-shaped finger. "All three victims are girls around the same age." He ticked off each point with another finger. "All three from good, strong families. All three healthy and well cared for." The hand fell. "First two found on back porches near the lake. And there are a couple of other details that we're not disclosing."

James felt sick to his stomach. But Cassidy claimed to be able to prove she hadn't taken Addison and Ella. If that was the case, then maybe it wasn't a copycat. Maybe the person who'd taken the two girls this year had also taken Hallie. Maybe she was telling the truth. So... "It still doesn't make sense. If she'd wanted to kill Hallie, then she wouldn't have been halfway to Manchester. She'd have done it here. And if she was a kidnapper back then, why now kidnap and murder?"

"All questions we'll ask her when we find her."

"But what do you think?"

Cote tapped fat fingers on the table. "Maybe Hallie's death was an accident." He didn't seem convinced. "Or maybe she lost her temper and beat your sister, and when she did, she got a taste for violence."

"No. No." He closed his eyes against the image. "You didn't know her."

"Seems to me you didn't either. And her mother—"

"You can't hold her responsible for her mother's crimes."

Cote shrugged his rounded shoulders. "Were they her mother's crimes? Linda Leblanc always claimed she hadn't hurt her daughter. Everybody thought Cassidy was one of her mother's victims, that her mom killed her little sister. But maybe Cassidy's guilty of her own sister's murder, too. Maybe her mother was trying to protect her."

James had never considered that possibility.

"Biggest reason we think it's her, though?" Cote rested his forearms on the table between them and leaned forward. "She ran. Innocent people don't run."

"Maybe when they don't think anybody will believe them, they do."

"If what she said is true, then by running she's allowed her kidnapper to snatch two more little girls, one of them my niece." For the first time, emotion clouded his words. "My brother's granddaughter is missing, and your ex-girlfriend's got her. So if you have any idea where she is, you'd better start talking or you're as guilty as she is."

## CHAPTER NINE

Two hours passed while Cassidy pretended to read. Some cars drove by, and many stopped at the office building.

Finally, Cassidy saw a man who looked familiar come from the road behind her. He looked to be in his mid-thirties, so too young to be Wilson. He walked around the far side of the building that housed the restrooms and disappeared from view. A moment later, he stepped out from the other side of the building carrying rolls of toilet paper. He entered the men's restroom, emerged seconds later with fewer rolls and, after announcing his presence, went into the women's room.

This had to be Eugene.

When he exited—free of toilet paper—he paused and gazed across the grounds. She lifted her novel when his gaze came her way, then lowered it a moment later to watch him.

He was about six feet and lanky. A beard and mustache covered much of his face. She recognized him not so much by his looks but by the guarded way he carried himself—hunched, eyes darting about as if waiting for an attack. He'd been picked on enough in school that she supposed he'd earned that defensive posture. He wore a red baseball cap emblazoned with the name of the campground, a light green T-shirt, and dark green shorts that went halfway to his knees. Looked like uniform pants, like those that might be worn by a park ranger or a Boy Scout.

He emptied trash cans in the dumpster at the perimeter of the common area and returned them to the restrooms. Then he walked up one of the narrow dirt roads toward the campsites.

Cassidy snatched her things and followed. If she could just hear his voice... And then she'd have to go into the office building to hear Wilson's. If she could get up the nerve.

Tents and cars dotted the landscape, flashes of bright colors amid the greens and browns of the forest. She walked among them, picking up snatches of conversations, the low hum of voices that sounded like they were coming from TVs. People must be watching on tablets or phones. Who went camping to watch a screen? Wasn't the point to get away from that stuff?

Music came from one tent, snoring from another. Little kids chased each other. One boy was jumping for the lowest branch of a pine but couldn't quite reach it.

Ahead of her, Eugene hurried up the road, despite an incline that had her panting. He didn't speak to anyone on the walk. When someone called out a hello, he raised a hand in greeting but didn't say anything. Not very helpful.

She tried to act like she belonged, though the deeper they went, the sparser the tents became. When Eugene passed a small wooden sign nailed to a tree that read *No Campers Beyond This Point,* she stepped into the forest and wandered toward the lake, though she couldn't see it from there. When she was far enough away that one would have to be looking for her to see her, she turned to study the small building at the end of the road.

It was smaller than a single-car garage. There was a window beside the door on the front. On the side beneath an attached over-hang, a green cart, like a golf cart, was parked.

Eugene went inside.

The forest floor was clear here, and she had no trouble giving the shack a wide berth as she rounded it. When she'd gone to the far side and faced back the way she'd come, she realized that the road had carried them higher than she'd originally thought. Through the pines, she could see the tops of tents, the restrooms, the volleyball court, and the beach far below.

Her focus shifted back to the shack. There were no windows on the rear side, but a door led to three steps that, were Eugene to come out, would lead him straight to her. But why would he come out the back? There was nothing here but forest.

And nobody for him to talk to. How was she supposed to hear his voice if he never talked to anybody?

Only the occasional shout from the campground reached her. Otherwise, just the sounds of the forest kept her company.

Now what?

She turned and climbed higher on the hillside. If she walked a mere fifty or seventy-five yards toward the highway, she'd intercept the trail. Perhaps this was how Eugene or Wilson had gotten to her and Hallie that winter day. Perhaps he'd been out for a leisurely walk and happened upon them. In fact, if the trails were as close as Cassidy believed, was it possible he'd heard Hallie's laughter? The girl had always been exuberant, but especially that day. After an illness had kept her homebound for a week, she was feeling better and eager to go outside. And, thanks to the warm weather—mid-forties, a scorcher for January in the mountains—she'd insisted they play outside.

Cassidy stilled and listened but could hear nothing from above, very little from below. The low hum of people and engines, cars and motorboats, though hardly noticeable, would drown out all but the loudest shouts. In the wintertime, when nobody was about... It's possible one of the Cages had heard Hallie's laughter or Cassidy's calls for the girl to slow down, wait up.

She should never have let Hallie out of her sight. If only she'd been smarter, made better choices.

After fighting the regret and self-recrimination for a decade, Cassidy'd learned how to shake it off, and she did so now.

It was possible Wilson or Eugene had heard the laughter, wondered who was up there in the middle of winter, and gone to investigate. He'd likely not had evil plans when he'd set out, only curiosity and boredom. She knew the kidnapper hadn't planned anything because he hadn't been prepared. Armed, yes, but it was likely he always carried the gun and the knife. He'd had no water, no food, no blankets.

So, he'd happened upon them, made the snap decision to kidnap them. And then he'd taken them to his mountain hideaway rather than back here. Why?

Because, whichever one did it, he didn't want the other to know. It made sense.

A voice jarred her from the memories, and she spun toward the shack, fully expecting to see Eugene standing there, watching her.

He wasn't, but it had to have been his voice. She hurried back to the shack to better hear.

"They were clean enough," Eugene said. At least she assumed it was Eugene. Surely there weren't two men in that small space.

A pause, and then the same voice said, "Someone musta... musta messed it up." Another pause, then, "Yeah, okay."

Then, nothing.

Did the voice sound familiar? She closed her eyes, tried to pull up memories she'd spent a decade trying to forget.

She wished he'd say something else. When he didn't after a few minutes, she gave up. This wasn't the guy. The kidnapper had been scared and jumpy, but not like Eugene. She didn't think Eugene was the man she was looking for.

There was nothing else to learn here, and she needed to hear Wilson's voice next.

She rounded the cabin, figuring she could jog back to the first tent in two or three minutes. Faster than the route she'd taken here, via the forest.

She was walking by the overhang and cart when the shack door opened.

She froze, backed into the carport, and prayed Eugene would head down the hill.

But he turned her direction.

She searched for a way to escape between the cart and the shack, but there was no room. She'd have to go over it.

"Hey!"

She spun and found Eugene behind her, eyes wide, mouth slack. He stepped closer, stopped a few feet away. "Yur not s'posed to be here. No campers past the sign."

"Oh. Was there a sign? I was looking for the bathroom."

"Bathrooms're back that way." He gestured with his head but didn't take his eyes off her. "Don't nobody come up here looking for bathrooms."

Though her heart pounded, she worked to keep her voice level, lighthearted. "To be honest, I was just exploring. Is there a way to get to the trail from here?"

"Trailhead's back that way too. There's signs on the trees. You gotta look fer the signs."

"You're right. I'm sorry to bother you."

He took a step closer. "You're pretty."

She leaned away. "Could you point me in the right direction?"

She hoped he'd back up and point to the sign on the road, but he only waved with his hand, never taking his gaze from hers. "Down the hill, you'll see 'em."

"I guess I'd better go then."

"I have some Pepsi inside. You want a Pepsi?"

She turned just enough for him to see her backpack. "I have a drink. Thanks, anyway. I probably better get going. My brother will be looking for me."

Eugene's eyes narrowed. "You got a brother? Where is he?"

"Back at our campsite."

"Which one's yours?"

Which one? Had they been numbered? Lettered? "I forget. It's not far. Near the lake."

"Don't think so. I'd 'a seen ya there. Your camp must be on the other side of the bathrooms. But then you woulda seen the bathrooms and not come all the way up here."

"Like I said, I was exploring. If you'll just let me by."

"My name's Eugene. What's yours?"

"Mary Beth." The name of one of the girls in the program where she worked.

"Those're pretty names." He stepped closer and touched her hair.

She held her breath.

A phone rang.

She lifted her foot, felt behind her for the golf cart's floorboard. She needed to put distance between them. Would anybody hear her if she screamed? Surely, surely somebody would come running. If her voice carried that far. If the people who heard it realized it was a true call for help and not a child's game.

Eugene slipped a phone from his pocket and swiped it on but didn't speak.

Through his speaker, she heard a man's voice. "Where are you? I told you to hurry."

He backed up a step.

"See you later!" She slipped past him, feeling the brush of his hand on the back of her shirt. Trying to touch her? To grab her? To strike her?

She didn't know, only knew that Eugene didn't possess the gentle soul she'd assumed of him back in high school. She jogged down the road, praying she could reach the tents before the golf cart—and Eugene—caught up with her.

# CHAPTER TEN

The little town of Coventry, in the valley between the mountains, was as picturesque as any in New England. When James was a kid, he'd thought it was the prettiest place in the world. Of course, he hadn't shared that opinion with his friends, who all complained about living so far from "the real world." Back then, the kids he'd hung out with had been enamored with TV shows that took place in New York City and Chicago and L.A. Reid had vowed at the mature age of nine that someday he was going to live in a high-rise and work in Manhattan. He was going to be a big shot.

James had never had such aspirations. His family had lived in Coventry for generations, and the town had felt as comfortable to him as his favorite pair of pajamas.

It hadn't changed much since he was a kid. Old restaurants had been replaced with newer ones—except The Patriot, a Coventry staple. There was an ice cream shop within walking distance of the park and beach on the edge of town. A Dunkin' Donuts had been built on an empty lot about a block off the main drag. Thanks to its proximity to the HCI offices, its drive-through was backed up around the corner every workday morning. A Greek restaurant had gone in when James was in high school. Their pizza was so good, he hardly complained about the business they stole from his restaurant.

James steered his car toward his house, contemplating this town, these people. They were all so convinced Cassidy was guilty, and after the conversation with Detective Cote, James understood why. They didn't know her like he did. Any doubts he'd harbored slipped away again. If Cassidy were guilty, what was she doing asking James for help? Why had she come to him?

Except, she hadn't come to him. It was possible she'd only asked for his help to throw him off after he'd discovered her, to keep him from calling the police.

No. That didn't make sense. And anyway, if that were the case, he'd know soon enough. Surely, if she were guilty, after having been discovered she'd have taken off.

Would she kill Ella first? Or take the little girl with her?

No, no. He couldn't think that way. Couldn't let himself consider the fact that running into him could have stepped up her timeline.

Crazy thoughts, crazy talk. Cassidy wasn't a killer.

If she was, he was the biggest fool in history.

On a whim, he turned into the campground driveway just a few hundred yards from his own and parked in front of the building that held the offices in front, the Cages' home in the back.

Like all the structures on the property, the log building so blended into the environment, it looked as if it had always been there. From James's viewpoint, it had.

He pushed open the door, and the bell above jingled.

Inside, the walls were the same rough timbers as outside. An old plaid couch was pushed against the wall, a banged-up coffee table in front of it littered with magazines and newspapers. A spinner stand by the door held brochures from local attractions. He scanned the few facing him—The Polar Caves, Castle in the Clouds, the Mount Washington cruise ship.

A long counter separated the guests' space from Wilson, who

sat at a rolling office chair in front of a computer. He looked up when James approached, and a kind smile split his face.

"How are you, Mr. Cage?"

"Think you're old enough to call me Wilson." He came around the counter and pumped James's hand. "Considering you're our closest neighbor, we hardly ever see you." His gaze softened to the compassionate look so many gave James, the one that grated his nerves. "How you holding up? This's gotta be hard for you, what with the girl bein' your best friend's kid."

"Harder for Reid," James said. "But yeah, it brings back memories."

Wilson wore the same army green shorts and light green T-shirt he always wore during the camping season. His red cap emblazoned with the name of the campground was perched on the counter. He motioned to the couch. "You wanna sit?"

"I'm okay. I just wanted to ask you a couple of questions." Though, now that he was face-to-face with Wilson, he wondered what he was doing there. Of course this guy hadn't hurt Hallie. Except James was sure Cassidy hadn't, either. "I was talking to Detective Cote about what happened back when my sister was kidnapped. He said you saw her and Cassidy on the trail that night."

Wilson took the tiniest step back. "Yeah. I was up at the shack and heard some noises, so I climbed up to the trail. There's a little path there. Saw your sister. She was giggling and running. Cassidy was behind her, calling to her to slow down. They both looked like they were having fun."

"See anything else?"

"Wish I had. When I was sure there was nothing to worry about, I came back here and got ready for my date that night."

Not that it was any of his business, but he asked, "With who?"

"Lady I met in Plymouth on one of those dating apps." He leaned against the counter. "That was back when I thought I might meet somebody, not be alone the rest of my life. But no woman wants to move to a dinky town and take care of an overgrown kid, which is all Eugene'll ever be. Don't get me wrong—I love that boy fiercely. But nobody knows him like I do. He's always been big and strong, and I think he frightens some folks. Not a lot of people have ever tried to get to know him, to be honest."

James felt a twinge of guilt. He'd never tried. He'd always had plenty of friends and never had any use for the slow kid next door. And Wilson was right. Eugene came off as a little scary. Long arms and legs, strong, powerful, but without the intellect to know how to control himself.

"Where was Eugene that night?"

"Here, playing video games. And I know what you're thinking, but he's as gentle as they come. Besides, police checked out both our alibis. Gal I was with vouched for me, and the people Eugene played online with vouched for him."

"I'm not accusing you. Just trying to put the pieces together. My parents kept a lot of the facts of the case from me."

Wilson clasped his upper arm. "It was hard on everyone, I'm sure. And now that it's all happening again..." He didn't finish the sentence, just squeezed James's arm and dropped his hand.

"I wondered... You and Eugene have been on this mountain a long time. You ever seen a cave or any rock formations that might create a cave?"

Wilson ran a hand over his head. "Nope. Never seen anything like that. Why?"

"Just something I heard."

"About Ella's disappearance?"

"It's not important." James glanced at the door, ready to leave.

The older man leaned back against his desk. "You let me know if there's anything I can do for you. I don't blame you for trying to fill in all the blanks."

James started to turn, then stopped. "Do you think... You saw Cassidy that night. Did anything about her stand out to you? Did she seem afraid or nervous or... anything?"

Wilson's lips turned down at the corners. "I didn't know her at all. She seemed like a normal kid to me."

"Do you think she did it?"

"I never could figure out how. I mean, she's on the mountain, playing with your sister. And then... what? She snatches her on a whim? How'd she get away? Why'd she wait, play with Hallie, and then run? Lotsa holes in the story. I figure something happened, made her snap."

Wilson made good points, points James wished he'd made to Cote earlier. He'd need to ask Cote how he explained her lack of transportation.

He thanked Wilson and stepped out of the office, surveying the campground. Looked like business was excellent. Wilson and Eugene would be busy with all these campers. Neither of them would have time to pull off two kidnappings. Probably.

But James wasn't willing to concede that they were innocent. Not if it meant conceding that Cassidy was guilty.

He caught sight of a woman running toward the common area down the middle of one of the narrow roads leading to the campsites. She wore a baseball cap and sunglasses and kept glancing behind her as if someone were chasing her. It was the way she carried herself, the shape of her, that made him think of Cassidy. But she wouldn't be here. Coming here would be insane.

Yet, the closer she got, the more she looked like the most wanted woman in New Hampshire.

The woman shifted his direction.

He jogged toward her, realizing as she closed the distance that it was, indeed, Cassidy.

When she was about fifteen feet away, she veered off toward the path that led to the parking area where she'd left her car the day before. A single word left her lips.

"Eugene."

And then she jogged away, disappearing around the side of the building.

A moment later, one of the camp carts motored down the narrow road, Eugene at the wheel, scanning the campground.

Looking for Cassidy?

James watched as Eugene parked the cart near the playground. He stepped out, still looking around. After a moment, he seemed to concede that he'd lost her—assuming he'd been following her—and entered the rear door of the restroom building.

James waited another minute to ensure Cassidy had time to get to her car, then climbed into his own. As soon as he slid inside, he dialed the number Cassidy had given him the night before.

She answered on the second ring, out of breath. "I'm safe."

"Eugene stopped at the bathrooms. What happened?"

Through the phone, he heard a car door slam, then a long exhale. "It was probably... I don't know."

"Meet me at my house."

"I don't want to get you in trouble." In the background, her car dinged, and the engine rumbled to life.

"Too late for that," he said. "See you in five." He ended the call before she could argue and headed home.

At his house, he lifted the garage door but parked behind his Jeep. He'd replaced the tires and started it that morning, thinking that, if he did go with Cassidy, he'd rather take the old off-roading vehicle than his new car.

When she pulled in a few seconds later, he directed her to drive in, then lowered the door behind her and moved his car into the empty space so nobody would think a car was parked inside.

Paranoia in action.

He opened his front door, walked through the house, and then opened the door that led to the garage.

She stepped inside. "I'm just going to have to pull it back out when I leave."

He swiveled and walked to the kitchen, where he leaned back against the counter and tried to calm his racing heart.

She followed and sat at the kitchen table.

"What were you thinking, going over there?" His voice came out too loud, but he didn't lower it. "You trying to get arrested?"

"I'm trying to figure out who took Ella. Last night, you

73

suggested it might have been one of the Cages, so I thought I'd go over there, see if either of them looked familiar. Or sounded—"

"What happened?"

As she explained, his anger only got worse. "You followed him? Are you insane?"

"I just thought, if I could overhear him talking, maybe I'd recognize his voice. I heard him on the phone."

"And?"

"It didn't ring any bells. And Eugene was too unsure. The guy who took us was afraid, but he knew what he was doing. Even though he probably hadn't planned anything, once he had us, he was confident in his course. I can't imagine Eugene being confident in anything."

"But he cornered you."

She settled back against the chair, her shoulders relaxing. "I think he didn't understand that he was scaring me. He's just socially awkward, and maybe I panicked. I ran, and then I went into the woods and walked through people's campsites, which got me a lot of looks."

"Think anybody recognized you?"

"I don't think so. But I think Eugene was looking for me. He'd drive a few seconds, then stop and look around. Then drive again. So I stayed out of sight. He'd been stopped a while when I gave up trying to hide, got back to the road, and ran."

"All those people at the campsites, you could've just yelled for help."

"And gotten all those eyes on me, maybe had the police called?"

Made sense.

He didn't know what to think. She didn't think Eugene could be the kidnapper, and he was pretty sure Wilson couldn't be, either. The man was kind and gentle. But maybe beneath that mask, he was a killer.

Or maybe Cassidy was the one wearing the mask.

All he knew was that the best way to find Ella would be to join

Cassidy in her search. He'd study her words, her actions, to figure out if she was telling the truth. It was possible, wasn't it? And maybe she could lead him to where she and Hallie had been held back then. Maybe Ella was being held there now.

If Cassidy was playing him, trying to pretend to be the hero, then she could definitely lead him to where Ella was being held.

Either way, the police could sort it out after Ella was safe again.

Between now and then, James would keep Cassidy close, and he wouldn't fall for anything. He had to let this play out. Whatever it took to save Ella.

# CHAPTER ELEVEN

Ella startled and sat up straight. The world was empty and black. Even the crickets were silent. Usually when the man left, he turned on a lantern he kept deeper in the cave. "To chase away the shadows," he said, but they really just made different shadows on the moist walls. She never liked those shadows, but they were better than the dark.

She lifted her hand in front of her face but only saw its outline against the faint light coming from outside. It was dark out there, but not as dark as inside. Like... like the crayons in her box at home. When she pressed hard, she could make the reds redder and the yellows yellower. Someone was pressing down really hard on the cave, 'cause it was blackest of all. There probably wasn't a crayon in the whole word this dark.

Where was the man? Usually, the crickets stopped singing to warn her he was coming. But maybe something else had scared them.

The wind whistled through the trees, but that wasn't what woke her. The wind didn't sound like coyotes to her anymore. More like Nana's singing when she used to tuck Ella in for a nap when Ella was a baby. She could almost hear Nana's soft voice in the wind asking God to watch over her while she slept.

Was Nana praying for her now? Was Daddy?

A low sound reached her, like her daddy's snoring, which sometimes carried through the walls of their house. Except it came faster. *Whomph whomph whomph.*

What was that?

A dog? A dog could find her and go for help. He could bark at a policeman until the policeman realized something was wrong and then follow the dog to the cave and save her from the bad man and take her home to Daddy.

The sound was getting louder, though, too loud for a normal dog. It must have been a huge dog, like Clifford in the books Daddy read to her.

*God, please send Clifford to save me. Let him find me.*

Except Clifford wasn't real.

The *whomphing* was getting louder. Closer.

Something moved in front of the cave entrance. Something... humongous. It *whomphed* at the opening, then lumbered inside.

A scream bubbled up in Ella's tummy, crawled up her throat and got stuck where her tonsils used to be. What was that? An animal. It was on four legs but too big to be a dog. Tall and wide and fat with big feet...

It turned, and she gasped.

A bear!

She scrambled as far away as the chain would let her and pressed against the wall and hid behind her hands and held her breath. Maybe it wouldn't see her. Maybe it would go away.

Maybe it was like Clara and would leave her alone if she ignored it. Even though that didn't work with the man, who always came back. But what if he didn't this time? What if the bear ate him?

What if the bear ate *her*?

The *whomphing* got closer. She could hear its heavy steps on the stone floor, hear it sniffing around.

She peeked out from between her fingers and saw its huge back outline. She couldn't see what it was doing, but she guessed it was eating her breakfast. The granola bars and Pop-Tarts and bread the man had left.

Minutes passed while she listened in silence, too scared to even breathe, while the bear gobbled it all up.

And then the box tumbled to the side. The bear scrunched the cardboard, sniffing again. It hit something metal. The bucket she used as a toilet. The smell of it released into the room, and she thought maybe the bear had knocked it over.

Maybe the stink would send the animal away.

Except it didn't, and the bear got closer, and the scream she'd been holding down pressed against her mouth. But she held it in.

The bear came close enough that its terrible breath blew against her head and fingers. It smelled like rotten vegetables and dirt and probably dead animals and her strawberry Pop-Tarts.

It growled.

The scream got out. Just a little, like a squeak, but once it started, she couldn't stop it.

She screamed and screamed and screamed.

The bear roared back, the sound echoing off the walls and mixing with her screaming and making a terrible sound.

She covered her ears and screamed again.

She was gonna be bear food.

But the bear scrambled out of the cave.

And Ella hid under her blankets and pulled them up over her head and cried.

Where was Daddy? Why didn't he come to save her?

IT FELT like forever later when the man came back. He crept into the cave, flashlight bouncing on the walls and floor. It hit the box of gobbled food and paused there.

Then, the light flashed in her eyes.

She squinted and covered her face.

"Maryann! What happened?"

Her terror returned, and she screamed as if the bear had come back, letting out all the terror she'd been holding in for hours.

The man scooped her up and held her close. And even though she hated him, and even though she knew she wasn't his sister and she wanted to go home to Daddy and away from this terrible place, she buried her face in his chest and cried. She hated him, but she was happy to see him. Happy the man hadn't been eaten by a bear, and she hadn't either.

"Can you tell me what happened?" he asked.

"It was a b-bear."

"Oh, Maryann. How scary. I'm so sorry." He sat on the floor and rocked her gently. "I'm sorry I wasn't here to protect you. You know I always try to protect you. From bears and bad guys and Mommy. You know I'll never let anything happen to you."

"I wanna go home."

"We will. Soon, I promise. We'll go to a new home where there are no bears and no caves, only beaches and waves, and I'll never leave you again. It's going to be perfect."

# CHAPTER TWELVE

C assidy had worried for hours.

This could be the end of all of it. Ten years of running could end with a single phone call from James to the Coventry PD. When he'd called that morning and said he'd pick her up for the trek up Mt. Ayasha, she'd wanted to refuse to share the address of the cabin she'd rented. But this was James. Her James. He wouldn't betray her.

He hadn't yet.

*Lord, please, please...*

Cassidy stared out the front window of the dingy cabin. Either James would show up or a whole bunch of cops would. She wished she knew him like she had in high school. She wished she could guess what he'd do.

God had this all in His hand. The question was, what was He going to do with it?

She could take off, disappear, and never return. But... Ella.

The thought of that little girl, all alone, kept her rooted to the scratched linoleum floors, staring at the window, willing James to arrive.

She'd collected some clothes and toiletries in the only backpack she owned, just in case James decided to come. Just in case they'd spend the night on the mountain. Her backpack wasn't large enough for a sleeping bag, but that wouldn't matter. It wasn't as if she'd sleep.

A glance at her watch told her it was six-fifty.

Two minutes later, his old Jeep turned into the driveway and parked. She shoved a credit card and her keys in her jeans' pocket —always prepared to run, just in case—and jogged outside, still half-expecting to see cops squeal in behind him. But the morning was quiet and peaceful.

Backpack in hand, she made her way toward him.

He stepped onto the gravel driveway. "That all you have?" he asked, nodding to her small pack.

"I wasn't sure what I needed."

She barely caught his smirk before he rounded the Jeep and opened the tailgate.

She peeked through the Jeep's windows. She'd spent a lot of time in its passenger seat in high school, and she let the memories fill her now, hoped to get past them. This would be weird enough without their past as an awkward third passenger.

James hefted a huge backpack from the Jeep, the kind... Well, the kind backpackers wore. "Turn around. Let's get it fit right."

"Whose is it?"

"Mine."

He owned two backpacks, one sized for a woman? Perhaps this had belonged to James's mother, and he hadn't wanted to bring it up.

James's had always been an outdoorsy family. Did things like backpacking and camping and hiking together all the time. As she slipped the backpack on, she wondered if Mrs. Sullivan had ever gone backpacking or camping after Hallie's death.

"How's it feel?"

"Strangely comfortable," she said.

"I added some necessities." He adjusted a few straps, then tugged on the back. "Think you can handle that?"

The backpack, no problem. Going back up to the mountain—that was a different story.

She emptied the contents of her little backpack into the larger one. Already in there were a sleeping bag, a small pillow, and a fleece sweatshirt. Apparently, he'd assumed she hadn't brought anything warm enough. She did have a sweatshirt but conceded that the fleece would be better. There were also a few other things she didn't recognize, backpacking accessories, no doubt.

"Where's your knife?" he asked.

She looked up from where she crouched beside the packs. "What do you mean?"

"You have to have a hunting knife."

"For what?"

He shook his head. "Just... lots of things. What if you need to skin an animal? Or a fish? Or you need firewood or to make a sharp point on a limb for—"

"Spearfishing?" She couldn't help the teasing tone.

"Just saying, you should never go into the woods without a good knife."

"I'll keep that in mind for next time. This time, I presume you have one?" When he nodded, opening his mouth as if to continue the lecture, she said. "Do we need food?"

He took her backpack and stowed it in the Jeep. "I got everything we need." He slammed the tailgate shut. "Ready?"

"I guess."

"Don't sound so enthusiastic."

He rounded to the driver's seat and climbed in.

When they'd dated, he'd always opened her door for her. Silly that she'd think of that now, but there it was.

When she was settled, he opened an Ayasha trail map and pressed it against the dash so they could both see. "Here's the trailhead." He pointed to the map. "Any idea where you've already explored?"

She'd never been very good with maps. Or directions. She

traced the trail. There was just the one. She pointed to where she thought she'd gone.

"You've barely scratched the surface." He folded the map and angled to face her. "Just... How do you know it was Ayasha, not Coventry or another mountain?"

"I know the difference."

"I'm just saying... I don't know what happened that day. If you drove over—"

"I didn't own a car."

"But you're saying you and Hallie were taken. Were you put in a car?"

"No. I took your sister for a walk. She said she wanted to go on the mountain, so we went that way. It's something you and I did with her a lot. I didn't think your parents would mind."

James pressed his lips together but said nothing.

"We were on the trail, not very far up. It was deserted."

"It was cold."

"But sunny, and Hallie'd been cooped up—"

"It's fine. You took her for a walk. Then what?"

"She was running ahead, and I... I fell behind. I wasn't... I thought we were alone. I thought we were safe there."

"And then, what? Someone snatched you?"

"Her. He snatched her, and I followed, screaming for help. Screaming at him to put her down. But he didn't. Just kept going."

"Did he have a weapon or something? Why did you stay with him? Why not run away?"

"He had a gun. And then..." He'd had Hallie. If Cassidy had run, he might have hurt her. Even if she could have gotten away, how could she abandon Hallie to save herself?

James didn't want to hear the story, and, truth was, she didn't want to get into that now. Not with him staring at her with his narrowed eyes, his suspicion. And what if he took the information as an invitation to ask more questions? She wasn't prepared for that.

James watched her, waiting for her to continue.

Cassidy pulled her thoughts back to James and his original question. "We never got off Ayasha."

He paused, seemed to be waiting for more. "How long was the walk?"

Forever and ever. Emotion clogged her throat at the memory. She breathed through it. James didn't need that right now. She didn't need it. When she could speak, she said, "We walked a long time. Stopped for the night, and he built a fire, tied us up, and told us to sleep. Not that we did. Then we walked a long distance again the next day."

With narrowed eyes, James studied her. "How did you think you could find it in one day?"

"With your sister, progress was slow, really slow. We got started late, after six in the evening. I figure we hiked three hours that night, around four the next day. I was moving faster than we did back then. And I have more hours of daylight now that it's summertime."

"And you're scared to stay on the mountain alone."

Terrified. "I thought if I could get close, I could call the police, report something. Not as me, but anonymously. Lead them in the right direction."

"Why was progress slow? With the... the kidnapper?"

"Your sister was little. She couldn't move very fast, and she was crying and—"

"Got it." The grief on his face made her wish the words back. He took another map from the console and opened it. "This is Mt. Ayasha, and these"—he pointed to a tiny portion on the north side of the mountain—"are the trails. From what you said, you probably explored around this area."

She followed his finger. Seemed about right.

"Obviously, there's still a lot of ground to cover. Would you say you were climbing a lot or moving across level ground? Or even... do you remember going down?"

"Climbing and level, I think. We never went down, at least not very far."

"Did you cross any roads? Any streams or rivers?"

She considered the question. "There was a stream, but nothing so wide it was hard to get across. Of course, it was below freezing, and there was snow on the ground. It's possible we crossed a frozen stream and didn't realize it. There were no roads."

"What else?"

She closed her eyes, forced herself back. "We had to go over rocks, like... like big boulders. There was one section he wanted us to climb, but Hallie couldn't do it. Most of the time, he carried her, but he couldn't carry her up that hill. We had to go around. Which I think must have taken longer. We left the trail right away, but it wasn't like we were forging new ground. It was a path, a very narrow path. I had the impression he'd gone that way before, many times." There'd been trees, trees, and more trees. Bare branches, stark against the snow-covered ground and gray skies. "Everything looked the same."

"When you walked in the morning, do you remember the position of the sun? Was it shining on you, or—?"

"Yes. Yes! There were thick clouds, but a few times the sun poked through."

He studied the map. "You must've been on the east side or the southeast side."

"That was until the snow started."

He looked up. "The snow didn't start until late that afternoon. It rained most of the day."

"It didn't rain on us. It was snow."

He gazed at the map again. "You must have climbed pretty high. Did you see the lake?"

"Never in the morning. It might have been visible at night but—"

"Too dark to see." James tapped the map on the south side of the mountain. "There are some old logging roads over here. Let's see if we can get started higher up."

About a half hour later, they turned off the state highway onto a narrow opening that most passersby would never see. Though the day was dry, about a quarter mile up, a stream cut across the road. James splashed through it and drove until it dead-ended in a wide opening.

He used the area to turn around and headed back down.

"Wait," she said, "where are we going?"

He was peering into the woods on both sides of the path. "We don't want anyone to see the Jeep."

"But—"

"Trust me, Cassidy."

It seemed the least she could do.

She feared he would drive all the way back to the highway by the time he found a spot. Then he did, bumping between the trees and over the bracken, finally coming to a stop a good twenty yards from the road.

"Somebody obviously uses that road," he said.

"How do you know?"

"Otherwise, it'd be overgrown. Could be anybody, but we ought to assume this is the killer's route."

The killer. The last thing she wanted was to run into him again.

She touched the Glock in the holster at her waist. This time, she'd be able to defend herself.

"What's that?"

She lifted her shirt to show him the pistol.

His eyes widened. "You know how to use that?"

"Of course."

"Back in high school, you were anti-gun all the way."

"I've since learned more than once how vulnerable I am."

He lifted his own T-shirt, and she got a glimpse of the handgun he carried there. "I wasn't going to show you because I thought you'd be mad."

"Relieved, more like."

"Good." They climbed from the Jeep, and James took the backpacks from the rear. Then, he reached for something else, something big and plastic and camo.

A tarp.

He pulled it over the Jeep, tying the corners to keep it in place.

"You think of everything."

"Sullivan family motto: Be prepared."

"I think the Boy Scouts took that one."

He turned from his work, a smile tugging at one corner of his lips, and she got a brief glimpse of the boy James used to be.

But the closed-off man was back immediately. "Ready?"

She hefted her backpack and strapped it on as James had shown her at the house. "Ready."

James kicked leaves and twigs to cover his tire tracks, and they set off up the road.

Already, he was considering things she'd never thought of. She let herself believe they might really do this. They might really rescue Ella, bring the kidnapper to justice. And then... And then she could be herself again. She wouldn't have to live her life in hiding. She wouldn't have to live with the guilt anymore.

Except, the guilt wouldn't go away, not until she told James everything. And maybe not even then.

# CHAPTER THIRTEEN

At the top of the road, James walked to the edge of the clearing, looking for a path. On the first pass, he found nothing. He stepped into the woods and again circled the clearing until he saw some pressed-down leaves and needles. He was no tracker, but he knew the woods. He'd spent his life in the woods. With a little luck and a lot of divine help—the kind other people talked about but he'd never experienced—he might be about to figure out where... whoever'd been here had gone.

From the clearing, Cassidy said, "What'd you find?"

"It's possible someone went this way." James started walking. Another ten yards, and he saw a broken branch on the ground. And from there, a path opened up. James followed it, and Cassidy followed him.

"Weird that the path starts way back here," she said.

"Maybe he takes different routes from the clearing so as not to show the way."

"Like he's trying to keep it hidden."

"Assuming we're following the kidnapper's path. For all we know, we're tracking a hunter. Heck, it could be someone scouting for good real estate. Could be kids."

"Kids wouldn't work so hard to keep it hidden. Neither would someone looking to build a house."

True.

Trees towered over them on every side. Pines, birches, oaks, and maples. The leaves and needles beneath them cushioned and quieted their steps. The slope was gentle at first but grew steeper. They walked in silence, the melody of the forest the only sound. Birds twittering, twigs snapping, animals skittering about. The rustle of leaves, the sway of branches in the breeze above. The weather would warm into the eighties today, but the higher they went, the cooler it would be.

They reached a stream, and he stopped and pulled out his phone. No service here, but GPS still tracked his location. He checked his coordinates on his screen, then checked the paper map he'd stuck in his back pocket and made a note.

"Whatcha doing?"

"We need to track our route. If we find her, we'll need to tell authorities where she is. If we don't, we'll need to know where we've been so we don't cover the same ground."

"It's like you've done this before. I'm impressed."

A wash of pleasure bubbled up, but he tamped it down. He wasn't here to impress Cassidy. He wasn't here to feel anything for her.

He folded the map and shoved it back into his pocket. "I thought it through last night, tried to figure the most efficient way to do this."

"Smart. I was just looking at landmarks and trying to remember. Of course, I'd never have even found this road, so we're already way ahead of where I'd be by myself."

He looked beyond the towering trunks to the blue sky. "Except you said sunlight reached you." He gazed at the shade all around them.

"We'd started from a different place. It's not going to feel familiar for a while."

"Good point."

They followed the stream, which climbed and circled toward the east. Brightness beckoned them forward.

"What made you decide to come with me?" Cassidy asked.

The path he'd been following—hardly a path, but it had seemed the right way—suddenly ended. In front of him, a boulder. The stream to one side, to the other...

Trees.

"What is it?"

"Lost the trail."

She stepped up beside him, then passed him and rounded the rock that was taller than she was. He followed, saw no sign of a path.

He hopped over the stream and looked around, but again, no sign of anybody having gone that way.

Had the kidnapper—or whoever—stopped here? Was the boulder their destination?

James looked down but saw nothing to recommend this place over any other. No beautiful vista. Just forest all around.

"Could he walk in the stream?" Cassidy stared up the mountain, and he followed her gaze.

"Staying hidden worth wet feet?"

"If you're a kidnapper."

Good point. He hopped back over to her side.

They'd walked ten minutes when she asked, "You going to answer my question?"

He'd hoped she'd forget. "I figured I had three options. I could turn you in, pretend I hadn't seen you, or go with you."

"Three good choices," she said.

"Not really. My best friend's kid is missing, so pretending I hadn't seen you wasn't going to work."

"You could have turned me in."

"Except I think you're right. I think everybody believes you're behind the kidnappings."

"Whoever did it is trying to make it look like it was me."

"If they'd caught you and you'd told them about the cave—"

"I've told them. Twice. They haven't looked. Though I never called it a cave. It felt like a cave, but it wasn't, not really. Just boulders positioned so that there's space beneath. Giant rocks with space under them."

"Whatever you called them, they've looked," James said. "Just haven't found anything."

They walked in silence for a few minutes, and James hoped the conversation was over. But then she disturbed the silence once again.

"You believe I'm innocent?"

He clenched his jaw. "Innocent is a strong term."

She grabbed his biceps. He could have easily shrugged her off, but instead he turned and faced her.

"What's that supposed to mean?" she asked.

"Why'd you run?"

"I told you. I was afraid they wouldn't believe me. I was afraid—"

"Guilty people run. Innocent people don't. It's that simple."

She dropped her hand. "Nothing is *that simple*."

"What were you afraid of?"

She shook her head and trudged past him.

"What?"

She said nothing.

He followed her. "Come on, Cassidy. What aren't you telling me?"

"Two days ago, you said you didn't want to hear it. Now you do?"

He started to respond but held his tongue.

She turned, arms crossed. "Well, do you or don't you?"

"I do. But... Not right now."

She swiveled and started climbing again. "You have no right to distrust me when you refuse to hear the story."

"Do you want to tell it?"

He followed as she climbed. "I need you to understand."

He wanted to understand, but not right now. Not yet. When

they weren't moving. When he wouldn't be distracted. When he could focus and study her face and weigh her words.

"Let's talk about the kidnapper," he suggested. "What can you tell me about him?"

"He wore a thick parka, but I got the sense he was slender underneath it." Her words were measured, emotionless. "He was tall, but not..." She turned, glanced at James. "How tall are you?"

"About five-eleven."

"I think he was taller than you."

"How old?"

She grabbed a tree trunk and hoisted herself up a small rise. "He wore a mask."

"The whole time you were with him? That's weird."

He climbed up behind her and saw she'd stopped and turned to face him. "Why?"

James thought back to Cassidy's words Monday evening. "You said he planned to kill you, right?"

"I said he didn't expect me to be there." She started hiking again. "I thought he'd kill me. But... I don't think he planned any of it. I think it was... It was a spur-of-the-moment thing. He saw Hallie, he snatched her, and then I came along and—"

"Then why the mask?"

"I guess he didn't want Hallie to see his face, either."

"No, I mean... If he didn't plan to kidnap you guys, why would he have a mask?"

"I don't know. How would I know?"

"It doesn't make sense."

"It was cold. People wear ski masks when it's cold." She skirted a huge rock blocking her way and climbed the gentle rise beside it.

"It's not that I doubt you." He did, but it wasn't only that. "I'm just trying to understand."

"Okay."

The stream beside them went from gentle to quick, falling over stones and terrain in mini-waterfalls.

Above him, Cassidy stopped and looked up. "Not sure this is the best route."

He followed her gaze and saw what she meant. The hillside was getting steeper, rockier. "Let's move sideways a bit. I think we want to get more to the east anyway." He led away from the stream. The slope was steep, and he picked his way to the side, moving upward slowly and using tree trunks as handholds to keep his feet.

"I'm wondering about the timeline," she said. "Where do you think the kidnapper's been all these years, assuming it's the same guy?"

"You think he's been gone?" James asked.

"What else accounts for the gap in time? Maybe he was in prison."

"Possible."

When he added nothing else, she said, "Possible he moved away. Do you know anybody who moved away then and has now come back?"

"Besides you?"

He glanced back to see she'd stopped.

"I'm just saying—"

"I'm back because he's back."

They walked a minute or two in silence.

"Let's say he moved somewhere and has been doing this for years," she said. "What if the authorities were closing in on him, so he came back?"

"Police have been in contact with the FBI, who tracks these things. They say there aren't any similar crimes in the US. So I don't think that's it."

"Could have been a tourist," she suggested.

"In January?"

"There're winterized places," she said. "And now it's summer." They walked a few minutes in silence. Long enough that, when she spoke a few minutes later, he was surprised to find she'd fallen behind.

"You remember how we used to contact each other?" she asked.

She was studying a tree trunk. There was a knothole in the side. She stuck her finger in it.

"Careful. You never know what's made its home in there."

She smiled at him. "No notes."

He trudged ahead.

"You know what I'm talking about, right?"

How could he not? Cassidy hadn't had a cell phone, probably the only kid at their high school who didn't. Her foster parents were strict and didn't like her getting phone calls from boys. So, James used to leave her notes in a hole in a tree on the grounds of their high school, which was walking distance from where she lived. On those notes, he wrote times he could get away to meet. Invitations for dates. Eventually, love notes.

Stupid, teenage stuff.

She said, "Remember the time—"

"This isn't a stroll down memory lane."

"I know. I just thought..." But her words trailed. He shouldn't have been short with her, but he couldn't let himself recall how they used to be. How much he used to care for her.

Fortunately, the way got steeper, and Cassidy quit trying to make conversation, just followed a few feet back.

She kept up, her heaving breaths the only indication that she was having any trouble.

And then, a thump and gasp.

He turned just as Cassidy rolled ten, twenty feet down. She crashed into the trunk of an old oak.

He scrambled to her. "You okay? Cassy?"

She sat up slowly and propped her backpack against the tree. "Just like Disneyland."

He crouched beside her and studied her legs, her arms, her face. Saw no blood, no protruding bones. "What hurts?"

She touched the hip that had hit the tree. "Nothing serious. I'll have a few nasty bruises."

"Did you hit your head? Can you move everything?"

She did a quick survey, moving both arms, both hands, both legs, both feet. "Everything seems to be in order."

"I'm sorry. I should've—"

"It's a mountain, James. Not your fault it's steep. Definitely not your fault I lost my footing." She patted the space beside her. "Let's rest a minute."

He took off his backpack, pulled out his water and a granola bar. "Want one?"

"Sure."

He handed her one of each and sat beside her. They'd only been climbing a few hours, and already the trip felt fruitless. After finishing the bar in two bites and downing a couple of sips of water, he took out his phone and map and marked their coordinates.

She nibbled her snack, gazing at the map he'd spread in front of them. "We've hardly covered any ground at all."

"It's a big mountain."

She sat back, closed her eyes. "I didn't think it would be so hard."

He'd just been thinking the same thing, but... "We just started."

"I know."

"Are you really ready to give up?"

She gazed up at him with those mesmerizing eyes. "I'm not giving up. I can't. I failed to save your sister, and I didn't get here fast enough to save that little girl last month."

"Addison." He swallowed the emotion trying to rise. Another little girl dead. Another family that would never be the same. "Her name was Addison."

"I know." Cassidy's two words were solemn, as if she felt the weight of the girl's death as heavily as he did. "I'm going to keep looking until I find Ella. Or until I find that cave. It's possible this is all some copycat, that these recent kidnappings have nothing to do with what happened back then. But until I find that spot, see if anybody's been there, I won't know for sure. I can't quit until I know."

A sound carried from the direction they'd come from. A *bud-a-dud-dud. Thud.*

He turned that direction, gaze scanning the mountain, the trees.

Had a rock gotten loose, tumbled down the hill?

Not without help.

"Probably nothing." But he whispered the words. He stood and peered below, to the sides, and above. Nobody was there.

He stayed like that for a long time, watching. Waiting.

The forest was silent, too silent. Even the birds seemed to be holding their breath.

Cassidy got to her feet and whispered, "Do you see something?"

See? No. But feel...? Yes, something was out there.

"Are we being followed?"

"I doubt it." He forced a casual expression and looked down at her. "Lots of wildlife out here. Could be anything."

She stared at him, her gaze probing. "What's your best guess?"

It had been a loud noise. A falling rock, but, if so, it hadn't been a pebble. And little animals didn't move big rocks. "Probably something big."

"Like?"

He tried to shrug it off, but she wasn't going to let it go. "There're deer, moose, bears, bobcats."

Her eyes widened.

"I know it sounds cliché, but whatever it was is likely more scared of us than we are of it."

Her lips tipped up in an almost smile. "You're scared of it?"

"Obviously you are. I was trying to make you feel better."

The smile widened, and she patted his forearm. "It's okay, James. I'll protect you."

He chuckled. "We never did pick up the trail again. I thought if we just kept going, we'd catch it."

"The kidnapper must go a different way."

If James and Cassidy had even caught a human trail. For all he knew, the little path he'd found had been forged by wildlife, not humans.

But a cold chill skittered over his skin. He thought of the person in the woods by his house two days before. The person who'd been following Cassidy.

Who'd seen James talk to her. Who'd probably heard him call her name.

Was somebody out there?

Were they being watched?

# CHAPTER FOURTEEN

Cassidy might've downplayed her injuries a little too much. As afternoon turned to evening, her hip throbbed and her shoulder ached. She hadn't been thinking straight after her fall. She'd been discombobulated at the sight of James rushing to her aid. More than that, at the nickname, Cassy. James was the only person who'd ever called her that, and only after they'd started dating, kissing, falling in love.

Those old feelings had never gone far, and his tenderness had pulled them to the surface.

If this were a romance novel, now would be the time for her to remind herself of all the reasons she couldn't be with him. Buried secrets, a distrust of men, a desire not to get attached.

None of those defined Cassidy. She'd learned to trust good men. Having lived most of her life separate and alone, she desired attachment more than the average person. And, God willing, as much as it terrified her, her secrets would all be revealed when they found Ella.

In any possible romantic scenario between Cassidy and James —if he had any feelings for her at all—there was just one reason, one giant reason, they couldn't be together: her part in his sister's death.

If he could forgive her, if they could move past it...

Two giant ifs.

Giant enough that she tried not to hope. The problem was, hope had saved her and guided her and fueled her for a decade. She could no more tamp it down than she could darken the sun.

The God of Hope—that was the first name for her Lord that she'd latched onto. And she wouldn't let it go for fear she might get hurt. After all, He was the God of all Comfort, too, wasn't He? He could handle her hope and her heartbreak. He could handle it all.

As they climbed the narrow trail, hope and pain were in a battle. Hope that they'd find Ella.

Pain begging her to quit.

Another feeling pulled her attention, though. Fear.

Ever since that noise earlier, she'd couldn't shake the feeling that somebody was watching them. She'd brought it up once, and James had stopped and peered around. She'd expected him to brush her off or offer empty promises that they were safe, but he hadn't.

"It was probably an animal. But..."

The *but* was the part that scared her.

There was nothing to do but continue the trek. The exertion kept them from talking. Every so often, James would ask if the surroundings looked familiar. Not yet, though she felt they were moving in the right direction. She didn't know why, couldn't have identified the things that gave her that impression. God, perhaps? Or some instinct or long-buried memory? But what had felt futile after her fall no longer did. They'd find the cave, as long as they didn't quit.

She couldn't speak for James, but nothing short of death or serious injury would stop her. She'd overcome a lot of risk to get to this place, all to save Ella, to stop the kidnapper from destroying more lives. She'd keep at it until Ella was safe in her father's arms.

Meanwhile, though, here she was, on this mountain she'd sworn she'd never return to. As she gazed around at the wilderness, it was hard to imagine that she'd ever had a different life. Seattle seemed a world away from this secluded place, the counseling center where she worked almost like a different dimension. That dingy basement space with its plastic, straight-backed chairs, the water-ringed wooden table covered with coffee and soda and snacks the girls devoured as if they hadn't eaten in months. They'd sip their drinks and munch their store-bought cookies and tell stories that didn't belong there, didn't belong anywhere, stories of abuse so bad at home that life on the street was better. At least on the street, it wasn't fathers and brothers and mothers and sisters who did the abusing. And then there were the other stories, the girls who'd left home chasing drugs or guys or freedom, absolutely confident that what they found in the world would be better than what they had at home. They were the hardest to reach. They were the ones who had to admit that they'd been wrong, not wronged.

All the girls were unique, all wounded, all special. And all of them needed somebody to hold their hands and tell them that they mattered, that they were okay. All of them needed somebody to help them find their way home. Often, home wasn't where they'd come from, but it could always be where they were headed.

Cassidy had found her new home in Seattle. She'd found her place to belong in the family of God. It was her life's goal to help others find Him, find home as well.

Now, that home felt as elusive as the place they were searching for on this mountain. It was as if that counseling center back in Seattle no longer existed. Or maybe it never had. Maybe the little room she rented was a figment of her imagination. She smiled at that thought. If she were going to conjure a place in her mind's eye, it would be nicer than the dingy studio apartment where she'd lived since college.

But it wouldn't be on a mountainside. Nope, this rugged wilderness world was not for her. She followed James through areas so thick with undergrowth that they'd hardly been able to forge a path. As they climbed higher, the trees were sparser, the undergrowth easier to avoid. The sun had long since fallen to the opposite side of the mountain, and the air was cooling. Not that she was cold. Trudging mostly uphill kept her warm enough.

Finally, James paused in a small, flat clearing. "Let's camp here for the night."

"Oh, thank God." Only when he turned to her, concern etched in the lines on his forehead, did she realize she'd said the words aloud.

"You should have told me you needed to stop sooner."

"I didn't want to stop." She took off the backpack for the first time in hours, enjoying the lightness, the cool air against her damp T-shirt. She sat on a fallen tree on the edge of the pine-needle carpet. "Before we started today, I thought I was in shape."

He took off his own backpack and dug inside. "I'll set up the tent." He took out a blue silicone bag and laid it on the ground. "The Jetboil is in your backpack. Could you get it out?"

She had no idea what that was but opened her pack dutifully, figuring it would be obvious. She pulled out a black contraption that looked like an insulated cup mounted on top of a tiny propane tank. That had to be it.

"What am I making?"

"Open the bag"—he nodded at it from where he'd already begun unpacking the tent—"and pick whatever you want."

She found instant noodles, rice, and oatmeal, not to mention tea bags and coffee. Also, bagged tuna fish, little squeeze-packets of mayonnaise, peanut butter, and single-serving jellies.

She knew there was another bag of food in his pack—he'd gotten the granola bars from it—and searched for it now, finding pita bread, nuts, dried fruit, and hummus.

"You brought the whole store," she said.

"Bad habit. Even though I figure we'll only be up here a night or two, I packed all the food I could fit."

"I could have carried some."

"There was no need."

She boiled the water and, using collapsible silicone bowls she'd found in her pack, fixed the noodles. It would go well with the tuna, and they needed the protein and carbs. Plus, if they found Ella, *when* they found Ella, she could have the bars and peanut butter and jelly.

Before Cassidy finished preparing dinner, James had the tent up and his sleeping bag laid out on the ground beside it.

"Why are you getting that dirty?" she asked. "Doesn't the sleeping bag go inside the tent?"

"You'll sleep inside. I'll sleep out."

"Oh."

"Seems... wiser, don't you think?"

The unspoken suggestion that something might happen between them raised her heart rate. It meant he found her at least a little bit attractive. Her hope wasn't futile.

"It's your tent," she said. "I should—"

"I like sleeping under the stars."

She looked up and only saw the canopy of trees.

"You know what I mean."

Not that she'd thought much about it, but all day she'd assumed he'd sleep by her side. It wasn't as if they were together. They'd hardly touched since she'd first seen him Monday. She was pretty sure they could sleep in the same tent and keep their hands to themselves.

"It's nothing against you." He'd been watching her reaction. "The opposite, really."

She wouldn't think too much on that. "Hungry?"

"Starved." He settled beside her and took the bowl she offered. "Climbing takes a lot out of you."

She took a bite of the instant noodles. They were surprisingly good. "When was the last time you went backpacking?"

"I go all the time. How about you? You ever go hiking or camping?"

"The closest I've gotten to nature in a decade is the park near my apartment."

His eyebrows hiked. "Don't you miss it?"

How could she miss a place that visited her so often in nightmares?

When she didn't answer, he asked, "Where do you live now?"

"Do you believe me, that I would never have kidnapped or harmed your sister? Do you really believe me?"

He opened his mouth, then snapped it shut.

She waited, let the silence press the question.

When he said nothing, she shrugged. "I live far away."

"You're afraid to tell me?"

"I hope to return to that life when-this is over. When I do, I'd like to not be looking over my shoulder all the time."

"I don't plan to turn you in."

"You considered precisely that about forty-eight hours ago."

"But I didn't." He ripped off a bit of pita bread and popped it in his mouth. When he'd swallowed, he said, "Can you tell me what you do, or is that top secret as well?"

"I work with at-risk youth, mostly runaway girls who've gotten caught up in drugs and prostitution."

"Tough job."

"I'm uniquely qualified."

His eyebrows lifted, the question obvious.

"Just the runaway part," she clarified. "Not drugs or prostitution. But I understand the temptation. I understand how easily somebody can be enticed into bad decisions. I understand why toss-away children are willing to risk everything and do anything to find a sense of belonging."

"Toss-aways. Is that how you felt?"

"Most of my life. Even with foster families, it's hard to feel like you belong. Until I met your family..."

Something flashed in his eyes, something dark. Goosebumps rose on her bare arms, and she dug in her backpack, happy to have something to focus on besides James.

Hands elbow-deep, she continued. "It was wonderful to know your family, a good family. I mean, I know I wasn't a member, but I got to witness it, I got to enjoy it for a time. I've only ever known snatches of that feeling, but I've always longed for it. What I've learned, what I try to teach the kids I work with, is that we're all welcome into the family of God. With God, there are no toss-aways." She found the fleece sweatshirt James had packed for her and slipped it on, careful of her bruised shoulder. "When people are firm in their relationship with the Father, they're not only secure in their place in the best family in the universe, but they're in a position to find stragglers and pull them in." She settled back on the ground.

"Do the kids listen to you?"

She started to lift her shoulders in a shrug, but a sharp pain had her holding the left one.

"You're hurting."

"Not too bad."

But he was already digging in the pack for something. He found it—a medicine bottle—and handed her two pills. "Ibuprofen."

"Good thinking." She downed them, praying it would help. "I'll work with a girl for months, some I've worked with for years. Many will laugh at me, scoff at me, call me a liar, swear at me, tell me they hate me. Some'll disappear and never return. But most come back. They're afraid to believe what I say, but they need somebody in their lives to tell them they matter, they belong. I try to be that person. So... does it work? God works. I do my part. The results are up to Him."

"Healthy attitude."

"Years of practice."

He grabbed a handful of nuts. "Want some?"

"You don't happen to have any cookies in that pack."

He found a chocolate bar and tossed it to her. "You always had a sweet tooth."

"My hero." She ripped the package and ate the first square.

"So, some girls listen, and some don't," he said. "Any success stories?"

"I've had a few kids reunite with their parents. A couple have finished high school and gone on to college. Any girl who stays off the streets is a success story in my book."

"You're a success story." He held her gaze. "Look at all you've accomplished."

She ate another square of chocolate, let it melt in her mouth before swallowing. "This town..." She wasn't sure how to say what she needed to say. "Not this town. Your family taught me a new way. Your family taught me that I mattered, that I was valuable, that I could be trusted because I could be trustworthy. No matter how hard I tried to look tough and stand-offish, your mother saw right through me. She saw past the black lipstick and angry T-shirts. She saw me. My own mother..."

She didn't finish the sentence, but James knew. Everybody knew about Cassidy's mother.

"And your father," she continued. "I'd had father figures ignore me, brush me off, yell at me. I had a foster father who came on to me when nobody was looking, tried to kiss me."

James scowled at that.

"One of my mother's boyfriends used to hurt me when I didn't behave. He wasn't as bad as Mom, but still... Your father treated me like a daughter. He treated me with respect and courtesy. He listened when I talked."

"And you talked a lot," James said, a smile lighting his eyes. "Man, sometimes I thought you'd never shut up."

He was too far away to reach or else she'd smack him. Instead, she laughed. "Having people listen to me... You have no idea what a novelty it was. People who listened and responded and cared what I had to say. I'd rarely had that. And Hallie..." Her voice cracked.

"My sister adored you."

"I adored her, too. I'd have done anything, anything..." She swiped the sudden tears away.

James looked up at the darkening sky. What was he thinking? She didn't know this man the way she'd known the teenage boy. She'd loved that boy, loved his family, with everything in her.

"Anyway." Cassidy worked for a casual tone. "Unlike a lot of the kids I work with, I'd seen how good it could be. I'd seen what a real family should look like, and I'd been introduced to the God who wanted everyone to feel that sense of belonging. Of... mattering. I'm a success story not because of anything I did but because... because of you."

## CHAPTER FIFTEEN

The man came back earlier than usual, before the sun even went down. He carried a paper bag, which he set on top of the cooler. "I'm going to have to take the food out after dinner, in case the bear comes looking for it, so be sure to get enough to eat and drink."

That morning before he left, he'd cleaned up the bear's mess and rinsed out her bucket. Now, he sat beside her. "I have a surprise for you."

She didn't want any surprise that didn't include her daddy, but she didn't say that. She'd learned it was better to talk to the crickets and keep quiet when he was around.

"I'm going to build a campfire." He pointed to a black spot on the pale rock. The black was sort of like chalk. It'd come off on her fingers when she'd touched it. "Just big enough to roast marshmallows. You love roasted marshmallows."

She'd never had them, so she just shrugged.

"And I got graham crackers and chocolate so we can have s'mores."

"What's that?"

His eyebrows lifted and disappeared behind the mask. "Don't

be silly. It's your favorite." His lips parted, and she thought he was smiling behind his mask. "You're in for a treat. But first, I brought you another surprise." He turned his back to her, opened the sack, then spun with a flourish. "Ta-da!" He presented a McDonald's Happy Meal sack.

She loved McDonald's. She tried to pretend she didn't care, but she feared she'd let a smile slip through.

"Cheeseburger and French fries," he said. "Your favorite. And I even brought you a Coke. Remember that time I took a sip from Mommy's Coke, and she got so mad that she tried to throw a plate at me, but it slipped out of her hand and landed on her foot?" He cackled as if he'd told a joke, but that wasn't funny at all.

He handed her the Happy Meal bag, opened her Coke, took out another bag, and plopped down beside her. He lifted his mask above his lips and ate.

The meal was warm and salty and perfect. But as soon as she finished, it turned thick and icky in her stomach, and she felt guilty, like she'd stolen a quarter from Daddy's bedside table. Like, by enjoying what the man had given her, she'd done something very, very wrong.

"Ready for dessert?"

She shook her head, and his smile faded.

"What's wrong?"

"I'm full."

"Oh, you can eat one tiny little s'more. You used to put away dozens of them. By the time I'm done building the fire, you'll be hungry enough." He walked outside, returning a minute later with a handful of sticks and twigs. He arranged most of them on the ground not too far from her, added some leaves, and flicked a lighter.

The leaves caught first, filling the cave with thick smoke, which made her cough.

The man waved it away. He knelt and blew on the tiny flame until a few of the sticks caught on fire.

Even though there was a gap in the cave overhead and most of the smoke found its way out, some didn't, and it was hot and smelly. This fire wasn't anything like the pretty, cozy fires Daddy built in their fireplace.

He stood and clapped his hands together once. "Great. Let's roast marshmallows." He pulled a bag of them from the paper bag, stuck one on the end of a long stick he'd kept out of the fire, and handed it to her.

She held the stick, unsure what she was supposed to do with it.

"Go ahead!"

"I don't know what to do."

His smile faded. "Sure you do."

She shook her head. He squinted and studied her a moment. "What did that man do to you that you don't remember how to roast marshmallows?"

She didn't know what she was supposed to say, so she said nothing.

"That's okay. I'll show you." He stuck a marshmallow on the end of a second stick and held it over the flames. She watched as it turned light brown.

"Whoops. Got ahead of myself." He took his marshmallow out of the flame and handed her the stick. "Hold that a sec, would you?"

She did, and he went back to the bag and took out of a box of graham crackers and a bar of chocolate. He got both open, put a piece of chocolate on half the cracker, and took the stick back from her. He managed to get the marshmallow on the cracker and pressed the two pieces together with the chocolate, like a sandwich. "Look familiar?"

She shrugged.

"Your turn." He nodded to the fire. "Go ahead."

"I'm not hungry."

"Don't be silly, Maryann. It's your favorite."

She wasn't hungry, but she did sort of want to try roasting the marshmallow. She put it in the flames like he had, but she got it too low.

It caught on fire.

She squealed and dropped the stick, shooting a glance to the man to see if he was angry. But he only laughed as he picked up the stick and blew on the marshmallow. The flame went out.

"The burnt ones are the best." He made a marshmallow-chocolate sandwich and held it out to her.

"I don't want it."

His eyes got squinty, and his lips lost the smile. "Try it."

"It's burnt."

"You love them like that. It's delicious."

"You eat it, then."

He scowled at her, holding the food closer to her. "I said, try it."

She crossed her arms and looked at the fire. She wasn't going to eat that stupid burnt marshmallow. Her stomach hurt, and she didn't want it. She didn't like him or his stupid s'more.

He broke the sandwich in half, then broke it in half again and held out the smallest piece to her. "Please? Just a little bite?"

"No."

He stood so fast, she jumped.

She scrambled to the wall and pressed her back against it.

He looked down at her like he wanted to hit her or kick her. "I went to a lot of trouble to give you a special night, Maryann. I bought these things just for you. The least you can do is try."

"I don't feel good."

"*I don't feel good.*" His high-pitched mocking tone reminded her of the boys at school. "Don't be such a baby. Eat a bite."

She should. Maybe then he'd leave her alone. Except she thought she might throw up, and she hated him and his stupid marshmallow and hated that he was trying to have fun with her. She shook her head and mumbled, "You can't make me."

Before she knew what happened, he'd pinned her to the floor. He straddled her, squeezing her cheeks hard and forcing her jaw open. He shoved the bite of food in. Then he pressed his hand over her mouth. "Chew and swallow."

His hand was thick and hot, and she couldn't breathe. She struggled to get out from under him.

He let up just enough for her to inhale. "Do it. Now."

She could hardly move her jaw with his hand like that, but she did what he said, afraid of the wild look in his eyes. Wild as the bear that had visited the night before.

Tears leaked from her eyes as she swallowed the bite. The marshmallow tasted like dirt, and the graham cracker was too dry. Even the chocolate was yucky. She swallowed again when it wanted to come back up.

He climbed off her and stood looking down at her with a dazed look in his eyes, like he didn't know who she was or who he was or anything. "Maryann never said no to s'mores."

Her whole body was shaking. She was even more scared than when the bear was there. More scared than she'd been when he'd first slipped his hand over her mouth and stolen her from Nana and Papa's backyard. More scared than she'd ever been in her whole life.

"Maybe you're not her."

She wasn't her, and she wanted to say so. Maybe if he realized she wasn't Maryann, he'd take her back to Daddy. If she just told him...

But inside her head, someone said, *Shh.*

So she didn't say anything.

He snatched the ruined food off the cave floor and tossed it in the fire. "I should leave this out, let the bear find you again."

*Please, no.*

She tried to be very small and very quiet, hoping he'd forget he was angry with her. Hoping he'd leave her alone forever.

He walked back and forth on the stone floor, mumbling. "No. This is my sister. This is her. The other girl was the wrong girl, but this is Maryann."

There'd been another?

"She was a mistake. A big mistake. Maybe..." He looked down at Ella, and his eyes looked all weird, like he was looking through her. He unlocked the cuff around her ankle.

She was too scared to even be happy not to have it scraping her skin. He lifted her and carried her under his arm through the entrance. It was the first time she'd been outside since he first put her in there, and she wanted to enjoy it. To take in the fresh air and sunshine. To never go back in that terrible, terrible cave. But with him holding her like...like Daddy held a folded-up newspaper...and mumbling about the other girl and how maybe he'd made a mistake...

She wanted back in the cave.

She wanted her daddy.

He set her on the ground, spun her around, and kept his hands firmly on her shoulders. She looked out at treetops in front of her. The trees must've been growing from a long way below. Their leaves and needles were dark against the fading light.

She dared a glance down. They were standing at the top of a cliff, a tall, steep cliff. At the bottom were rocks like sharp teeth, waiting to gobble her up.

"I have no choice." His voice sounded funny, like he was hardly even there. "She isn't my sister. I have to find Maryann."

He lifted Ella, held her on his hip, and kissed her forehead. "I'm sorry, little girl. My sister loved s'mores, and you don't even know how to roast marshmallows. You must not be her."

He grabbed her under the arms and dangled her over the cliff.

"No! No, please." Her legs kicked beneath her, found nothing but air. "I am Maryann." The words were a lie, but she shouted them again. "I'm Maryann. Please, don't!"

He watched her a minute with those scary empty eyes. Then, he blinked and looked at her for real. He pulled her close and hugged her. "It is you. I knew it! You were playing a trick on me, silly girl. You almost fooled me."

She held onto him, terrified to let him go. Terrified to be in his arms.

"Silly sister." He backed up and pressed his nose against hers. "I want us to be happy. But we'll only be happy if we choose to be. So let's not fight." He carried her back to the cave, humming a cheerful tune.

# CHAPTER SIXTEEN

James forced his eyes closed, trying not to think about the root jabbing at his back through the thin pad he'd laid his sleeping bag on. Trying not to think about his conversation with Cassidy. He'd never tell her how his parents had blamed her, hated her, after Hallie's death. He'd never tell Cassidy how his parents had cursed the day she'd walked into their lives.

But thinking about Cassidy wasn't the only thing keeping him awake.

The noise earlier—the falling rock—had surely been caused by an animal. James had bundled their food and tied it on a branch a good hundred yards away, just in case it was a bear that had stalked them all afternoon.

Black bears weren't usually dangerous to humans. They could be if they were hungry, but there was plenty of vegetation on this mountain to feed them. And if they'd spooked a mama bear and her cub earlier, the animals would have stayed as far from him and Cassidy as possible.

Could've been a bobcat. Thing was, he couldn't imagine a bobcat inadvertently sending a rock careening down the hill. They were stealthy, careful on their feet. Unlikely to accidentally dislodge a rock and give their position away.

Honestly, if they weren't so secluded up here, James would suspect a human had done it.

And since they were, theoretically, on the trail of a human—a kidnapper and murderer—the idea wasn't so farfetched.

All his years of spurning God, and now, with Cassidy's life in danger, he recited Psalm four, verse eight, reminding himself that God did indeed make them dwell in safety. Despite all his losses and disappointments over the years, he believed it. Old habits? Or had he always believed and only pretended not to, insulating himself from more loss?

Either way, God's promises weren't far from his mind now.

He reminded himself of Psalm ninety-one, which promised protection from danger. He'd memorized those scriptures as a child. After Hallie's abduction and murder, he'd quit believing God was listening. Now, though... He needed God to be listening. Needed God to protect and guide them.

If someone was out there, someone who recognized Cassidy, someone who might believe she would recognize him...

If the killer knew she was here, she wasn't safe.

It was that simple.

He was an idiot for bringing her up here. Except, if he hadn't come with her, she'd have continued the search alone. If James thought she was vulnerable now, he didn't want to think about what could've happened to her if she were by herself.

A third victim of the same killer?

Assuming the recent kidnappings were related to what happened to Hallie and not a copycat.

And assuming Cassidy was telling the truth.

He finally drifted to sleep only to awake with a start. There'd been a noise. Not one of the natural noises of the forest. Those he was accustomed to. This had been sharper, like the snap of a branch.

In the tent beside him, just inches away, Cassidy's breaths were low and steady. Seemed she'd finally fallen into a deep sleep.

Except for that snap, he'd think they were alone.

A bobcat wouldn't be so heavy as to snap a twig. A bear, then. He closed his eyes, listened for the heavy whuffing of a bear's breaths. Only silence greeted him.

Maybe James had dreamed—

*Snap.*

The sound came from the hillside above. Above and to the east. Somebody was there. Moving.

Silently, James climbed out of his sleeping bag and put on his hiking boots. He grabbed his pistol, disengaged the safety, and got to his feet, staying low.

Scanning the forest in every direction, he listened.

He stood there five minutes, ten. Not moving, allowing the moonlight and shadows to define the forms around him. He wouldn't leave this spot unless he was sure where he was going and what he was looking for. He wouldn't leave Cassidy exposed.

If he were a stalker, where would he hide? Their campsite was on a flat bit of ground on an otherwise steep slope. Below, trees and brush and nothing else. Above, the hill was rocky. Behind them, the stream was close enough that, before the wind had picked up, he'd been able to hear the trickling water. Ahead of them, all he could see was forest. Who knew what else was out there?

Slowly, slowly he gazed at trunk after trunk, searching for a hidden form. Movement. The reflection of metal. Something.

He saw nothing, and the longer he looked, the more the shadows tried to trick him.

It was too dark to see if there were any indentations on the forest floor where a person could hide.

He watched a long time, but nothing moved.

"What is it?" Cassidy's whisper came from inside the tent. "James?"

"Yeah. Sorry. It's nothing."

The sound of the zipper warned him she was coming.

"Stay in the tent."

"Because of *nothing?*"

"Probably nothing. Just stay down."

The zipper moved again. He glanced and saw it was opening, not closing.

"Cassidy. Please."

"Either you get in or I'm getting out."

Exasperating woman.

She crawled out beside him. Her hair was pulled up in a messy ponytail. She held her handgun pointed at the ground. "What happened?"

"I thought I heard something."

"From what direction?"

He nodded toward the hillside and, together, they peered into the darkness.

"What should we do?" Terror laced her words. "Should we leave?"

It was too dark, the hill too steep. To hike an unknown trail—not even a trail—in the dark would be dangerous. One wrong move could prove fatal.

They were better off staying put, though the longer he stood there, the more exposed he felt.

"Get in," he said.

"But what if he comes?"

"We're both armed. If he comes, we'll protect ourselves."

She crawled inside. He snatched his sleeping bag and followed. The tent was just wide enough for two people to lie side by side.

She scrabbled into her sleeping bag, and he did the same, only then registering the chill of the night.

"Tell me what happened." Her whisper was low.

"It was probably nothing."

"Is that what you really think?"

He didn't know what to believe. "If someone wanted to hurt us, we just gave him a very good opportunity."

It was too dark to see anything in the tent, so he stared up at the cloth above their heads.

Chirping crickets. A bullfrog's croak. The hoot of an owl.

Something slithered over dry pine needles.

"All day," she whispered, "I felt like we were being followed."

He should probably say something to make her feel better, but how would that help? "Yeah. I'd hoped I was imagining it."

"Someone's watching us."

He wished he could take the fear out of her voice.

Moonlight shone on the treetops and sent shadows creeping across the tent.

"Let's just... start the day," she whispered.

The glowing hands on his watch told him it was three-thirty. "Sun won't rise for an hour and a half."

"But we can't just lie here. And we can't go back to sleep."

"I know."

"Who do you think it is? You think it's—"

"Shh." He lowered his voice until it was so low, he wondered if she could even hear it. "Let's not talk about it. Let's not talk about anything related to... all this. In case he's listening."

Her shudder was perceptible despite the thick sleeping bags between them.

He faced her, propping his head on his hand. "You live in a city or a suburb?"

"I can't make small talk when—"

"Just... try, Cassy. Let's just not think about it."

She turned his direction. "City."

"Expensive city, or—?"

"Pretty expensive, but..."

When she said nothing else, he asked, "But what?"

"Are we really going to lie here and chitchat like we've just met for coffee?"

"What else is there to do?" As soon as the words were out, his mind conjured a few images. Cassidy in his arms. Cassidy's lips against his.

He'd spent a decade trying not to think about this woman, and now she was lying beside him in the dark. But they weren't alone.

She fell onto her back and stared up. "There was a home for runaways in this city, a pretty good home. At eighteen, I was considered an adult. But I had to change my name anyway, so why not fudge my age? I told people I'd just turned seventeen. That bought me almost a year to build a new identity."

"How did you do that? Was it hard?"

"It's simpler if you're a minor. Nobody expects a minor to have a photo ID. All I needed was a birth certificate and a social security number. It took me months to earn enough money to buy those. When I did—"

"Wait. How did you work without a social security number?"

"There are lot of places that don't look too closely. How do you think illegals do it?"

He'd never thought about it.

"Anyway, I saved enough money, bought myself a forged birth certificate and a social security card with my new name on it. Then, when my fake birth certificate showed I'd turned eighteen, I got a driver's license. That was all the ID I needed to build a new life."

"Smart."

"Still, it was hard. People with families don't understand the challenges for those without. Did you know that twenty percent of kids who age out of foster care become instantly homeless? Twenty-five percent suffer PTSD. Sixty percent of men will be convicted of a crime, and seventy percent of women will get pregnant before age twenty-one."

"You do public speaking or something? That sounded rehearsed."

Her chuckle was low. "I guess it was. We're always looking for donors."

"But you managed to thrive."

"I got lucky. I repeated my senior year and graduated from the local high school with my new name. The home where I lived... The people were good to me. They have this program for adults who need a leg up, former runaways and foster kids who are trying hard to support themselves and stay out of trouble. Very few of the people they help get in, but I did. God's grace. I lived there while I went to college. They helped me with the tuition. They... they saved my life."

"It's why you do what you do."

"Yeah. And I'm good at it. I'm good at connecting with kids who are afraid to connect."

He couldn't imagine the goth girl with the high walls pouring her heart into at-risk girls. The Cassidy he'd known and loved in high school had been closed off and afraid, at least at school. When she was at his home, with his family, she opened up and let him see the girl beneath the mask. So unlike the teenage version, this woman was open and fearless.

"You've changed so much."

"Also God's grace," she said. "He taught me to hope for better. Taught me that, if my hope was in Him and Him alone, I would never be disappointed."

Sounded both faithful and cynical.

"You've stayed in that same city all this time?"

"Yeah. I'd love to move farther out where the rent isn't so high, but cars are expensive. People without cars have very little choice but to stay in the city."

"You have a car now, though."

"It's rented through one of those online car sharing services— like that Air B and B but for cars. On the off chance somebody runs the plates, they'll lead back to a guy who doesn't have my real name. Or... my real fake name, anyway. Seemed safer than going with Hertz."

"So," he said, going for casual, "back in this nameless city, is there someone who would mind you and me sharing a tent?"

"Like, a husband?"

"Or a boyfriend?"

"No."

That surprised him. Cassidy had always latched onto people, never felt comfortable alone. "Was there, ever?"

"Besides you?"

He rolled onto his back. He shouldn't have started down this road.

"I've made some mistakes in that department," she said. "Since then, I've learned to be alone, to be content in—"

Something slapped against the tent, and she gasped.

He sat up and grabbed his gun, looking for the silhouette of a man. A bear. Something. All he saw was a dark spot on one side of the tent fabric about the size of two hands, spread wide.

She sat up beside him. They both watched.

The wind whipped, and the dark spot lifted, blew away.

"A leaf?" she whispered.

"A twig, I think, with a few leaves attached."

She lay back down, and he did the same, though now his heart was racing.

They'd almost done it. Almost gotten their minds off the danger outside the tent. But, distraction or no, the danger hadn't gone away.

# CHAPTER SEVENTEEN

D espite the presence of whatever—or whoever—lurked just beyond the thin fabric of their tent, Cassidy had somehow fallen asleep for a bit. James made her feel safe. Or at least *safer*.

Thank God James had come.

After slipping on her sweatshirt and shoes, she crawled out of the tent. Where was he?

He had to be close. She'd awakened when she'd heard the zipper only a few moments ago. He'd probably gone to get the food.

She walked in the opposite direction and emptied her bladder behind a bush, hoping neither James nor their stalker would see her.

Was the stalker still out there? Walking back to the small camping area, she scanned the forest in the early morning light. If he was, what was he after? Certainly not trying to hurt them. He'd had the opportunity to do that last night and hadn't taken it. Trying to scare them away? Again, he'd missed his chance. In the daylight, she wasn't nearly as afraid. Except it wasn't so much that the fear had waned but that her determination had expanded again.

Little Ella was out there, somewhere. She'd been missing four nights now. The last little girl who'd been kidnapped had been gone nine nights. Her body'd been found the tenth day after she'd disappeared.

The clock was ticking on Ella's life. They had to find her. And no creepy stalker in the woods was going to stop them.

Well, stop her. She couldn't speak for James.

He tromped through the woods from where he'd left the food, but his hands were empty. When he saw her, he attempted a smile, but she wasn't buying.

"What's wrong?"

"Food's gone."

"Gone? Like... Was it a bear last night?"

"Not a bear." He lifted his hand, revealing the rope he'd used to tie the bundle of food to the branch. She saw the clean-cut end. "Someone stole it."

Someone who didn't want them on this mountain.

"We're going back," he said. "Now."

"What? No, we can't. Ella's out here. We have to—"

"Someone stole our food, Cassidy."

"We'll survive. We'll... forage."

"I'm not worried about eating."

At the thought of it, her stomach growled.

"Someone wants us gone."

"You said it yourself. If he wanted to hurt us, he could have last night."

Kneeling in front of the tent flap, he yanked her sleeping bag out and started rolling it up.

"James, we can't quit now. We're so close."

His head snapped around. "Close, are we? How do you know? You have no idea—"

"I just mean... we've come so far."

"This is a big mountain." He tossed her sleeping bag beside his own and yanked a tent peg from the ground. The fabric fluttered to the bracken. "We might be close. We might be nowhere near that cave. Assuming it even exists."

"What does that mean? Now you don't believe me?"

"I believe... I believe you believe what you're saying."

"Wow. So now you think I'm crazy."

"It was a long time ago. You can't remember everything. And it's not worth risking your life to possibly save Ella's. We'll go down, tell the police—"

"I've told the police!" Her shout reverberated off the rocky hillside. She lowered her voice. "More than once."

"But now we can tell them someone tried to scare us away."

"Someone is scaring *you* away."

He glared at her. "It's not safe for *you*, Cassidy. I have very little to lose."

Why would he say such a thing? James, who'd always had everything. Who'd always had such a strong faith. Someday, she hoped to delve into those questions with him. But not now.

"The police don't believe me. They think I'm a murderer."

He sat back on his heels. She waited for whatever words he was gathering, but he returned to the task of folding up the tent pole, then shoving it in the little fabric bag it had come in.

"What?"

"They're not sure you're a murderer. They think you kidnapped Hallie. They're not convinced her death wasn't an accident."

"Wow." She laced her voice with a heavy dose of sarcasm. "That makes all the difference in the world."

"I'm just saying—"

"I'm just saying that Ella is out here."

He rolled the tent fabric into a tight ball and shoved it in its protective sack, then attached it to his backpack.

She snatched her sleeping bag and shoved it in her own. "Do what you want. I'm not quitting."

Over his shoulder, he said, "You're not staying up here."

"It's a free country."

He stood and faced her. "Only for people who aren't wanted by the police." His voice was cold, steady.

"Is that a threat?"

"You're not staying up here by yourself. Someone's watching us. Someone wants us to leave."

He didn't understand. He couldn't understand.

"I swear, Cassidy. Either you come down with me, or I'll call the police myself and tell them where you are."

"Good. Do it. Then they'll come up here looking for me. At least it would get them on the mountain. They might even accidentally save Ella's life. I don't care how she gets rescued, James. I don't care if I end up in prison. I'm not leaving without her. I can't be responsible again—" She cut off her own words.

"Responsible." He stepped closer, peered down at her. "Do you feel responsible for Hallie's death?"

She put the backpack on and started walking.

He grabbed her arm. "Do you, Cassy? Are you responsible for my sister's death?"

She glared up at him. "A man took her. I told you—"

"You just said, 'I can't be responsible—'"

"Because I couldn't save her." She yanked her arm away. "I'm not going to live with it again. I'm not going to live with knowing I could've saved Ella, our friend's daughter, but didn't because I was too afraid. And Addison, too. If I'd stayed, if I'd faced it instead of running away, they might've caught the guy. But I didn't stay. I was afraid, and I ran, and now one little girl is dead, and another will be soon. So I don't care what you say. I don't care what you threaten. I'm not leaving this mountain without her."

James slipped his hand around her upper arm again, but, this time, the touch was tender. His hard expression softened. "I'm afraid for you, Cassy. Don't you understand? I'm not willing to risk your life."

"It's my life. You don't get to decide how I spend it."

He dropped his hand.

She turned to walk away.

"Wait. Just... wait a second, please."

When she turned, he pointed to the fallen tree-turned-seat.

She sat, and he stared above her head.

"I searched the area this morning," he said. "Saw signs of someone"—he pointed at the rocky hillside behind her—"up there."

"He's gone?"

James shrugged. "Maybe. Or maybe he knew I'd come looking when the sun came up, so he found a spot farther away to watch us."

Fear raised goosebumps on her arms, and she peered into the thick forest all around.

"You can pretend all you want that you're not scared," James said, "but you'd be a fool not to be. And you're no fool."

"Fear isn't a good reason not to go on. And before you say anything, neither is hunger."

Despite her words, hunger already gnawed at her stomach. How long could she last, climbing, without food? They'd eaten often the day before, and it hadn't ever seemed enough.

Jesus lasted forty days in the wilderness without food, though, and she was worrying about a day or two? Surely it wouldn't take longer than that to find the cave.

There were too many unknowns. What she did know was that she wasn't going to leave Ella on this mountain alone any more than she'd been willing to leave Hallie.

After a minute, James settled beside her.

"What are you going to do?" she asked him.

"I can't very well throw you over my shoulder and carry you down."

"You could leave me."

He bumped her shoulder gently. "You know I'd never do that."

Did she know? The James she used to know wouldn't have, but this man was very different from that one.

The James from her childhood had an easy laugh and an easier smile. He'd been relaxed, happy, filled with faith.

This man was brooding and solemn and suspicious, hiding behind the beard and the long hair and the anger he ducked inside like a turtle's shell.

He took out the map and laid it on the ground, crouching

beside it. "We've covered"—he tapped the paper—"a lot of ground here. We know you were at a high altitude because it snowed there long before it snowed in town."

"And the air was thinner. It got hard to get enough oxygen."

"Harder than now?"

She took a deep breath and blew it out. "Yeah."

"We're still a ways from the summit." He folded the map. "We'll keep looking for a little while."

She'd keep looking until she found the cave, but she didn't say that. One hurdle at a time.

"We can only do what we can do." James tucked the map in the backpack. "But, if our stalker thinks that, by stealing our food, he's forced us back down... He's probably gone. We can search a little more. But if he comes back, if he threatens you, we're leaving."

# CHAPTER EIGHTEEN

The man left not long after dinner. Ella had a tummy ache and spent the night squatting over the metal can, her legs trembling 'cause they were so tired. By the time the man came back, the cave was filled with the stink of her diarrhea.

He stepped inside, sniffed, and gave her a long look. "The McDonald's didn't agree with you."

Which was why she didn't want his stupid s'mores.

"Do you still feel sick?"

Her stomach felt empty and achy, like the time she'd been trying to climb a tree but had fallen on a branch and landed on her belly.

"You can tell me. I'm not Mommy. I won't get mad at you if you're sick."

Why would a mommy get mad? If that was how mommies were, she wasn't sorry hers lived so far away.

"I should have been here for you." He sat beside her and slid his arm over her shoulder. "Things are hard right now. It's taking a lot of time to get everything in place for our new home, but once we're on the beach, I'll never leave you again. That's what brothers do. They protect their little sisters. That's my job."

She wouldn't admit that she'd cried all night for Daddy. That she'd wanted somebody to promise that her tummy would stop hurting and she'd be better soon. That, during those last couple of hours when she'd hovered over the bucket, she'd wished the man were there to help her, to keep her butt from falling into the stinky poop-filled tub.

"Mommy wasn't a very good nurse, but I am," he said. "I should have taken care of you, like I did that time you got the flu. Your temperature was really high, but Mommy wanted you to go to school anyway. I snuck you back home after she left for work and took care of you all day long. Mommy was so mad when she got home, she smashed my head against the wall. But I didn't care. And I didn't let her hurt you. You never even knew, did you?"

He looked at her as if waiting for her to say something.

She shook her head.

"I kept her from hurting you then. She won't hurt you now, either. I promise, nobody will hurt you now."

# CHAPTER NINETEEN

Try as he might, James couldn't ignore the gnawing in his stomach. They'd been hiking for three hours, and for every minute, his hunger had grown. He hated that he needed food so badly. Hated the weakness that seemed more obvious as Cassidy followed him, seemingly unaffected. If he needed to, he could search for edible plants and berries, but he didn't want to take the time to do that. He wanted to find that cave, find Ella, and get off the mountain. Nothing else, not even the gnawing in his stomach, mattered as much as that.

He glanced behind him, and Cassidy tried to smile. "Everything okay?"

"Sure." She hadn't mentioned food, so he wouldn't either. "Anything look familiar?"

She looked around. "Not yet."

"Think we're headed in the right direction?"

She shaded her eyes and looked up. "Sun seems to be in the right place. Or close to it. I don't think we're high enough yet."

He continued the trek, and she followed. She'd been following all morning. Not leading. Not offering helpful suggestions or trying to guide him in a particular direction. She truly didn't know where they were going, only what they were looking for. Which tracked with what she'd told him. He was starting to believe she was innocent and back in Coventry only to try to save Ella. What other reason would there be for this climb?

Unless Ella were already dead, and Cassidy was trying to establish an alibi for herself and using James to do it.

Did that make sense?

It was all too convoluted, and he couldn't think straight.

Stupid hunger wasn't helping.

"Can we stop for a second?" she asked.

A rock was jutting from the slope just above, and he climbed it and held out his hand to help her up.

She let go as soon as she was steady on her feet and plopped down.

"My legs are shaking," she said.

He took out their bottles of water, which he'd refilled at the stream an hour past, and sat beside her. "Your shoulder still hurt?"

"Hardly. Hip hurt when we first started, but it's loosened up now."

She took a long sip of her water, then replaced the cap. "Doesn't exactly take the place of a stack of pancakes."

"With real maple syrup." He could practically taste the food.

"I prefer the fake stuff. Mrs. Butterworth."

He glanced her way to find her smiling. "Just sugar and artificial flavoring."

"We never had the real stuff, not at my mom's house, not at any foster home. I think it's too sweet."

"Too sweet? This from the queen of chocolate."

"Chocolate is the perfect amount of sweet." Her stomach rumbled, and he felt gratified that he wasn't suffering alone. She stood and brushed off her jeans, so he did the same, glad she didn't want to linger.

After he started climbing again, she said, "So, how about you? Anybody in your life who wouldn't like that you and I shared a tent last night? Girlfriend?"

"Nope."

"Why not?"

The slope was gentle here. No excuse not to talk. "Haven't met the right woman, I guess."

"Have you been looking?"

"Sure. Of course." A lie. He'd not dated anybody in years. After his mother died, he'd lost interest in dating. In everything.

"Where do you meet women?"

Women. Like he was on the prowl every weekend. "I don't know. Around, I guess."

They hiked for a few minutes before she started again. "What do you do for work?"

Was it not clear that he didn't want to talk? He tamped down the urge to snap at her that it was none of her business. He was hungry, not angry.

When he didn't speak after a few minutes, she said, "I'm sorry. I'm just trying to kill time."

He forced himself to breathe through the irrational irritation. "I still own The Patriot, but Tip manages it for me. In the summer, I give backpacking tours."

"On Coventry?"

"People who pay for guides are looking for more adventure than that. I take people on the Presidential Range. Four days, six days—just depends on what they want and where they want to go."

"That explains why you're so prepared for this trek."

He shrugged.

"Keeps you busy, I guess."

Kept him away from town, away from people who knew too much about his life, his past.

"And in the winter?" she asked.

"My dad used to collect coins. He used to spend a lot of time at it, but when he and my mom married and he opened the restaurant and the other businesses, he had less time for it." Dad had owned a number of businesses in town—two restaurants, the ice cream stand by the lake, a shop for tourists. After Hallie's death, he'd sold them or given them away one by one. He'd kept The Patriot, his first business, to pass on to James.

"What kinds of coins?" she asked.

"Rare coins. Just whatever spoke to him. That's how Dad put it —they spoke to him. He used to go to coin shows and spend hours looking through coins to buy one or two. He loved it."

"I never knew that."

"When I was a kid, he'd take them out and tell me their stories. It was something we did together. Even though he'd quit going to coin shows, he never lost his passion for them."

"Your dad was such an amazing man," Cassidy said. "So passionate about... everything he did, I guess. But mostly his family."

"Yeah." James let the wave of grief roll over him, allowing himself to recall Dad the way he'd been before Hallie's death. The bright eyes, the optimism that laced every word, the faith that undergirded their family. So much loss.

The hill got steeper, and he kept quiet until it leveled out. But her question was still hanging out there.

"After he died, Mom gave me the collection. I was trying to get close to him, to love something he loved. I went through it, spent a lot of time valuing what he had. I had no intention of selling them. I just wanted to see what was there. Then I realized it was more than just a few shoeboxes full of old coins. It was history. It was connection. Next thing I knew, I was going to coin shows, trying to see what Dad saw. I started buying and selling and..." He shrugged. "It's my job in the winter. I trade coins, mostly online. Most rare, but I also dabble in bullion. Buy low, sell high. You know."

Behind him, she chuckled. "Not really. What exactly is bullion?"

"Bullion. You know. Gold, silver, platinum, palladium?"

"Palladium?"

"It's a metal valued... well, usually around the same as gold, sometimes higher, sometimes lower. Sort of looks like silver. Used in jewelry and dentistry and catalytic converters."

She chuckled. "That's a strange list of uses."

"Yeah. Something about it cleanses exhaust or something. I don't know. I'm more interested in the value of the coins."

"You own a lot of palladium?"

"Nah. Traded it some, but it's not exactly plentiful. I'm more interested in the rare coins, but I've collected some silver and gold over the years. It's sort of my version of a retirement account, I guess."

"Ha. Retirement. I'm just lucky to scrape up enough money to pay my rent. I'll have to work till I die. Maybe I'll get lucky and die young."

He shot her a look. "That's not funny."

"I'm not trying to be funny. I know where I'm going after this life. I have no reason to want to put it off."

Her words raised his frustration again. "You have no idea what it's like to bury someone you love. If you had any care for the people who love you—"

"Quite the assumptions you're making there."

He let her words roll around in his brain, but they never ordered themselves in a way that made sense. "What assumptions am I making?"

"That I've never buried anyone I love. And that there are people who'd grieve me."

"Of course there are. The kids you serve, if nobody else."

"The few who would shed a tear wouldn't fill a church pew."

"People you work with?"

"Acquaintances. Friends, sure. But not... not family. Nobody whose life would be different if I weren't in it."

What a sad thing to say. To believe about your own life.

"It's just one more thing people with families don't understand. I'm not saying I don't have people who love me. And I'm not saying my life doesn't matter. It does. I make a difference in girls' lives. I'm just saying, when you don't have family, who's there to care? Who will the hospital call when I die? My best friend, I guess. But since she married and had a kid..." Her words trailed, but he could imagine. He'd been happy for Reid when he and Denise married and Ella was born. But he'd missed the friendship they'd had before. Even after Denise left, Reid had been too busy playing both father and mother to spend much time with James.

Selfish though it was, he grieved the loss. "I understand better than you think."

Silence greeted that statement. He didn't explain. Didn't have to. His family was gone. Sure, he had aunts and uncles and cousins, but they had their own lives. They'd be sad if he died, but they'd recover by dinnertime. Reid would care. Vince would care. Aside from that...

"I'm not trying to be morbid," she said. "I just believe that what's to come is better than what's here. Life is hard, but God is good, and I'm not afraid to face Him. I'm looking forward to heaven, where there'll be no more tears or pain or suffering."

He'd often thought of the world to come. When they'd buried his sister, some of his grief had been tempered by the idea that she was in a better place. When his father died, then his mom, he'd considered the peace they had. The reunion in heaven. He was the only one left here on earth, left to deal with their deaths—and the rest of this hard world—all by himself.

After they'd walked a few minutes, only the forest sounds and their grumbling stomachs to keep them company, she said, "Do you mind...?"

When her words trailed, he glanced in her direction. "You need to rest?"

"No."

He continued forward.

"I don't want to make you angry, but I'd really like to know what happened back then. From your perspective."

Memories he preferred not to conjure. "Why?"

"We can put together what I know and what you know and, I

don't know, learn something. And I'm curious, I guess, how everybody decided so fast that I was a kidnapper and a murderer."

"Not sure what I can add. You two disappeared on Tuesday night. Search parties went out, stayed out all day Wednesday."

"Even in the snow?"

"It was raining most of the day. The rain changed to snow Wednesday night. They kept looking, but there were no tracks. They had nothing to go on except the fact that you didn't have a car, so nobody figured you'd gone far. And Wilson Cage said he saw you on the trail."

"He did? I didn't see him."

James took in that information but wasn't sure what to make of it. Mr. Cage had told him he'd been in a hurry to get ready for his date. It made sense that, once he realized who it was and that they were fine, he'd ducked back onto the path and returned to the campground.

"I didn't get a look at him or to hear his voice yesterday. He could be the kidnapper."

"He had an alibi."

"So? People lie. Whoever took us tied us up and left us in that cave for hours at a time. He came back with supplies, so he had to live nearby, close enough to walk."

"The campground's not exactly near where we are right now. It's on the other side of the mountain. And anyway, it seems the kidnapper has a much faster way to get up here, an unmarked road or something. It's taking us forever to find this place, but your kidnapper must have known the area well."

"Even so, he had to have gone home. The things he brought were old. It wasn't like... like he'd just picked them up in town."

That made sense. They were on the far side of the mountain from town now. Not a lot of neighborhoods at the base on this side. Summer homes rimmed the lake, and a few cottages had been built onto the hillside, but most were empty in the wintertime. In fact, Hallie's body had been found at one of the few houses on this side of Mt. Ayasha that was occupied year-round—a fact Cassidy would have known because it was lived in by the school principal. Vice principal back then. Everybody knew where he lived, which he'd lamented more than once when teens had TP'd the trees in his yard.

James would ask Vince who else wintered here. His mother had lived on this side of Ayasha since before Vince was born.

"Anyway, Hallie's body was found Thursday afternoon. At that point, authorities became convinced you'd taken her. They called off the mountain search and focused on highways and interstates and bus stations." He wanted to ask her how she'd gotten away, but he couldn't quite force the words out. He'd thought his grief from those days was long buried, but it was all coming back. His prayers every night that Cassidy would be found, alive and well and with a good explanation for what happened. He'd believed her dead until Vince had assured him they knew she wasn't. And then... He hadn't known what to think.

"That's it," he said. "Because your body wasn't found, because the police had a credible reason to believe you were still alive— your phone call, but only the cops knew that at the time—you became the prime suspect in—"

"Stop."

"Sorry, but you asked."

"No, I mean..."

He turned to see her staring up at the hill beside them.

"What?"

"This is it." Her voice, now a whisper, quivered. "He wanted us to climb this, but Hallie was too little, and he couldn't do it with her on his back."

The slope was steep and littered with boulders as if a giant child had stacked them, one upon another. Green poked between the rocks, but very little vegetation grew here. Who would ever think to climb this?

Cassidy, apparently. She scrambled up the first boulder.

"You're gonna—"

"Shh!" She shot him a look and kept her voice low. "We can do this."

"Let's go the long way, the way you went that day with him."

She kept climbing.

"Wait." When she turned, he shrugged out of his backpack. "How much farther from here?"

"It's just"—she waved toward the top of the hill—"up there."

He looked around, found a large boulder below where they stood, and scrambled downward to it, motioning her to follow.

She did, and, after marking their location on the map and shoving his flashlight in his back pocket, he stowed his backpack and reached for hers. "It'll be easier to climb without these."

She shrugged hers off and handed it to him, then returned to the slope and started climbing toward the cave and, he hoped, Ella and a kidnapper and murderer.

## CHAPTER TWENTY

*D*on't think about it.

*Don't remember.*

All that mattered now was finding Ella. What happened back then...

*Don't think about it.*

But the memories were as solid as the boulders that scraped against Cassidy's hands.

She should have listened to James. To come this way was only stubbornness. They could have found the other path. But it would've taken time, time they might not have.

Ella. She had to focus on Ella, on saving this girl's life. Not on the one she failed to save.

She reached for a handhold and gripped. Ignoring the pain in her fingers, her shoulder, her hip, she hoisted herself up, tried to settle her foot in the crag of the rock. Her boot slipped. Her knee jabbed into the stone. She tipped back, and her hand lost its hold.

Her arm flailed, found nothing to hang onto.

Memories flashed, all the things she never wanted to see again. Hallie's terror, Hallie's trust.

Hallie's lifeless eyes.

A strong hand pushed Cassidy forward. James whispered, "I got you."

She managed to get her foot on the crag, her hand in a hold. Pulled herself up.

Only a little part of her wished she'd fallen. Wished for all this to be over.

*Lord...* But there were no words. Because to live meant to face it. To die meant freedom.

Definitely not the kind of thoughts she should be harboring while she climbed this dangerous slope.

James came up beside her. The hill wasn't that high—she guessed sixty feet—and the worst was below them.

He studied her face, and she worried her thoughts would be as obvious as the concern in his expression. He whispered, "You okay?"

"Just lost my grip. Thank you for that."

"Glad I was there."

She steeled her courage and continued.

James lifted a staying hand and went ahead of her.

He scrabbled up the remaining fifteen feet or so. When he reached the summit, he crouched down and held out his hand to help her up.

She followed, gripped his hand, and joined him on the hillside.

They rested a moment, breathing heavily. It was silent. Even the birdsong was muffled. Or maybe her fear was roaring too loudly for her to hear anything over it.

The hill gave way to a level area covered in vegetation. A natural path led to the right from where they'd climbed, but she pointed to the left, where the mountain rose steeply toward the summit.

Now that she was here, she remembered it vividly.

She took out her handgun and started to the left. The broad grassy area narrowed until the path was only about a foot wide. The mountain rose on one side, fell on the other. Bushes and short trees grew from the stony soil, blocking the sunshine. She made her way forward, feeling James behind her. But she couldn't look.

They rounded a bend, and there it was.

A giant boulder, rounded by years of weather and covered with vegetation. It was flattish on the bottom and propped against a pile of other boulders, also covered with vegetation. Beneath the large boulder, a gap.

It would be impossible to see from any other direction, completely hidden from above. But here, the opening was obvious.

When she paused to listen, James gripped her upper arm and motioned that he wanted to go first.

She pressed her back against the steep hillside, and he slid past her and crept closer.

No noises came from within. Not a whimpering child or a threatening man. But Ella had to be here. She had to.

James stepped around the corner, crouched down, and moved into the opening, gun drawn.

She followed him into the darkened cave, her own gun pointed at the ground rather than at James's back, which she nearly bumped into.

She moved to his side and let her eyes adjust to the darkness.

Empty. The scent of feces hovered in the air.

Though outside the sun shone, inside, the only light came from the narrow opening they'd just come through. James flicked on the flashlight and aimed the beam around the space.

It illuminated dirt floor, stone walls, boulder ceiling. No little girl huddled in the corner. No man prepared to defend himself.

James shined the flashlight along the walls, but Cassidy went straight to the back, got on her hands and knees, and looked at the only hiding place the cave offered.

Ella wasn't there.

She made her way to a familiar spot against the wall and sat. With Hallie on her lap, Cassidy had spent hours upon hours here, praying for help. Waiting for a rescuer. No deliverer had come. Though she desperately wanted to be that deliverer for little Ella...

She had failed.

Ella wasn't here.

*Oh, Father. Now what?*

Was the kidnapper a copycat? Somebody who knew just enough about the event a decade earlier to make it look like the same person?

Or had the kidnapper found a better hideout?

What if Eugene had seen her and told his father, and Wilson had figured out who she was. It was possible Wilson had moved the child last night, knowing Cassidy was back in town.

Or had it been the kidnapper and murderer who'd followed Cassidy on the trails two days before. Had he moved Ella then?

Was that why their stalker hadn't tried to kill them? Better to have Cassidy find the cave and be discredited when Ella wasn't there.

She didn't know. She only knew she was hungry and tired and in pain, and for what?

For nothing. All for nothing.

*Lord, I can't do this anymore. I can't... care so much, not if she's going to be lost too. Ella is in Your capable hands. You didn't see fit to let me find her, so... please, rescue that little girl. Please, don't let her suffer the same fate Addison did.*

She didn't want to see it, didn't want to imagine what it had been like, but the images were too real. She'd been the recipient of beatings the first decade of her life. Her mother always stunk of the whiskey she drank with orange juice for breakfast, on the rocks at lunchtime, and straight by the time dinner rolled around. The scent of whiskey accompanied all of Cassidy's early memories. Mom and whiskey and a fist. Mom and whiskey and an empty bottle-turned-weapon. Mom and whiskey and a cigarette butt and the scent of burning flesh.

It had been bad enough when Mom's rage spent itself on Cassidy, but when Mom turned her rage on Cassidy's little sister, Becca, it had been horrible. Little Becca, too small to take the beatings, would beg for help. Cassidy would fight back then, push her mother away and yell at Becca to run and hide.

Mom was usually too drunk to pursue.

If only Cassidy had been home that day. When she was ten, the neighbors had invited her over to play, and Mom had been passed out on the couch. After Cassidy'd fixed Becca breakfast, she'd kissed her good-bye and gone next door. The neighbor had gotten a new Barbie Jeep, and they'd played with the dolls for hours.

Too long.

When she realized the time, a pain grew in the pit of her stomach that told her something was wrong. She didn't know what, she didn't know why. She only knew she had to check on Becca.

She walked in to find Mom kneeling over Becca, eyes glazed over and wide. Confused.

Becca hadn't been breathing.

Cassidy called an ambulance, but it was too late.

Becca died.

Mom claimed Becca had fallen, but the injuries weren't consistent with that story. And Cassidy had told the truth. For the first time, no matter the threatening scowl Mom gave her, Cassidy had looked the scary policeman in the eyes and told him the things her mother did. How she pushed her. Hit her. Burned her. Cassidy told the policeman how she'd tried for years to protect her sister. And she told him how she'd failed her sister that day because she'd been playing with a Barbie Jeep.

But even as she'd blamed herself, she'd known, deep down, it was Mom's fault.

Mom went to prison. Cassidy ended up in foster care, swearing she'd never, ever be like her mother.

And then, after promising Hallie she'd protect her, promising she'd never leave her...

She'd stood over Hallie's body.

No matter how hard she tried, she couldn't save her sister and she couldn't save Hallie and she couldn't save Ella.

Why was she here? Not here in this cave, surrounded by the most terrifying memories of her life. Not here in Coventry, the town that had never accepted her. Not here in New Hampshire, the state that had failed to protect Cassidy and Becca from an abusive, alcoholic mother.

Here, on the planet.

No family. No loved ones. No real home.

As she'd flown from the West Coast to the East, she'd convinced herself that this was why she'd survived a decade past. So that she could come back and save Ella.

That there was a purpose for all the pain. That God could use the worst parts of her existence to bring life to someone else.

She'd been wrong.

And all she'd done for the first twenty-eight years of her life was to prove, over and over, that she couldn't save anybody.

And here was more evidence.

Why was she here?

# CHAPTER TWENTY-ONE

The cave existed. Standing in its center, James tried to push away all the questions and images—his sister and his girlfriend and a killer. Right in this spot.

What had happened to Hallie here? To Cassidy? James might never know all the facts, could never know all the fears, but he could feel, somehow, a sense of... darkness. The murderer might've abandoned this cave, but an aura of wickedness lingered like the scent of sulphur after an extinguished match.

James tried to shake it off, that oppressive evil that seemed to permeate his skin and fill his heart with despair. But the truth was the truth. Evil things had happened here.

His search of the cave, limited though it was with the narrow beam of his flashlight, gave further evidence that, at some point, somebody had been here. Earth disturbed by hands or bodies. Black marks on the otherwise gray walls that led up to the ceiling and out a narrow gap in the rocks. Somebody had lit a fire here. What that proved was that, though those who claimed to know this mountain better than anybody swore no caves existed, somebody knew about this place. Somebody besides Cassidy.

The kidnapper.

Where was he now?

If he'd seen Cassidy and James the night before and guessed their destination, he could have moved Ella. That was possible, but the guy was a killer. Why not just kill them?

Perhaps he only liked to kill little girls. Perhaps he had no stomach for murdering adults. Did that make sense?

Not really.

More likely, he figured two more missing people would raise suspicion, pull more people onto the mountain. But... he'd stolen their food, which also raised suspicion.

James didn't understand, and the gnawing in his stomach wasn't helping matters.

Cassidy was seated against the cave wall, arms around her bent legs, head on her knees. She was silent, but her heaving back told him enough.

He sat beside her and wrapped his arm around her shoulders. "Hey, it's okay." He pulled her close, and she shifted, pressing her cheek against his chest.

Both arms around her, he said, "You were right about this place."

"She's not here, so it doesn't matter."

It mattered to him. Though back in high school, Cassidy had learned to love the outdoors as much as he, she'd been a city kid before foster care, never one for hiking or backpacking. She'd never have come this far from town on her own.

Somebody had brought her here. Of that, he was certain.

A monster. A killer.

A man who'd ruined his parents' lives. James's life.

Cassidy's life.

All because some man, some nameless, faceless man, liked to steal little girls.

Hallie and Mom and Dad were gone now, but Cassidy was here. Alive and brokenhearted.

He rubbed his hand up and down her back. "It's okay."

"She's not here."

"But maybe she was."

Cassidy looked up, eyes wide. "You think so? Did you see something?"

"Nothing specific, but somebody was here. The kidnapper could have moved her."

"If she was ever here at all." The despair in Cassidy's voice frightened him, especially after her remarks on the hike up about how nobody would grieve her.

He would grieve her. If something happened to Cassidy... He couldn't even finish the thought.

"If we were on the wrong track," he said, "then why did someone steal our food?"

"It doesn't matter now."

He ignored the hopeless words. "When they figure out who did it—"

"They never will." She straightened, staring at the cave wall not five feet across from them. "They'll never find out the truth because they think it was me."

She made a good point.

They sat in the cool air. What was she thinking? Would she turn herself in now? He could vouch for the existence of this place, but would that deter Vince and Detective Cote, who were sure she was guilty?

One thing was certain. He couldn't quit looking for the kidnapper. He wouldn't. Now that he was convinced Cassidy was innocent, he had to keep searching—for Ella's sake, Reid's sake, and Cassidy's sake.

And Hallie's and Addison's as well. They deserved justice.

She shifted beside him, lowered to a prone position, and pointed toward the rear of the cave. "Do you see that?"

He glanced in the direction she pointed but saw nothing.

"You have to get down here."

He lay beside her. Sure enough, from this angle, he saw something deep in the cave. A...glimmer of light. "What is it?"

"I saw it when Hallie and I were tied up, but I didn't know what it was." She stood and walked that direction. The ceiling lowered, and she crouched, then crawled forward. "When he came back, he untied us. I guess he felt safe because he stationed himself at the mouth of the cave. There was no way to get past him."

The ceiling lowered more. James had noticed this place but hadn't explored it in his perusal of the cave because Cassidy had gone straight to this spot and looked. He got on hands and knees and followed.

In front of him, Cassidy wiggled, doing something, but he couldn't tell exactly what. Then, she twisted around until she faced him and handed him her handgun. "I don't think I'll be able to squeeze through with that on."

He took it, studied it. A Glock 9mm. Good gun.

Cassidy crawled backward. To where, he didn't know. It seemed they'd reached the end.

Except she kept going.

"What is it?" he asked.

"A way out." She disappeared down a shaft so narrow, he hadn't noticed it and was sure he wouldn't fit. He crept forward and looked. The ground gave way to an opening. The stone over-hang lowered here, so that the space was barely wide enough for Cassidy's thin hips. No way he could go forward. But she was gone.

"You okay?" he called.

"Can you make it through?"

"No chance."

"Back up. I'll just come around the other direction."

The thought of her out there, alone, sent acid to his stomach. "Can you just come back through?"

"Hard enough getting out. Not sure I can get back in. Hey, while you're in there, will you look around? I lost... something special to me back then. I think it came off when we were getting away."

We?

As in, her and Hallie?

He'd ask her about that later.

He took out the flashlight and backed toward the mouth of the narrow passage, eyes open for whatever Cassidy had lost. There was nothing—

"Wait!" She called. "I found—"

A gunshot cut off her words.

# CHAPTER TWENTY-TWO

"Cassy!" James's shout reverberated off the narrow stone passageway as he crawled out. It widened and he hurried on hands and knees until he crawled into the cavern, jumped to his feet, and bounded out of the cave. He held her gun at the ready, running too fast along the narrow path between the steep wall and the sharp drop-off. He sprinted past the spot where they'd climbed up and around a bend, then slid down a short slope and around another corner. He skidded to a stop behind the thick branches of a pine that grew out of the hillside below.

Cassidy lay facedown on the ground, arms covering her head. A protective posture, which suggested she was alive.

He lurched forward. "Cassy! Are you—?"

"Get down!"

He hit the rocky soil just as another gunshot rang out. He peeked up from his prone position beside Cassidy. Aside from the occasional treetop, this area was exposed. The shooter had to be below them on the mountain. On this side, with the lake between Mt. Ayasha and Mt. Coventry, there were no other ridges with a vantage point. James should be safe if he stayed low. He crawled to Cassidy's side. "Are you hit?"

She lifted her head to face him, blood gushing from her hair.

He tried to get a better look. "What happened?"

"I don't... I don't know."

"Can you flip over?"

Keeping low, he gently turned her onto her back so he could examine the wound. Just behind her ear, an inch-long gash had blood pouring from it.

His first aid supplies were in his backpack at the bottom of the hill.

Cassidy had wrapped her sweatshirt around her waist, so he tugged it off and pressed the fabric to the injury.

"Did you see anyone?" he asked.

"No." She was shivering, and he wrapped his arms around her, trying to warm her. She couldn't go into shock, not now. They had to get out of there.

"You're okay." He moved her hand to the sweatshirt. "Hold that in place."

She did, and he slipped off his T-shirt and tore a strip off the bottom. Gently, he lowered her hand and pressed the T-shirt over the wound, getting a better look at it. It was still bleeding heavily, but... "It's just a flesh wound. It'll heal." He tied the T-shirt in place.

As soon as he was finished, she cuddled in beside him as if she were considering a nap. As if she felt safe there. But they weren't safe.

He kissed her temple. "We need to get moving."

She nodded, then closed her eyes and tensed as if the slight movement had brought pain. If a nod hurt, what she needed to do next would be torture.

"Let's get this sweatshirt on you." He set her away from him and lowered it over her head, careful of the wound and bandage. She was all but limp in his hands as he worked her arms into the sleeves.

How was he ever going to get her out of here?

He pulled his cell from his front pocket hoping that, since they were near the top of the mountain, they might have service.

Nope. Zero bars.

He pulled up the navigation screen and took a screenshot. That would suffice until he got back to the paper map and plotted their location.

Aside from the occasional birdsong, the mountain was silent. It was too much to hope that the shooter had given up. Was he making his way closer? Looking for a better vantage point?

"We're going to crawl back to the hill we came up. You think you can get back down?"

Her eyes widened. "No. I can't go down that way. We'll take the other path, the longer path."

He didn't like that idea, but only because he didn't know that way. He knew this one, and his backpack and all their supplies were at the bottom of that hill. How much time would the long way around take? How much time did Cassy have before the loss of blood affected her ability to move, to think?

"Can you find it?" he asked.

She swallowed, started to nod but stopped, and then flipped onto her stomach and crawled.

He followed, staying low. In this direction, the forest thickened again, and, when they were safely away from where the shooter had to have been perched, they stood.

Cassidy seemed firm on her feet, thank God. He handed her gun to her, and she slipped it into its holster. She hurried forward, still crouching low, whether from instinct or pain, he didn't know.

He'd have led, but she seemed to know where she was going.

They followed a very narrow path, but more of a path than what they'd taken to get up there.

It wound downward until, suddenly, Cassy stopped.

"What's wrong?"

"I don't..." She looked around, then back up the slope. "It's been so long. I don't know how to get back to where our stuff is. I only went that way the one time."

Did they need their backpacks? He didn't care about the packs themselves. His sleeping bags, his tent, his Jetboil... None of that mattered. But the map with the coordinates of where they'd been was in there.

That didn't matter now. They'd found what they were looking for.

But the medical supplies.

In the silence, he listened for any sounds that didn't belong. Only forest noises surrounded them.

Where was the shooter?

What should they do?

He urged Cassidy into the cover of trees, easing her to a sitting position against a maple out of sight of the path. "Rest a second while I figure out where we are."

She didn't argue, leaning her head against the trunk and closing her eyes.

He didn't ask if she was in pain. The answer was written in the tension on her brow, the hunching of her shoulders.

Looking at her, thinking what could've happened...

Averting his gaze—better to concentrate—he studied the too-small map on his phone, trying to figure out where they were in relation to the bottom of the rocky cliff they'd climbed. He needed his map with the markings. This digital one showed nothing but green. Useless.

He crouched beside Cassidy, set his handgun on the ground, and gently lifted the fabric from her wound. Fresh blood filled it, but less than before. He returned the bandage and pressed. "How're you holding up?"

"I'm all right."

"Did you see anyone?"

"No. Nothing."

He gazed into the forest all around them. No signs of another human being. But someone was out there.

They needed help. They needed protection and guidance. Needed what only God could offer right now. Not that he had the right to ask anything of God after his years of silence, but he took her hands and closed his eyes. "Father, we need help. Hide us from the shooter. Guide us back to our packs and my Jeep. Please stop the bleeding in Cassy's wound and protect her from further injury." He opened his eyes to find her watching him. "Anything to add?"

"No. Just…" Her eyes filled with tears, and she shook her head as if to rid it of the overflowing emotions.

He kissed her temple, and a scripture welled up in him until he couldn't contain it. "God is our refuge and our fortress. He'll cover us with His feathers."

"We'll find shelter under the shadow of His wing."

James couldn't help the smile crossing his face. Apparently he wasn't the only one who'd studied the Psalm. "We won't fear the terror of night or the arrows—or bullets—that fly in the daytime."

"I don't remember the rest," she said. "Something about no disaster coming near our tent."

"We needed that one last night."

She sniffed, her own smile breaking through the fear in her expression. "He brought us this far," she said. "He'll get us safely through."

James sat beside her and studied the map with fresh eyes. *Lead us, Lord.*

He closed his eyes, pictured the paper map, pictured the route they'd walked to get to the cave, the one they'd just come down. If he weren't mistaken…

"I think we need to head back up a little ways."

"Okay." She leaned on one arm to prop herself up.

He jumped to his feet and helped her stand, worried about the wooziness that had her gripping the tree trunk for more support.

*Lord, infuse her with strength.*

He snatched his gun from the bracken, laid his free hand on her back, and led her to the path. They climbed up, him alternating between studying the map and gazing at the surroundings, looking for any sign of a shooter.

It was impossible to know where to go, but somehow, they made their way around the hill where the cave was hidden and to the base of the rocky slope.

He pulled her off the path to the rock where they'd hidden their backpacks.

But the backpacks were gone.

He settled Cassidy against the rock. "I'm going to look around. They have to be here. I must have forgotten where—"

"He took them, James."

He wasn't willing to accept that answer. He needed his map.

He walked around, checking behind trees, in a depression, around rocks. The backpack, his map, the medical supplies—all gone.

Settling beside Cassidy, he leaned against the rock, and once again, studied the woefully deficient map on his phone. The last thing he wanted was to go back the way they'd come. There had to be a faster way to the Jeep—or any road—from here.

Yes. There was a road—not the one they'd come in on, but another one—that seemed like it wasn't too far down. "If we can make it down to here"—he pointed to the spot—"we should have service enough to call the police and—"

"What? No. You can't do that. They'll arrest me."

"You were shot. We need—"

"I was grazed."

"You could've been killed."

Her eyes filled. "I know. I know."

"We need to report it."

"When I'm safely away, you can call the police. I'm not going to jail today."

Surely they wouldn't take her to jail. Rather than argue, he stood and held out his hand to help her up.

Gun in its holster, gaze on the map, he led Cassidy in the direction of the road. One way or another, they needed to get back to his Jeep. He didn't know how they'd do that if she refused to let him call the police. It wasn't as if he could call his friends for a ride.

Neither Vince nor Reid would look kindly on the fact that he'd gone on this journey with Cassidy.

*Lead us, Lord.*

They needed all the help they could get.

## CHAPTER TWENTY-THREE

The loud bangs had scared Ella, and she'd tried to scream, but the gag the man had shoved in her mouth kept the noise from coming out.

She lay still on the ground, waiting for another bang, but none came.

The man had tied her hands behind her back, her feet together. And he'd wrapped her chain around a tree trunk so she couldn't get away.

She'd asked him what was wrong, and he'd only said that the cave wasn't safe anymore. Could it be more dangerous than when the bear got in? What kind of monsters were there now?

He promised he'd be back for her and left her in the woods, all alone. Where was he? What was he doing?

Why didn't Daddy come?

She laid there a long time, her tummy still feeling yucky. Bugs crawled over her skin. Icky bugs, not her crickets. She felt them in her hair and on her back. But with her hands tied, she couldn't swipe them or her tears away. They were probably gonna eat her up while she laid there. And then wouldn't the man be sad. His *sister* dead because she got eaten by ants.

Two squirrels chased each other in the tree limbs above her

head. Up and down, round and round the trunk, acting all silly and free. She wished she could play chase with them. She wished she were a squirrel and could run away. The man could never catch her if she were a squirrel.

Ella and her friends liked to race each other in her backyard sometimes. Everybody always wanted to play at Ella's house because she had the best daddy. He didn't sit inside and ignore them when they played like other parents did. No, he came outside and played with them. Once, when it was really hot and they were all sticky and sweaty, her daddy snuck outside and attacked them with a giant water gun, and all the kids laughed and giggled and begged to be shot next. And then he turned on the sprinkler, and they played until the backyard was a muddy mess. When Papa came over that night and scolded Daddy for ruining the yard, Daddy said, "My daughter is infinitely more valuable than grass, Pop."

What was Daddy doing now? Was he missing her? Was he crying like she was crying? Or was the man right? Did Daddy not want her anymore?

No. Daddy loved her. He loved her, and he wanted her back. He was probably lost without her. Who was he eating Cheetos Puffs with? Who was he playing games with? Who was he kissing good-night now that she was gone?

*Dear God, please. I wanna go home. I want my daddy.*

The first squirrel hopped to another tree, and the second one followed, and they disappeared, leaving Ella alone with the bugs.

# CHAPTER TWENTY-FOUR

Cassidy's head pounded, her stomach roiled. She could hardly walk straight, much less think straight.

She followed James, trusting he had some idea where they were going and making no effort to help guide them. It took all her energy to stay on her feet. But she wasn't about to tell him that. What she needed more than anything was food. And water. And an Ibuprofen or four.

When she was sitting, when she could put together complete sentences, she'd tell James why he couldn't call the police. Because their having been shot at didn't prove anything. It certainly didn't prove Cassidy wasn't a killer. For all she knew, somebody'd shot at her because he recognized her as the girl wanted in connection with Ella's kidnapping. Maybe the shooter wanted justice for Addison or Hallie. Maybe it was a crazy out-of-season hunter.

Being shot at didn't prove she was innocent any more than being the victim of a mugging would make someone innocent of a bank robbery.

The police would probably consider her murder sweet justice. Meanwhile, they'd think they had their kidnapper, and Ella would still be in danger.

Assuming the girl was still alive. Except... there was something, something she was forgetting.

She trudged through the woods behind James, focusing on his feet to keep her on the path.

One thing was certain now, one thing she hadn't been so certain of before. She didn't want to die.

Nothing like having a bullet graze your head to remind you of the innate desire to live.

*Father...*

James had lifted logical prayers. All she could manage was a mantra of *Father, help* and *please, please...*

He heard her. He knew.

It was late afternoon, hours after they'd first climbed the cliff to the cave, when they stumbled out of the woods and onto a narrow paved road.

James turned to her. "You okay? You've been awfully quiet."

"Concentrating." On not falling down. On putting one foot in front of the other.

"How's the head?"

Pounding. Throbbing. "Fine."

The slight narrowing of his eyes showed he wasn't convinced.

But that didn't matter. "You can't call the police."

"You need medical attention."

"I need Neosporin and a bandage. And an aspirin."

"Tylenol. Aspirin's a blood thinner."

Good point. If she'd eaten today, if she hadn't been mountain climbing on an empty stomach, if she hadn't been shot, she'd have thought of that.

He turned his attention to his phone.

"Please, James. Please don't call the police until I'm safely away from you. I need to rest. I need a bed, not a jail cell."

"Don't have service anyway." He lowered the phone and started walking along the edge of the asphalt. "Someone'll come along."

She fell in step beside him. "How far are we from the Jeep?"

"Miles."

Miles. She'd never make it.

She started to wonder if she'd be better off if she were arrested. At least the police would take her to a hospital, and a doctor might make her stay, and she'd be given a nice, warm bed and a good meal and a potent painkiller. If she could just sleep, then she could think straight. Then she could figure out what to do next.

Of course, in that scenario, the "next" would be jail.

They'd walked ten or fifteen minutes when the distant sound of an engine broke through her muddled thoughts.

Before she had a chance to react, James pulled her off the road and behind a tree. "I'll get a ride to my Jeep and come back for you. Stay here."

She lowered to the ground, happy to comply.

James walked back to the road. She couldn't see him from here, but she heard the engine approach, then slow down.

"You all right?" a male voice called.

"My friend and I were hiking when she took a bad fall. Any chance you could give us a ride to my car?"

What was he doing? Why bring her into this when he'd just told her to hide?

"I can call someone for you." The driver's voice dripped with suspicion.

"My name's James Sullivan. I live right next to the campground on Highway 23. I'm just gonna grab my ID." After a pause, she heard, "Here you go. Feel free to take a picture and send it to someone you trust. I mean you no harm, just need to get my friend to safety."

"Where's the car?" the stranger asked.

"A couple miles from here." Then James shouted, "Ellen?"

Ellen. Cassidy's middle name. Good memory.

She stepped out from behind the tree and walked toward the silver sedan. It had Massachusetts plates. Not a local. Not someone who'd recognize either of them. Of course, he could've seen her photo. It'd been plastered all over the state. But it was an old photo and looked nothing like the new Cassidy.

There was a man behind the wheel, another in the passenger seat. Both dressed for a day outdoors.

The driver gazed at her through the windshield, then said, "Okay. Get in."

James helped Cassidy into the backseat. The air conditioner must've been working overtime, because the air was chilly against her sweaty skin.

James settled beside her and scooted close.

The driver hit the gas while the passenger, eyeing the sweat-shirt she was still gripping, asked, "What did you do?"

She was trying to formulate an answer when James said, "She took a nasty fall and gashed her scalp. I left all our stuff and carried her out. Any chance you guys have some water?"

The passenger handed back a cold bottle, and James palmed it open and handed it to her.

She gulped greedily, forced herself to stop, and handed it to James. He took a reasonable sip.

"Where'd you go?" the driver asked.

While directing the driver to his Jeep, James chatted with the guys in front as if he and Cassidy had enjoyed a relatively peaceful hike punctuated by a terrible accident.

Just a few minutes later, the sedan turned onto the narrow logging road where they'd begun this journey. "Didn't even know this road was here," the driver said.

"Helps to be a local. If it's too rough, we can walk it from here."

The driver slowed, but the passenger said, "Better drive 'em all the way up. She doesn't look like she can walk."

Cassidy considered opening her eyes—when had she closed them?—to argue but realized the guy was probably right. Even if she could walk it, she definitely didn't want to.

"Jeep's there."

The sedan braked, and Cassidy opened her eyes. Oh, yeah. James had hidden it from the road.

The driver turned back. "Why'd you hide it?"

"Teenagers come up here to drink. Didn't want to invite vandalism."

The guy squinted as if he weren't sure.

James opened his car door and slid out. A minute later, her door opened, and he helped her stand. She waited while James shook the driver's hand through the window. "There's a turn-around just ahead on the right. You'll see it."

While the sedan inched forward, James swept Cassidy into his arms.

She wanted to protest that she could walk, but she couldn't seem to make her voice work.

He carried her to the Jeep, then set her down gently and clicked it unlocked.

After yanking off the tarp, he settled her in the seat and put her seatbelt on her, though she could've done that herself if only she could've gotten her eyes to stay open.

The Jeep bounced back to the dirt road, then turned onto the state highway.

Next thing she knew, the car slowed and turned. She forced her eyes open and saw James's house ahead.

He opened the garage door, drove inside, and then helped her into the house, where he settled her at the kitchen table and got two glasses of water. "Drink."

She did, letting the cold liquid soothe her aching throat.

He opened a box of crackers, took out a handful, and set the box in front of her. "Munch on those while I get us something more substantial."

The first bite of the tiny orange square and she was sure she'd never tasted anything so good. It'd been less than twenty-four hours since she'd eaten, but between the physical exertion and the injury, it might as well have been a week.

Next, he handed her a bowl of yogurt with some berries in it and a piece of cheese. "We don't want to overdo and make ourselves sick."

She started with the cheese—provolone, she thought—then dug into the blueberry yogurt. It tasted delicious with the raspberries he'd added.

She ate every bite, then sat back and let the food settle in her stomach.

"You okay?"

She nodded.

He crouched in front of her and gazed at her face. "You sure? You're pale as death, and you haven't spoken in... a while."

Hadn't she? She started to say something, but her voice rasped out. She cleared her throat and tried again. "I'm okay."

He sat back on his heels. "You scared me there for a minute."

"I was feeling a little..." Sick? Dizzy? Tired? All of the above. "I needed food."

"Yeah." He gazed at the sweatshirt she'd dropped on his table. "That was a lot to take, between the loss of blood, the fatigue, the hunger."

"I'm okay now." She already felt better. Not a hundred percent, but better.

He squeezed her knee. "Sit tight." He left the room and came back a minute later with a plastic shoebox that looked vaguely familiar.

He set it beside her, and she realized it was the same box that Mrs. Sullivan had stored first-aid supplies in years before.

With a wet paper towel in one hand, he met her eyes. "I'm going to clean it, okay?"

"Can you do that without touching it?"

His smile was slight. "I'll be gentle."

She braced for pain. It wasn't as bad as she'd expected, though. James dabbed at the wound, then added antibiotic ointment. "I think, since the bleeding has stopped, you don't need stitches. Or... staples, I guess. That's what they do for head wounds, right?"

Staples? "I'm not letting anybody put staples in my head."

"I don't think they would anyway. The gash is too wide. But it's not bleeding anymore."

James pressed a bandage over the wound, which pulled uncomfortably against her hair. "How do you feel?"

"Better."

"How about the head? Does it hurt?"

"Not too bad. It's not throbbing like it was before."

He opened a cabinet and returned to the table with two tablets. "Tylenol."

"Thanks." She downed them.

Seated beside her, he leaned forward, one arm on the round table. "Can you tell me what happened out there? If you saw anyone or...?"

She closed her eyes, thought back. "We were in the passage-way, right? And I...I turned around, went feet-first." James said nothing while she tried to put it all together. But... "I don't remember anything after backing away from you toward the opening except thinking how grateful I was that you were with me. I felt...safe."

She opened her eyes to find his gaze on her. She wasn't sure what she read in that expression. More than curiosity, more than concern. She was afraid to name it, afraid the name would raise her hopes higher than they should be.

"What happened next?"

Again, she closed her eyes. She couldn't think with him so close, looking at her like that. "The next thing I knew, you were there. You were making me crawl away. And then we were running down the hill."

"You didn't see anybody?"

He was so close when she next opened her eyes. "No."

He wrapped her hands in his and squeezed. "Thank God..." He swallowed, bobbing his Adam's apple.

"I know." The bullet had been centimeters from ending her life. She didn't know what James felt for her now, but even if it was only friendship, she was grateful he wouldn't have to bury her. James didn't need to lose another person he cared about.

The thought that she might have lost him... She didn't even want to consider it.

She pushed back her chair. "Mind if I use the restroom, get cleaned up?"

He cleared his throat and dropped her hands. "I'll go upstairs and do the same. When you're ready, I'll drive you back to your cabin."

"Not calling the police?"

"After you're safely away, I'll tell Vince everything."

"Vince is... who?"

"Detective working on the case, and my friend."

James was friends with the cop who was searching for her, who thought she was a murderer? How did that work?

She hobbled into the downstairs bathroom. What she really needed was a shower, but she'd do that when she got back to the cabin. For now, she washed her hands and splashed some water on her face.

She'd lifted the bandage and was trying to get a look at the wound in the mirror when the doorbell rang.

James's footsteps rumbled down the stairs. He knocked once on the bathroom door. "Stay there. I'll see who it is."

Probably nobody to be afraid of, but her heart hammered anyway.

"Hey, man. What brings you by?" James's voice was faint through the walls and wood that separated them.

"Is she here?" The voice was muffled, the words clear.

Adrenaline whooshed through her veins. Who was it?

"She who?" James said.

Footsteps pounded on the hardwood.

"Sure, come on in." James's voice was laced with sarcasm.

Cassidy rushed to the window and raised the sash. Her hands trembled as she worked to lift the screen on the decades-old window. Finally, she got it up. She stuck her head out, half expecting to see cops surrounding the property, guns drawn. But the backyard was empty.

She hoisted herself onto the sill and out the window, dropped between the rhododendron bushes that lined the back of the house, and ran across the grass.

Where should she go?

The campground. She had no other choice. She bolted through the woods, pulling out her phone on the way and thanking God she hadn't stored it in the backpack. She opened the Lyft app and ordered a ride, praying the driver wouldn't recognize her.

She hid in the woods between the campground and the trailhead and waited until her ride was close. Mercifully, just a few minutes later, she jogged to meet the little Volkswagen with the Lyft placard in the window and slid into the backseat.

"How you doing?" the young driver asked.

"Too much sun." She angled her back to the window and closed her eyes as if she couldn't keep them open another minute, hoping the guy wouldn't notice the bandage on her head.

If only she had her sunglasses, her baseball cap. They were in her backpack.

She had the feeling the driver would be asked about this ride, so she couldn't go straight back to the rental. As desperately as she needed to rest, she settled in for the long drive to Plymouth, the first town that had come to mind when she'd ordered the Lyft. When she was dropped at the supermarket, she'd order an Uber to take her to her rental. She just needed to throw off the police long enough for her to collect her things and disappear. Again.

# CHAPTER TWENTY-FIVE

While Vince searched the house. James deleted Cassidy's phone number from his contacts and recent calls. Someone at the station would be able to retrieve that information, but hopefully by then she'd have dumped her phone.

He shoved her sweatshirt deep in his kitchen trash, then slipped her glass and bowl into the dishwasher.

He sat and sipped his water as if his insides weren't balled up like a fist.

He wasn't sure what to hope for.

He'd convinced himself on their long trek down the mountain that the best course of action would be to call the police, report the shooting, and tell them everything they'd learned. But now, as one of his best friends stomped through his house, gun drawn, James wondered if Cassidy had been right. It seemed that Vince and the rest of the Coventry PD were so sure she was guilty that they might not listen to reason. When James had opened the door, Vince's face, contorted in rage, had shocked him. He'd never seen his friend wearing that expression before. If Vince had that much fury built up, James worried what he would do if he found Cassidy.

With a gun in his hand.

On the second floor, a door slammed. Vince's footsteps pounded on the stairs as he descended. A moment later, he banged on a door. "Open up, Cassidy."

*Please, let her be gone.* Because the angrier Vince got, the more James was convinced she wouldn't get fair treatment.

Vince ran out the front door.

James followed and saw his friend at the tree line on his phone. At least he holstered the gun. As James approached, he picked up the words "suspect escaped on foot." Then Vince turned and glared at James. "I'll learn what I can. Be ready."

He ended the call. "Where did she go?"

James wouldn't deny she'd been there. He wasn't prepared to lie to the police, or to his friend. Fortunately, he could honestly say, "I don't know."

Vince's overlarge ears turned red, and James fought the urge to step back. "To the house. Now."

If he'd hoped for special treatment because of their friendship, he'd have been disappointed. Vince gripped his upper arm like he thought James would bolt, but James yanked away. "I don't need your help."

"You're gonna need that and a whole lot more if you don't start talking."

Inside, James started for his kitchen, but Vince grabbed him again. "To the bathroom. I want it open."

James glared down at the hand on his arm. "If you'll just let me get a tool."

Vince let him go, and James went to the kitchen. Vince watched as if he might snatch a cleaver and attack.

As if they hadn't been friends for a decade.

He tamped down the anger, snatched a harmless knife, and lifted it for Vince to see. "Stand back or I'll butter you to death."

Vince said nothing, just followed James to the bathroom door, where he used the utensil to turn the simple lock, then stepped back. "Help yourself, *friend*."

Vince shouldered past him into the small room. Water on the vanity, the hand towel askew.

The window wide open.

Vince turned and glowered. "Start talking."

James swiveled and headed for the living room, where he settled in the La-Z-Boy Dad had bought nearly two decades before. Dad had watched countless games from this chair, pounding on the arm when he got angry, cheering when things went well. He'd fallen asleep there almost every night after dinner. The chair still reminded James of his father, and he settled into it and tried to be comforted by the familiarity.

He could almost see his mother on the sofa, catty-corner to him. She used to sit on the end, a cross-stitch project on her lap, only half paying attention to whatever Dad had chosen on TV. Sports, movies, sit-coms—Mom never seemed to care as she followed pretty patterns one stitch at a time.

What would his parents think of him now? They'd blamed Cassidy for Hallie's death. They'd been wrong—as had Vince and the rest of the town of Coventry. But they'd been certain in their wrongness. They'd see James's alliance with Cassidy as a betrayal.

That was the problem, though. Everybody had jumped to the same conclusion. And, over the years, they'd become more and more convinced of their rightness, doggedly hanging onto an idea that simply wasn't true.

To argue a different opinion, even one based on fact, made you the enemy. Even to *listen* to a different opinion, to consider it, was a betrayal. Even though James's sister had been the first victim of this kidnapper, by considering that Cassidy might not be guilty, he wasn't only betraying the idea, he was betraying all who held that idea close.

Vince propped on the arm of the sofa. Based on the look on his face, he saw James as a betrayer too.

James prayed for wisdom. For justice for Hallie and Addison. For rescue for Ella. He prayed for freedom for Cassidy. Jumbled, incomplete prayers he trusted God understood.

"Talk."

"She didn't do it, Vince. She doesn't have Ella. She didn't take Addison. She didn't kill Hallie."

Vince sucked in a breath through his teeth as if barely holding himself together. "Where is she?"

"I don't know."

"Best guess."

James swallowed the lie that wanted to come out. Best guess—back at the cabin she'd rented. But he couldn't tell Vince that. He needed to give her time to...

Would she run away again? Would she disappear forever?

New, jumbled prayers bounced around his brain. He couldn't lose Cassidy now, not when he'd just gotten her back.

"Where. Is. She." Vince's hands clenched into fists. His whole face took on the color of a ripe autumn apple.

"She didn't do it."

"I trusted you. You know that? Cote wanted to swarm your place with cops, but I talked him out of it. Told him you'd tell us if she contacted you. Told him there was no way you'd harbor the fugitive suspected of killing your own sister."

"She didn't—"

"We're going to find her." Vince seemed to force a deep breath in, then blew it out through his teeth. "It'd be better for her if I found her, not one of the guys in uniform. Emotions are running high right now. I'd hate for your girlfriend to get hurt."

Was Vince serious, or was that a threat? The anger that infused Vince's every word told James that Cassidy wouldn't be any safer with him than with any other cop that got his hands on her. Even Detective Cote, Ella's uncle, would display more restraint than Vince was showing right now.

Vince's phone rang, and he grabbed it. "House is clear. Search the forest, the campground, and the trails. And canvas the campers and hikers, see if anybody saw her."

He waited through a response, said, "I'm working on that."

When he hung up, he leaned forward, perched his elbows on

his knees, and held his phone between his hands. "Fine. She didn't do it. Not that I believe you, but if you're right and she's telling the truth, then it won't hurt her to come in and answer questions."

"You guys all think she's guilty. No way she'll be treated fairly."

"That's her excuse for not turning herself in? Come on, James. You're smarter than this."

"How did you know to look for her here?"

Vince rubbed his lips together, then settled onto the sofa and sat back. "Somebody saw you two on the mountain. I got a call early this morning. We've been keeping an eye out for you. Cote wanted to station someone here, but I convinced him you'd call us when you came in. Told him you'd do the right thing." He shook his head, disappointment clear in the set of his lips.

"Who saw us?"

Vince gave James a cop-stare that was probably supposed to intimidate.

"Somebody followed us last night," James said. "Somebody stole our food. And somebody—"

"Stole your food? Gee, lemme write up a report." Vince launched himself to his feet. "A child is missing, James. Your best friend's daughter! She's going to be dead if we don't find her fast. Dead. Do you get that? And you're worried that somebody stole your food?"

James resisted the urge to stand toe-to-toe with Vince. Friend or not, Vince was a cop. He deserved James's respect. "If you'd please let me finish."

Vince crossed his arms. "Finish."

"Somebody shot Cassidy this morning." He tapped his head where the wound was. "Grazed her right here. An inch to the right, and she'd be dead. Cassidy, the only person who survived this guy. The only person who knows what really happened to my sister, and the only person who can shed light on what's going on right now. Who do you think would have done that, if not the real killer?"

Vince practically fell in the chair, his breath coming out in a huff. "Why didn't you call it in?"

"No service. But we'd considered calling the police. I was just cleaning her wound." Nearly true. "We found the place, Vince."

"The cave?" Some of the anger leached from his face. "You found it?"

"I can tell you the coordinates, and you can check it out."

Vince sat back, focused on the floor. His hands were pressed to his knees.

James prayed Vince would see reason, quit focusing on finding Cassidy and start looking for the real kidnapper.

But Vince's expression was all hard lines and anger again. "Where's Ella then? Didn't you rescue her? That was the point, right?"

"You told me there were no caves. Everybody told me there were no caves, but I saw it. Cassidy was—"

"Blowing smoke. And you were sucking it up like a pothead. So, your girlfriend found a cave on the mountain."

"But there were clear signs of a fire. Someone had been there."

"So what? Ella wasn't there."

"But that's just it. If the kidnapper saw us the night before—"

"Wasn't the kidnapper. It was Eugene Cage. I guess him and his dad got in a fight the night before last about some woman prowling around. Wilson said Eugene's been known to follow women hikers. He's gotten some complaints."

Had Eugene followed Cassidy the day she'd stumbled into James's yard? That would make sense.

Vince continued. "Wilson didn't realize it was Cassidy, only that Eugene had creeped someone else out. He saw a woman running away from him who looked afraid. Said the woman ran into you. Eugene got mad at his father, took off onto the mountain the next day, and saw you guys. Didn't have a phone, but when he came down, he told his dad. Wilson realized who it had to be and called it in."

Eugene. Had Eugene stolen their food? Had Eugene shot at Cassidy?

Had Eugene kidnapped and murdered Hallie?

James had never wanted to suspect his neighbors, but it looked like a possibility. Carefully, he asked, "What did Eugene tell you?"

"I know what you're thinking, but it wasn't him."

"How can you be so sure?"

"What were you doing over there yesterday? Wilson said you went to talk to him about his alibi back when Hallie was taken, but were you really there to check on her?"

"I had no idea she'd be there. I just saw her running—from Eugene."

"Why was Cassidy there?"

"The guy who kidnapped her wore a mask the whole time, so she never got a look at his face. But she thought, if she could hear his voice, she'd recognize it. She went to the campground to try to get close enough to hear Eugene's voice. And Wilson's."

"And?" Vince's eyebrows rose as if he already knew what James was going to say.

"Eugene's voice didn't sound familiar, but—"

"It couldn't have been him."

"His only alibi was fellow gamers online. That can't really pass for an alibi."

"Eugene isn't clever enough to pull this off and get away with it. Cote checked with a few online gamers. They confirmed he'd been playing online the whole time. He was satisfied with the alibi, and so am I."

Of course they were. They'd decided Cassidy was guilty from the get-go.

And Eugene... was that some kind of discrimination or reverse discrimination? People suspected him because of the severe learning disability, and they discarded him for the same reason. But being learning disabled didn't make a person good or bad.

"What did Eugene tell you yesterday?"

"He saw you two and followed you for a while."

"Why didn't he call it in the day before?"

Vince blew out a long-suffering breath. "You're here to answer my questions, not the other way around."

"I'm just trying to put it together."

"I didn't interview him, but my understanding is that he didn't realize it was her at the time. He and his father had the fight, and he took off."

That made sense. But... "I thought you were heading the investigation. Why didn't you interview him?"

"Had a lead elsewhere. Turned out to be nothing."

"And you won't consider, after everything, that Eugene is guilty?"

Vince lifted one shoulder. "It's possible, I suppose, that Eugene is our guy. Hard to believe, considering how busy the campground is in the summertime. If he was going to do something like this, you'd think he'd do it when he was bored, not busy. What time were you shot at today?"

"It was about... one o'clock. It took us some time..."

Vince was already shaking his head. "Eugene was at the police station about then. I'll call 'em, and we'll confirm it, but, seriously... you really think he could pull off three kidnappings and two murders?"

"Four kidnappings. Cassidy was kidnapped, too. Where was Wilson when Eugene was at the police station?"

"At the campground, I assume." Vince's lips pressed together until they turned white. "I'll look into it, see if anybody can put Wilson at the campground this afternoon."

"And find out if he stole our food. I think it's worth digging into. Eugene's got a learning disability, but he's not stupid. And he can shoot. Wilson and Eugene go hunting every fall. Have ever since they bought the campground from Dad when I was a kid. We used to keep an eye on things when they were out of town."

"None of that changes what I have to do right now."

The gnawing feeling in the pit of James's stomach that had

been growing ever since the first loud knock expanded. "Which is what?"

"Cassidy Leblanc is a fugitive from justice. There's a warrant out for her arrest. I warned you to tell me if she got in touch with you. You didn't do that."

"She's not guilty, Vince. She didn't do anything wrong."

"That's not for me to decide, and it's not for you to decide. You had a responsibility to report it when she contacted you. You've left me no choice. Stand up."

James stood, and Vince clamped a hand on his shoulder. "You have the right to remain silent…"

# CHAPTER TWENTY-SIX

Ella was asleep, back in the cave, when the man returned. It was dark again. He shook her shoulder. "Maryann, wake up. I wanna show you something."

She wanted to tell him to go away, but she sat up, blinking in the light. One of her braids had come loose, and her hair was scratchy on her face. She brushed it away as he brought the lantern closer. He sat beside her on her blankets and pulled a bunch of papers from his pocket and handed them to her. "We're all set."

On the first paper was just a bunch of letters and numbers she didn't understand. "What's this?"

"That's the information for our flight. It leaves in less than twenty-four hours. Isn't that exciting? We'll have a long drive before we get to the airport, though, so we have to leave later today. I just have a few things I have to take care of first."

Today? They were leaving *today*?

"Remember how we used to dream of going on an airplane, flying far away to somewhere Mommy could never find us? We're finally gonna do it."

Daddy had taken her to California once to visit her mother. She'd loved looking out the windows at the clouds below. And, when they were landing, the cars looked like ants at a picnic.

The man tapped the paper in her lap. "I got us IDs, so we'll have no trouble getting into Canada and on the plane. And guess what?" He looked at her like he was waiting for her to guess.

She shrugged.

"Sleepy girl." He bumped her shoulder. "Mommy won't have any idea where we went. Isn't that awesome?" He took the papers from her, flipped through them, and found another one. "And this is where we're going." His voice was filled with joy, as if he'd just presented a strawberry birthday cake, not another flat piece of paper.

She looked at the picture. A beach with palm trees and a pretty building beside it. It was hard to make out much in the dark cave, and she didn't care. She didn't want to go to his beach anyway.

"That's our new home. Isn't it beautiful?"

She popped her thumb in her mouth.

"Admit it, Maryann. It's beautiful." His voice suddenly wasn't joyful but scary, like he was about to get really mad. "I've gone to a lot of trouble to do this for us."

She took her thumb from her mouth, thinking that if she did what he asked, he might do her a favor. "It's very pretty, and I can't wait to play in the waves."

"And body surf! That's the best."

"Uh-huh. First, can you take me to see my... the man who isn't really my daddy? I just wanna tell him good-bye."

He snatched the papers from her hand and shoved them back in his pocket. "He doesn't want to see you, Maryann. He's forgotten all about you."

She sucked her thumb again, but he yanked it out of her mouth. "Don't do that. You're not a baby."

Daddy'd told her the same thing, only he'd said it nicer. *Let's quit doing that, precious girl. You're getting so big.*

Daddy was nice. Not like this man.

The man blew out a long breath. "Time to sleep. I'm gonna have to leave really early and take care of those bears so they don't scare any other little girls. You need to be very quiet while I'm gone. Bears are attracted to noise, and you don't want them coming back. You need to be quiet, no matter what happens, okay?"

She nodded, imagining bears all around her little cave. "Are you gonna kill them?"

His lips pressed together, and his eyes got all squinty. After a moment, he said, "If they come back around here, I'm gonna have to." He kissed her forehead. "Hang in there, little sister. It's almost over."

# CHAPTER TWENTY-SEVEN

This couldn't be happening again.

At the grocery store in Plymouth where the Lyft driver had dropped Cassidy off, she'd ordered an Uber.

While she waited for the car, she'd purchased food for the road, enough for a few meals. A prepared sandwich for dinner, plus protein bars, crackers, a few fresh apples, and a bag of individually wrapped mozzarella cheese sticks that should last until the next day. She'd also bought another burner phone.

On the ride from Plymouth to her cabin, she'd removed the battery from her old one so it couldn't be tracked.

Had James been arrested?

She didn't want to think about how much trouble she'd caused him.

When she stepped into the rented cabin, all she wanted to do was fall into bed. But that wasn't an option. She had to figure out what to do next. And she couldn't do that until she had time to process all that had happened. Until she ate a decent meal and got some sleep and managed the headache that had been building in intensity ever since she'd jumped out James's window, she couldn't do anything but keep putting one foot in front of another. She wouldn't think about the fact that she'd been shot in the head. She wouldn't think about how close to death she'd come, once again, on that mountain.

No. She had to focus.

And she couldn't stay here. James had picked her up here. He'd have to tell the police about this place. James wasn't accustomed to being on the wrong side of the law, and he'd said the detective working on the case was his friend. She only hoped he'd give her enough time to gather her things and leave.

She was a fugitive and, by asking for his help, she'd put him in a terrible position. It would have been one thing if they'd found Ella, but they hadn't.

She wouldn't think about that yet. Not yet.

After packing her belongings, she threw the suitcase in her trunk and left. She drove toward Laconia, following road signs to an airport. She needed to park in a place where her car wouldn't stand out—so in a parking lot—but also in a place where nobody would notice her sleeping in the backseat. Or, if they did, where she could come up with a good reason why she was there.

The regional airport seemed like a good bet. It was quiet. No commercial flights, as far as she could tell, only private aircraft. If anybody questioned her, she could claim to have come to pick someone up but found they'd been delayed. Made sense, as long as nobody dug too deep.

Better still would be if nobody noticed her at all.

By the time she parked between two SUVs, the sun had gone down over nearby Lake Winnipesaukee. She ate the sandwich, washed it down with a bottle of water, and then hunkered in the backseat to sleep. She wished she'd thought to buy a blanket and pillow, but neither had crossed her mind. No matter. If nothing else, being a foster kid and then a runaway had taught her how to be resourceful. She pulled enough clothes from her suitcase to keep her warm and use as a pillow. With the lump between the seats and no bedding, Cassidy wasn't sure she'd sleep. Still, she closed her eyes and prayed that God would shield her from discovery. That He would tell her what to do next. That He would give James wisdom as he dealt with the mess she'd gotten him into.

Mostly, that God would protect little Ella, who was still out there, somewhere. Ella desperately needed a rescuer. *Lead them to her, Lord. Or lead me. Keep her safe until she's returned to her father.*

~

CASSIDY HAD LIVED a lot of bad nights in her life. Nights hiding her little sister from her mother's drunken rages. Nights hiding herself from her mother's lecherous boyfriends. Nights in new foster homes where she didn't know where a threat would come from, but knew one would. Nights on the run, all alone, after Hallie's death.

But she'd never had a night like this one.

The nausea hit an hour after she'd settled in to sleep. The sandwich hadn't settled well, but she blamed the nausea more on the pounding headache. And she blamed the headache on the strain of trying to think. And the gunshot. And the lump she'd discovered on the back of her head.

Even though she told herself a hundred times that thinking about what happened could wait until morning, the fuzzy memories wouldn't let her go.

Between bouts of throwing up, she'd closed her eyes and drifted to sleep, only to be yanked awake by nightmares and images and phantom sounds. The noises they'd heard the first day. The missing food. The feeling of being watched. The terror of climbing the cliff. The empty cave.

And suddenly, it came back to her. The gunshot.

The horrifying crack, the searing pain. The way she'd fallen back, her head bouncing against the stone wall behind her. The shock of hitting the ground. All of it had been overridden by the terror in the moment, but now that she was safe, it seemed her mind needed to process it all.

A thousand times, she relived it.

Over and over, she prayed and slept and awakened with a gasp, covered in sweat, until, finally in the small hours of the new day, she'd fallen into a deep sleep.

The sound of knocking woke her. When she moved, everything hurt. Her side. Her back. Her head. Her stomach. Realizing where she was, she bolted up to find a uniformed man looking down at her, his expression hard. Groggy, she pressed the button to lower the window. But the car was off. She unlocked the door and opened it.

"Ma'am, you can't sleep here."

When she looked up at him, she blinked in the rising sun behind him and tried to think through the fog of sleep and the fear pounding in her chest. Did he recognize her? She should've donned the sunglasses. Now, she'd go to jail. Ella... Ella would die. All because she'd slept too long.

"You'll have to move along," the man said.

"I was waiting..." What was her story? Where was she? "A flight. A friend was supposed to... I was supposed to give someone a ride."

The cop didn't seem to care. At least he'd come to the clean side of the car. She'd thrown up out the opposite door. "You'll have to wait somewhere else," he said. "There're plenty of hotels in Laconia."

Wait. He wasn't asking for ID? Pulling out handcuffs?

She read the patch on his uniform and realized... Not a cop. A security guard. He worked for the airport.

*Thank God. Thank God.*

"I'm sorry. I thought it would be an hour or so, but I guess... I'll find somewhere else. Sorry about that."

He nodded and stepped away.

She breathed through the fear pounding in her head. Fear and... pain.

She'd deal with that in a minute. She climbed into the front seat, started the car, and drove away, one eye on the security guard in her rearview mirror, who watched until she turned the corner.

Mercifully, there was a Dunkin' Donuts nearby, where she used the restroom, cleaned up, and got a cup of coffee. Her stomach growled, but she'd bought granola bars at the grocery store. After the nausea, the last thing she needed was a donut.

Back in her car, she ate a protein bar, sipped her coffee slowly, and then followed Route 3 south, thinking it would take her back to the interstate. She'd lived in New Hampshire for the first seventeen years of her life, but she'd never owned a car and didn't know her way around. She needed a place to rest for a minute, a place away from the rent-a-cop at the airport, who might, at any time, realize hers was the face of the woman wanted in connection with a kidnapping and murder.

Finally, she reached I-93 but stopped at an outlet mall before getting on the highway, parking between two cars and praying nobody would notice her.

Praying the airport security guard hadn't made a note of her license plate.

Praying for guidance. What should she do now?

The day before, she'd told herself that today, she'd process what happened on the mountain, and that after processing it she'd have direction. Now, after hours of nightmares and not enough sleep, she only knew that she was forgetting something. Something very important.

She closed her eyes and allowed her mind to return to the cave and the passageway. She'd climbed out, just like she had years before, only this time, she hadn't had to coax Hallie to join her.

She forced herself to think about, only about, the day before. She'd climbed out and dropped from the cave opening to the ground. Then, she'd called back through the passage to James, who'd said he wouldn't fit. They'd decided to meet, and then...

She'd seen something. A flash of color on the ground. She'd bent, picked it up, called to James.

And then the boom. The pain. But the thing she'd found...

She leaned back in the driver's seat and dug her hand in her pocket and felt something soft that didn't belong. She pulled it out. It was a hot pink hair tie. Clean and bright and dry, as if it hadn't been exposed to even a single night on the mountain. It wasn't large enough to fit Cassidy's hair. It was smaller. Made for a child.

*Ella.*

Cassidy imagined the photograph that had been circulated of Ella. The girl had worn a huge smile in the picture, her head tilted to the side, her shoulders up just a bit as if she were embarrassed. She had long brown hair braided in two strands.

This hair tie would be perfect to secure a braid.

Ella had been in that cave. This hair tie was proof. If only Cassidy had thought of it in time to tell James. Then, he could have told the police.

But what had it been doing there, near the secret entrance? Cassidy considered the area. If the kidnapper had taken Ella out of the cave and down the other path, the slow way, he'd have had to pass that spot. Had Ella dropped the hair tie on purpose? Had she hoped someone would find it?

Cassidy pulled the new no-contract phone from her grocery sack and turned it on. It was a cheapie, but the map would get her back to Coventry and Mt. Ayasha. She didn't know yet what she'd do when she got there. She'd figure that out on the way.

# CHAPTER TWENTY-EIGHT

How come James could sleep better on a rocky hillside than on a thin mattress?

Because no bars had kept him on the mountain.

He shifted on the crappy bed and squeezed his eyes closed, telling himself to go back to sleep.

There were no windows in this cell, but the clock on the far wall told him it was seven o'clock. Despite the thoughts buzzing like flies, he'd slept for a few hours.

Had Cassidy? Where was she?

Not for the first time since he'd last seen her, he lifted a prayer for her. When he'd been tossed into the cell, when he'd heard the click of the lock, he'd understood the fear he'd heard in her voice when he'd suggested they call the police. He understood in a way he never had before. The bars, the charges, the people in authority looking at him as if he were a felon...

He had to get out of there.

But he couldn't leave. That was the most stressful part. Not the angry looks he'd gotten from the cops, most of whom he'd known all his life, but the fact that he couldn't leave. Being in jail was like the longest, most boring high school class in history, only he had no idea when the bell would ring.

And what a... a foolish, childish way to look at it. James had thought himself an adult, but one night in jail had broken him.

No.

He sat up. Unbroken. Alive and well and determined to do the right thing. *Lord, what is the right thing?*

No answer. Not an audible one, anyway, but James wasn't surprised. He'd hardly been on speaking terms with God for a decade. That he was now was a testament to his desperation. And his hope. Because, while these walls seemed to be closing in on him, they weren't. And while Ella was still missing, her body hadn't turned up. She was out there, and God knew exactly where she was. And while Cassidy had disappeared again, the police hadn't found her. If they had, she'd be in the jail cell next door. God was good and had a plan for all of this. He had to. *Right, God?*

Again, no answer, but Scriptures James had memorized years before had been flitting through his brain all night long. Promises like *I will never leave you or forsake you* reminded him he wasn't alone. Promises of justice and righteousness reminded him that God cared as much as James did, more, he figured, that Hallie's murderer be held accountable for what he'd done. That Ella be rescued. The verse he kept coming back to was from John. Simple, powerful words. *The truth will set you free.*

What was the truth, though? Cassidy hadn't kidnapped Hallie, but who had? And where was that person now? Where was Ella?

He didn't know, but he was going to find her. If he ever got out of there.

At eight-thirty, he was taken by a uniformed police officer he'd never met to appear before the judge in the courthouse next door. The attorney he'd called the night before entered a plea of not guilty, and the judge, after hearing arguments on both sides, set his bail at fifty thousand dollars.

Because, apparently, they feared James would skip town with Cassidy.

Never mind that the judge had been a friend of his father, that James had known him as long as he could remember.

Never mind that he'd graduated with the city's attorney.

Never mind that he owned property and a business in Coventry. He was associated with Cassidy. Therefore, he wasn't to be trusted.

While his attorney filed paperwork, James tried to decide whom to call to post his bail. He couldn't very well call Reid.

Vince was the one who'd put him in there in the first place.

He had no family nearby.

He'd *felt* alone since his mother had died, but he'd never truly *been* alone. He'd had an entire town full of people who cared for him. Again, Cassidy's plight felt more real to James than ever.

He thanked his lawyer before the uniformed officer led him out of the courtroom. They walked the short hallway connecting the courthouse to the police station. When they entered the other building, another cop called, "Don't bother locking him up. Someone's posting bail now."

James looked sideways at the cop who held his arm in a tight grip. "Who?"

"I guess you'll find out in a minute."

It was more than a minute, but James didn't complain as he sat, handcuffed to a bench, and waited.

Finally, he was freed from the cuffs and led through the doors and into the police station's entry.

Vince pushed himself off the wall. "You ready?"

"What are you doing here?"

Vince opened the glass door that led outside to freedom. For now, anyway. Though, accessory-after-the-fact was a serious charge. It was likely James would be back in jail—no, prison—when this was over.

"I put you in here as a cop," Vince said. "I'm bailing you out as your friend."

James hadn't been sure where their friendship stood the day before. As he stepped out the door onto the sidewalk in downtown Coventry, gratitude rose up. He turned to thank Vince but was yanked around by a solid grip on his arm.

The fist came out of nowhere.

He stumbled back, crashed into Vince. Face on fire.

The stream of curse words shocked him more than the voice that delivered them.

"I should kill you!" Reid lunged toward him again, but Vince shoved Reid away.

Reid lifted his fist.

"Back off." Vince's voice carried the same authority he'd used the day before with James. "Unless you want to end up in jail for assaulting a police officer."

Reid stepped back, shaking his right hand.

James rubbed the jaw he felt sure was broken. Didn't seem to be, but it probably hurt a lot worse than Reid's knuckles.

Reid was still glowering at him over Vince's shoulder. "You let her get away!"

"We were looking for Ella." But Reid wasn't listening to James any more than Vince had the day before. "Cassidy didn't kidnap your daughter."

"Then where is she?" Reid's gaze flicked to Vince, who stood aside but seemed ready to jump in again if necessary. If not for the cop, James was certain he'd be feeling another right hook. And he wouldn't fight back. Not against his best friend, not considering everything Reid was dealing with.

"I don't know," James said. "Probably still looking for Ella. She's determined—"

"She murdered your sister." Reid's voice, no longer shouting, was filled with vitriol. "She murdered Addison, and now she's gonna murder Ella. And you had her."

"She didn't—"

"If my daughter dies, I'll kill you."

"Careful, Cote." Vince squared up against Reid. "The last thing I wanna do is throw you in jail, but I will if I have to."

Ignoring Vince, Reid glared at James. "You better watch your back." He turned and stalked away, pushing his way through the crowd James only now realized had gathered.

Townspeople looked on. People he'd considered friends the day before glared at him. He could feel their disappointment, their hatred. It was as hot as the morning sun beating down on them. He feared, like the sun, it would grow hotter before it cooled.

If he and Cassidy didn't find Ella, his friends' feelings of betrayal would never cool.

"Move along, people." Vince grabbed James's upper arm and led him to his SUV.

They were halfway to James's house before Vince spoke. "You ticked I didn't arrest him for assault?"

"I'd be ticked if you had," James said.

"Everybody who knows anything about this case thinks your girlfriend did it, James. You're the lone holdout."

"She didn't—"

"And it's possible"—Vince continued as if James hadn't spoken —"that you're biased in her favor. I'm not saying you're wrong and I'm right, but I want you to consider something."

James watched the familiar landscape slide past the windows and waited.

"Isn't it possible that those old feelings you had for Cassidy and the guilt I know you felt after Hallie's body was found—guilt because somebody you'd trusted had killed her—have deceived you? Isn't it possible you don't see what the rest of us see because you don't want to?"

"Thank you, Dr. Phil, for that insightful analysis. I feel much healthier now."

"I'm just trying to help, man."

"Isn't it possible that you guys all decided Cassidy was guilty not based on any real evidence but based on the fact that her mother was in prison for murdering her little sister? Isn't it possible that this town's bias against her has clouded everyone else's judgment?"

"Could be, if she hadn't run away."

"Seems to me, based on how everybody is behaving, that she was smart to run. There's no evidence linking her to Addison's disappearance or Ella's, only the fact that the crimes are similar, and yet she's suspect numero uno. But you accuse *me* of bias?"

When Vince parked in James's driveway, James yanked open his door. He started to slam it, but paused to say, "Thanks for bailing me out."

"Don't you wanna know what we found on the mountain?"

"You went up there?"

"Believe it or not, I want to find Ella as much as you do."

James glanced at his front door. He wanted a shower, a cup of coffee, and a meal.

Vince climbed from his car, and James walked toward its rear, not eager to invite Vince inside. When he passed the SUV's cargo area, he glimpsed a rifle sticking out from beneath a tarp-covered mound.

Vince saw him looking. "Unfortunately, we didn't find anybody up there, though I went prepared."

"What'd you find?" James leaned on the back of the truck. Birds sang overhead, celebrating what seemed would turn out to be another beautiful day. Sunshine, puffy white clouds. Tourists would enjoy the lake and mountains, fill the restaurants, spend money in the tourist traps as if all were well.

Vince perched beside him. "The cave, right where you said it would be. Empty, just as you claimed. Recent footprints, but nothing usable, and they were probably yours and Cassidy's." James didn't miss the quick look of censure before Vince faced forward again. "Outside the passageway you said Cassidy squeezed through, though I can't imagine how—"

"She's pretty slim."

"We found a spot a bullet might've hit. A hole, a little blood. We got samples of everything. Shooter must've retrieved the bullet. We also found blood on the ground nearby."

The memory of that moment filled James's empty stomach with acid. Where was Cassidy now? Was she safe? Was she well?

Vince continued. "We looked but never found where the guy took the shot from. I mean, I think I know where it was, but there were no casings or footprints. Whoever he is, this guy's smart."

"But you know she was shot."

"I know *somebody* was shot."

"You think I'm lying?"

Vince said nothing.

"He's out there," James pushed off the tailgate and turned to face Vince. "He saw us on the mountain. He recognized Cassidy as the only person who knows what happened ten years ago. She's the only person who can identify him. So he tried to take her out."

"You may be right. If you are..." He looked down, shook his head, looked up again. "If that was where the killer kept his victims, there'd have been some trace. And, even if the killer is *that* good, good enough to hide all evidence he'd been there, he's gone now. He won't go back."

"In other words, we blew it," James said. "By going into the cave, by showing our hand..."

Vince lifted one shoulder, let it drop.

"If you'd listened to me... You said you'd been looking for that cave for years. How did you never find it?"

"I'm not rising to your bait." Vince crossed his arms, stared straight ahead. "I looked. I missed it. I did the best I could."

James settled against the tailgate again. He wasn't mad at Vince. He was mad at himself. Had they tipped the killer off, sent him running?

How would they ever know?

"Turns out Eugene was at the police station yesterday about noon. Let's say he left the police station and went up to the mountain and tried to kill Cassidy." Vince's voice held more than a hint of skepticism. "What I understand, he had Cassidy cornered at the shack at the campground. Why didn't he kill her then?"

The campground? Had Eugene realized who Cassidy was when he saw her the first time? Based on what Cassidy had told him, James didn't think so.

"When he saw you two on the mountain," Vince said, "why not shoot then?"

James had asked himself the same question. "Maybe he didn't want to kill me. Maybe he didn't want me to catch him. Maybe he didn't think we'd find the cave, and when we did—"

"Lots of maybes."

"Isn't that your job, to look into maybes?"

"I'm doing my job. I just don't want to..." His words faded, and he crossed his arms. "Look, I'm not discounting anything you're saying. Eugene's on the list. Wilson's on the list."

"Where was he yesterday afternoon?"

"Says he was at the campground, but nobody checked in or out during that time. He can't seem to corroborate the story. He swears he'd never leave the place unattended."

"Even to take out somebody who could put him in prison? Not sure I buy that."

"We've not ruled anything out. But my money's still on Cassidy, I could be wrong. Everybody could be wrong. Which is why"—he pushed off the back of the truck and paced a few steps away—"I pressed for charges against you."

"Gee, thanks. Nothing like a little prison time between friends."

"If you're right, then somebody tried to kill your girlfriend."

"She's not—"

"Whatever Cassidy Leblanc is to you, you're saying somebody shot her. Somebody wants her dead. It's possible it was the real killer or just a vigilante who thought he'd put this town out of its misery."

"But Ella's still missing. Killing the kidnapper wouldn't bring her home."

"Vigilantes aren't known for being the most logical, level-headed sorts. The point is, you may be right, and I may be wrong. If Cassidy isn't the killer, then you and she are his biggest threats. Cassidy has vanished... again. But you're here. Right now, I hope, if this guy exists, he thinks we aren't taking you seriously. I hope he believes you've been taken out of the equation. The charges lend credence to that idea."

"Credence? You get one of those word-of-the-day calendars?"

Vince chuckled, but it died fast. "What you gotta do is lay low. Stay outta sight. Go back to your normal life."

Not that James had any idea what his next step was, but he was pretty sure it wasn't going to involve hiding at home. "Anything else, boss?"

"You swore upside-down and backwards you don't have a way to contact your girlfriend."

"She's not—"

"If you're lying, if you can contact her, tell her to call me. I don't want her marching into the station. I'm willing to hear what she has to say, but I can't guarantee her safety with the rest of the force. If you get her to contact us, it'll go a long way toward getting these charges dropped. And it'll help us find Ella. Will you do that?"

"I don't have any way to reach her. Even if I did, she won't call you."

"Then *you* call me. If you know where she is, you call me and I'll take it from there. I promise I won't let anything happen to her. I just need to hear her story from her mouth. Okay?"

"Let me just clarify here," James said. "Are you saying you're willing to concede that Cassidy isn't involved in the two recent kidnappings? Or are you saying you aren't sure she was involved in Hallie's?"

Vince's smile seemed about as authentic as Ernie's Mexican food. "I'm saying I'm willing to listen."

Right until he threw her in jail.

The bail, the hand of friendship, the words of concern... James didn't believe any of them. This was all about Vince collaring Cassidy.

Vince was telling James to get on board or get out of the way.

AFTER A SHOWER AND A MEAL, James called Reid. Not surprisingly, his friend didn't answer the phone. James had counted on that. If anything happened to him, though, Reid would listen to his message.

He was counting on that too.

"I have a theory about what happened to Ella." For the next few minutes, he told Reid's voice mail what he believed, including details that supported his idea. "Maybe I'm way off. But I needed you to know." He wanted to add something mushy about how Reid was his best friend, how James would never betray that friendship, how he was doing everything in his power to bring Ella home. But he didn't. He'd get the opportunity to say all those things to Reid's face. He had to believe that.

He disconnected and left his cell phone on the kitchen counter, fearing the police were tracking it. He grabbed his keys and headed for his Jeep, trying not to think the thoughts that had started bombarding him soon after Vince left. But they were there, begging for attention.

It was a long shot, but he needed to reach Cassidy. He didn't think she'd call him, not if she worried somebody was listening in on his phone calls. Which...they probably were. The cops could do that, right? Get a warrant to monitor him, hope he'd lead them straight to Cassidy?

He checked his rearview mirror. Nobody was back there. Would there be a tracker on his vehicle?

Was it possible he'd slipped from healthy fear to clinical paranoia?

Where was the real Dr. Phil when he needed him?

He passed Coventry High School and turned on the next street, where he parked between two older homes set on acre-plus lots. He locked his Jeep, and after checking to make sure nobody was watching, darted between the houses, through the woods, and to the fence behind the school.

He'd been back to Coventry High many times since graduation. Town meetings, school plays, and recitals were held in the high school auditorium. He'd been to a few of the latter since Ella had taken up dance. Nothing like watching five-year-olds twirling in tutus.

Every two years, he went to the school cafeteria to cast his votes. He'd even come to watch a few baseball games over the years.

But he hadn't been to the football field behind the school since graduation.

Though the forest was thicker than it had been a decade earlier, he had no trouble finding the tree, the knothole. The first time he'd seen it, he'd been on the other side, having jogged across the field when he saw Cassidy at the fence. He thought about the sadness he'd observed in her expression back then. He hadn't known much about foster care but worried about her treatment in a house filled with other foster kids. Everybody knew the story of Cassidy's mother. At school, Cassidy'd been teased to her face, gossiped about behind her back, and bullied more than once. James, Reid, and Denise had put an end to the bullying, at least. But seeing her at the fence that day, staring across the empty football field toward the baseball diamond, he'd worried.

Her tears had been evident in the streak of black makeup down her cheeks. Nothing serious had happened, and she didn't explain, only said she'd been thinking about her sister.

At the time, he'd suspected there was more to it. How could the grief have held on so long? Her sister'd been gone for years.

Now, he understood how grief could hit you like that. Time didn't fix it. Nothing fixed it.

Or James had been looking in the wrong places for freedom from his grief. Maybe, if he hadn't turned his back on God, he'd have found peace long before.

James found the old knothole. It was over his head an inch or two, so fearing he'd be as likely to get bitten as to find anything, he reached inside and felt around.

And pulled out a folded piece of paper with nothing written on it but a phone number.

He jogged back to his Jeep, again looking around to see if anybody was watching.

He hit the state highway and drove all the way to the interstate, then drove south to Plymouth. Paranoia in action again, but if they tapped his phone, they could tap local payphones, right?

He had no idea how those things worked.

After peering at gas stations and grocery stores and finding no payphones, he finally gave up and bought a no-contract phone in a Rite Aid, got it going, and dialed the number.

It rang twice before it connected. The person on the other end said nothing.

"It's me," he said.

He heard an exhale, then, "You found it."

Obviously, but he didn't say that. "Smart place to leave it."

"Smart place to look for it."

Before that week, he'd gone a decade without hearing her voice. He'd told himself over and over that he didn't miss her, didn't ever want to see her again. What a liar he'd been.

"You're okay?" he asked.

"Still alive. Still not in custody."

Her voice sounded strong enough. "I guess that's all we can ask right now. Can I come get you?"

"I'm worried someone's following you."

He glanced around the parking lot. Didn't see anybody suspicious, not that he would. "What do you want to do?"

"We'll meet. I'll drive. I found something I think belonged to Ella. Right before the gunshot."

"What is it?"

"Just a little hair tie, but it proves she was there. You have a plan?"

Not a plan, but an idea. An idea that, if he was right, could lead them to Ella. He warred between the desire to save Ella and the desire to protect Cassidy. Unfortunately, to do the first, he might not be able to do the second.

But Ella was five years old. And Reid... Reid needed his daughter home.

*Father, lead us. Forgive me for... for all of it. I need You now. We need You now.*

No flash of light. No writing on the wall or windshield. But James felt a sense of peace that defied the situation.

"We'll figure it out," he said. "Where are you?"

# CHAPTER TWENTY-NINE

Cassidy waited at the end of the narrow dirt road. Finally, James's Jeep bounced up and turned into the woods, where he'd parked the last time they'd been here. She drove down to meet him, and, after he laid a rifle across the backseat and tossed a small backpack in behind it, he opened her door.

"You planning an assassination?"

A muscle ticked in his jaw. "If I find the guy who killed my sister..."

She squeezed her eyes closed, let the words roll over her. One thing at a time.

James took her hand and tugged. "Can you get out, just for a second?"

When she did, he swept her into his arms and held her tight. "Thank God you're here. Thank God you're all right."

*Oh.* She savored the feel of him. He'd supported her the day before, gotten her safely off the mountain, tended her wounds. But not like this. Not like... like he cared. Like he felt something for her. Even if it was just friendship.

She couldn't speak for the lump in her throat.

He leaned back enough to study her face, then turned her head to look at the wound. "How does it feel?"

"Tylenol helps."

He probed it with his finger, and she winced at the pain.

"Sorry. Just... It's an ugly wound. You probably need to keep it covered."

"Band-Aids don't exactly adhere to my hair. I suppose I could shave my head."

She'd expected a smile, but his expression was solemn. "It doesn't look infected. I brought some antiseptic wipes." He dug into his backpack and came out with a little square package, which he ripped open.

The sting had her yanking away.

"Hold still."

Easy for him to say. But he finished quickly and dug into the backpack again. "I found this at the pharmacy." He held out a red-and-white bandana. "I thought you could wrap it around your head to keep dirt out of the wound."

She took the square cloth, tamping down the vanity that had her wanting to refuse. She wasn't exactly the bandana type. She was touched he'd bought it for her, touched he'd thought of her. She folded the cloth, wrapped it around her head, and tied it in the back. "How do I look?" Ridiculous, she was sure.

The quirk of his lips, the tenderness in his eyes, told her he wasn't thinking she looked ridiculous.

After a moment, he cleared his throat and looked away. "Let's clean it often. Anything else hurt? Between the tumble down the mountain Wednesday and being grazed by a bullet yesterday, you must be in pain."

"Nothing serious. I bumped my head after the bullet... maybe got a concussion, which explains how out of it I felt coming down the mountain."

"Show me."

She touched the spot, and he looked. "Pretty big bump." Gently, he kissed it, then pulled her close again. "When I heard that gunshot..."

Tucked against his chest, she felt his quickening heartbeat beneath her ear.

"And then I worried you'd disappear again." He backed away and laid his hands on her face. His gaze, filled with sincerity, with affection, met hers. "You didn't murder my sister. I knew it. Deep down, I always knew it. I'm sorry I ever doubted you."

Those were the words she'd longed to hear for a decade. That James understood. That he believed in her, despite everything.

The truth churned in her stomach. She had to tell him. For them to have any real future, she had to tell him everything. If that ended whatever was brewing between them…?

Then she'd deal with it. She wouldn't have a lie between them. She couldn't. James deserved to know.

He brushed her hair back from her face, tenderly avoiding her wound, and bent his head. He kissed her forehead. The corner of her eye. Her cheek.

Finally, his lips met hers.

She opened up to him, wrapped her arms around his neck, and pulled him closer. This, this is what she'd wanted. This is what she'd spent a decade longing for.

Everything else faded until all she felt, all she experienced, was James. The boy she'd known ten years earlier faded. The man he was now, with the whiskers, the past she knew little about, even the haunted eyes… All of it. She loved all of it.

All of him.

How could those feelings not have faded, disappeared, after so much time? They hadn't. Now, the years slipped away. Her current life in Seattle slipped away. All that mattered was James. This man who cared for her. And, if that changed after she told him the truth, all the more reason to savor the moment.

Too soon, he angled away, then hugged her. His heartbeat was racing. So was hers.

It was absurd, this moment. A child's life was on the line, and they'd paused for a kiss. Except… except love was never absurd.

"I've been fighting that since the moment you stumbled into my backyard Monday."

"I thought you hated me."

"God knows I tried." He rubbed her back. "But I never let go of the hope that everybody was wrong."

She pushed away from his chest. "We need to—"

"I know. I know." He stepped away. "Ella is still out there."

She leaned against the car, worked to shift mental gears. "But where? The kidnapper knows we found his hideout. Surely he's long gone by now." She tapped the back window where he'd stowed his stuff. "You seem to have a plan."

"Come on." James rounded the car and climbed in the passenger seat.

She settled in beside him. "Catch me up. It was a cop at the door, right?"

"Yeah. Did you recognize his voice?"

"Why would I have?"

"Vince was new to the force when we were in high school. He was the guy who gave the *Don't do drugs* talks. Whenever there was a problem, he was there. I just thought..."

She was shaking her head. "I vaguely remember who you're talking about. I paid even less attention in those stupid assemblies than I did in class. I doubt I could pick him out of a lineup. And anyway, the door muffled his voice."

James told her what happened after she climbed from his window. That he'd been questioned. Arrested. Arraigned, because of her.

She buried her face in her hands. "I'm so sorry. It's all my fault."

Gently, he urged her hands down. "I could've turned you in. I could've sent you away. I didn't do those things, and not for your sake. I did them because I wanted to find Ella."

"But we didn't. And you're saying the police searched the cave and the surrounding area and found no sign of her." She dug her hand in her pocket and came out with the hair tie. "I found this and stuck it in my pocket right before I was shot. I remembered this morning."

James took it from her. "It looks like something she'd wear. She was there."

"She'd definitely been there, but now she's gone. And we have no way of knowing where. Eugene was the one who stole our food?"

"I never got confirmation of that."

"Do you think he shot at us? Or the father—"

"Wilson."

"Yeah. Maybe... maybe he did it, and Eugene told him we were up there, and he went up the next day."

James was nodding. "Or, if Eugene didn't do it, what if Wilson thinks he did? What if he's trying to protect his son."

"That makes sense."

"Except they reported having seen you. Why do that if they planned to kill you? Eugene was at the police station yesterday around noon. He'd have to have left there, driven up the mountain, hiked to the cave, and been there to shoot at us. I think it was around one, right?"

Cassidy thought back. "It's all so fuzzy now."

"It could be either one of them." James's tone, though—devoid of the anger she would expect—told her he didn't think his neighbors were the culprits.

"Or it's somebody else entirely." Though the thought that they could still be so far from knowing the real killer made her sick to her stomach. "It could be somebody not on our radar. I wonder if Eugene told anybody besides the police he'd seen us."

"Eugene keeps to himself," James said, "but he told Wilson. I guess Wilson could've told someone."

"Or the killer saw us. He obviously knows the mountain as well as anybody. Maybe he saw us in time to get Ella out of there, and the fact that Eugene saw us on the mountain is unrelated."

"Possible." James faced forward, took a long breath and blew it out. "Truth is, I have an idea, but I'm not sure. I have zero proof, zero evidence. Really, zero reason to believe it's true except a gut feeling."

"What is it?"

"We need to check the cave again."

"Why would he go back there?" Cassidy shifted to get a better look at James's face. "He knows we've found it. The cops searched it."

"Exactly for that reason. What place would be safer now than the mountain?"

"A hotel. A house."

"Too easy to be spotted in places like that. Especially with a little girl."

Cassidy hated to suggest it, but... "Safest thing right now would be to kill Ella and dump her body."

"But he hasn't done that. For whatever reason..." Those words hung in the air. She considered what he might be thinking.

"The kidnapper wasn't cruel." Not to Hallie anyway.

At her words, James turned her way, a grim expression on his face.

"I never got the impression..." She tried to think how to express this. "He never hurt your sister. He treated her like... like a little sister, I guess. He wanted her to be happy. He was kind to her."

James turned back to the window.

"And Addison wasn't molested."

"I know."

"I think it's logical to assume Ella isn't being mistreated, at least not in that sense. I know it's not everything—"

"It's something, though." His Adam's apple bobbed. "Did he hurt you?"

Now it was Cassidy's turn to look away. "I wasn't molested, either."

He must've seen the truth in her expression, because he said, "Tell me what happened."

She shrugged, tried to swallow the memories. The kidnapper

had hurt her. When Hallie had slept that first night, he'd crawled on top of her, pinned her down.

She could almost feel the heat of his breath against her cheek, the pain of his grip on her arm, the weight of his body on top of hers. His hand... He'd touched her, pinched her. When it hurt so badly she wanted to cry out, he covered her mouth with his hand. All he said was, *You wake her, you die. You don't want pretty Hallie to watch you die, do you?*

The message had been clear. He could do whatever he wanted to Cassidy. If she wanted to survive, if she wanted to protect Hallie, she had to take it.

Both the night on the mountain and the night in the cave, when Hallie slept, he'd climbed on top of her. Never going farther than the threat, but the threat was enough to keep her quiet.

He'd hit her once when they were climbing. He'd grabbed her and squeezed hard multiple times to get her to do what he said. But it wasn't the pain that had plagued her through the years. It was the fear.

She tried to explain it to James without causing him further distress. She must've succeeded because, when she finished, he said, "I'm glad he didn't hurt you too badly." As if physical pain were the worst thing that could happen to a person. Her bruises had healed. The memories visited her almost every night. Someday, when this was over, if he forgave her, if they were still together, she'd try to explain the rest.

"We need to return to the cave," James said. "I think this guy's arrogant enough to go back there."

"But, now that we have the hair tie, we could call the police, get them up there looking for her. The hair tie is evidence, and... and we could use the help. This guy's a killer."

"You're kidding, right?" His eyebrows hiked up. "Yesterday, you were terrified to call the cops."

"You could call them, and I could"—she shrugged—"you know, make myself scarce. You could tell them you were searching alone. It just seems safer than us going up there by ourselves."

James stared past her. A long moment passed before he shook his head. "I don't think that's the best plan right now."

"Why not?"

He squeezed her hand. "They won't believe me. There's not enough time for me to have hiked up there again today, found it, and returned to report it. They know I was with you yesterday. If I suddenly turn up with evidence, they'll believe I got it from you. It'll be about finding you, not about finding Ella. I just... I don't know that it'll work. And right now, the most important thing is finding Ella. I think... I think I should return to the cave and see what I can find out."

"Okay, to the cave. Where do we park?"

"I know the perfect spot."

# CHAPTER THIRTY

They parked on the edge of a narrow side road halfway up the mountain. "Is this wise?" she asked. "The car sort of sticks out here."

"There are some hunting cabins nearby mostly used by tourists. Nobody'll worry about the car except Bart Bradley, who lives up the road."

"My gosh, is he still alive?"

James's chuckle had her grinning. "He's in his mid-seventies."

"You're kidding. He seemed older than that ten years ago."

"I think he likes his crusty-old-man persona." James yanked his bag from the backseat, dug inside, and pulled out a slip of paper and a pen. He scribbled something down.

"Whatcha doing?"

"Leaving a note saying the car broke down. Hopefully, that'll keep it from getting towed or drawing too much attention."

They each donned their backpacks. Grumbling about the loss of his backpacking equipment—the canteens, particularly—James pulled out two water bottles and a box of granola bars. "Will you carry these? This little backpack is crammed full."

She shoved them, along with her phone, into her backpack, ensured her gun was loaded and ready, and locked the car.

They'd been hiking for fifteen minutes or so when she broached the subject on her mind. "Tell me about this gut feeling you have."

"I don't think so."

"Seriously?"

He said nothing, just continued the trek.

"Why not?"

"If I'm right, we'll know soon enough."

"You're a stubborn man, James Sullivan."

Without turning, he said, "If I weren't, you'd be in jail."

A fair point.

He turned to help her up a particularly steep rock. As she took his hand, she caught his smile. At least he wasn't annoyed with her for pressing him.

"I've been meaning to ask you..." James's voice faded, and he glanced around to see her.

"What?"

"You ever talk to your mother?"

Cassidy's stomach swooped like it did every time anybody asked about Mom. "Nope. I can't figure out how to contact her without telling the authorities my name. I tried to call once, but I used a fake name, and she refused the call. Maybe she knew it was me and didn't want me to get in trouble, or she knew it was me and didn't want to talk to me. Or she had no idea it was me."

Guilt pressed in, but Cassidy pushed it away. She could only do what she could do. If she got everything worked out, she'd be able to contact Mom, see her again. Tell her about the hope she'd found in Christ.

"What's your life like back in...?" James's words trailed off.

"Seattle," she supplied.

He shot a grin over his shoulder. She loved that she'd made him smile. Amazing what trusting a person could do. "Why Seattle?"

She shrugged, though he was in front of her and didn't see. "It was far. I don't like hot weather. I spent a few days in Chicago, but it was too big. Too crowded. Overwhelming. I was targeted by this guy... Probably a pimp."

This time, when James shot a look her direction, his eyebrows were lowered and angled together.

"I got away from him. I was old enough and scared enough not to trust anybody. At that point, I decided Chicago wasn't for me and kept pressing west. When I hit Seattle, it felt like the end of the world. I'd met this woman—sweet, motherly type. She let me use her phone for a little while. I found a home for runaways and went straight there when I got off the bus. After my experience in Chicago, I knew I'd need help."

"So you weren't homeless or anything?"

"Nope. I should've been, though. If they'd known the truth, they'd have reported me to the police, not given me a home. I lied about my name, my age, my background. I made up this whole story about abuse and..."

Regret pressed in, as it so often did. If she could go back in time, go to the authorities after Hallie's death instead of running away, what would her life be like today? Would anybody have believed her? Would they have found the killer back then? Would Addison still be alive? Would Ella be safe at home with her father?

Probably. Probably she could have prevented all of this. If only she'd had the courage.

She didn't realize she'd stopped until James turned and gripped her arm. "Hey. You okay?"

"I've asked forgiveness for lying to everyone, but does it count if I haven't told my friends and coworkers the truth?"

"You were trying to survive."

"I should've done the right thing. I did what felt like the easier thing at the time, but running proved to be very hard. Facing it would've been hard, too. I know that. But it would have been the right hard thing, not the wrong hard thing." Cassidy focused on the treetops overhead, where the leaves danced in the slight breeze. Where everything seemed so simple, so natural, so... ordered. Her life felt just the opposite. "When this is all over, I'm going to tell them everything. I'll probably lose my job, but I can't live like this anymore, pretending to be somebody I'm not..Telling kids to overcome while my life is shrouded in lies."

When she returned her gaze to James's face, his scowl had her stepping back. "What?"

"You're going back?"

"I live there. It's my home."

"But if..." He swallowed, stepped nearer. "We're going to get this all straightened out. Everybody's going to know you did nothing wrong." He settled his hands on her hips. "You don't have to leave again." He leaned closer, and his voice softened. "I don't want you to leave again."

He wanted her to stay? To stay as in... forever? She couldn't imagine. "My job is there. My friends are there. My life is there."

"You told me nobody would grieve you if you died. That you had no family. You told me—"

"I have friends. It's not the same as family, but..." It was all she had. They were all she had. "There's nothing for me here."

His hands slid off her hips. He stepped back.

She reached out, but he backed out of her reach.

"I don't mean it that way. You're here, and someday..." She wanted nothing more than to be with James, but she didn't know if that would be an option once he knew the truth. Staying here would be risky.

"Someday what?"

"You could come visit me. Seattle is beautiful. You'd love it there."

"This is my home. This is where my parents are buried. This is where my sister is buried."

"They're gone, James. Would you really choose your deceased family over..." But she didn't finish the sentence. Because he probably would. Why would he choose her over his home? His friends?

Though she'd dreamed of reuniting with James for years, she'd never considered returning to Coventry for good. In all those dreams, James had found her, had come to her, had given up everything to be with her. They'd only been fantasies, though. Childish fantasies.

She knew that now, knew James was as much a part of Coventry as this mountain, as Lake Ayasha. James wouldn't give all this up for her. It was foolish that she'd ever thought otherwise. She was just Cassidy, the toss-away kid.

With a breath for courage, she said, "You have a life here, and the people in your life aren't going to accept me. Nobody in this town will accept me."

"Once they know the truth—"

"I'll always be the foster kid, the girl whose mother killed her sister, the girl who took off rather than face what happened. They'll never believe anything better of me."

"You're so certain you know how *everybody* in Coventry will feel. The arrogance of that—"

"You have no idea what you're talking about. You have no idea how it feels to be the outsider."

"There you go, playing the victim card. You were always so good at that. Here I thought you'd matured. You wiped off all the stupid makeup, you wear colors other than black"—he waved toward her pale pink tank top—"but you're still the same scared, walled off girl you were a decade ago."

"I'm not. I just know what I know. I know how small-town people are."

"Small town, small minds? Is that what you think? Of me? Of my family?"

"No. Not you. But everybody else—"

"You've been gone ten years, Cassidy. We're not in high school anymore. The people of this town are good and decent and kind. They assumed you were guilty because there was a lot of evidence pointing toward you. And because you took off. If you'd stayed—"

"I know, okay. I know I should've stayed. I know I shouldn't have run, but I did. And now it's too late to undo it. I can never fix what I did." No matter what happened with Ella, no matter if they caught the killer, no matter what, she couldn't fix her mistakes. No amount of apologies would ever bring Addison back. Nothing would ever restore Ella's innocent faith in her safety, even if they rescued her. Nothing would ever return Hallie safely to her family. A sob rose with the horrible truth, and she dropped her gaze to the ground, tried to pull it back before the tears started. If they started, she wasn't sure they'd ever end.

Maybe she and James could save Ella and prove Cassidy's innocence, but she would never be free to come home.

And James would never leave this place.

She could go back to Seattle, tell everybody there the horrible truth, fess up to the lies she'd lived for a decade, and then, hopefully, resume her life.

It had been good enough before. But, now that she'd seen James again, now that she'd felt his arms around her, felt his lips on hers, that old life would never be enough.

"Hey." He pulled her against his chest. "I didn't mean to make you cry."

Though she should push him away, begin the process of separating herself now, she let him comfort her, savoring the feeling of being in his arms.

He leaned back, tipping her chin up. "I don't want you to go back to Seattle."

"I can't stay here."

"You might be right about the people in Coventry. The last couple of days have shown me that old prejudices die hard, and people who buck against them do so to their peril. But I believe that, when faced with new facts, the people of this town will accept them. I believe the people of Coventry will realize that they were wrong to accuse you. Maybe, if you give them the chance, they'll accept you and care for you, just like I do." His lips tipped up at the corners. "Well, maybe not *just like*." He closed the space between them and kissed her. Too soon, he ended it. "Either way, you and I aren't done. I'm not ready to say good-bye to you again, Cassidy. I don't think I'll ever be ready for that."

She allowed him to pull her close again, tried to believe his words. Wanted so badly for them to be true.

He pulled back. "We need to—"

"I know. Sorry. I didn't mean..."

He took her hand and squeezed. "You don't need to apologize to me, Cassidy. You're here, risking everything to save a little girl whose father thinks you're a killer. Whatever happens here, you're a hero, and if we survive this, I'm going to make sure everybody knows it.

A hero. Not even close.

Two more hours they trekked up the mountain. This route was different from the one they'd ascended the other day and the one they'd descended the day before. Hills, boulders, rocks, and trees, trees, and more trees.

As they climbed, their conversation dwindled. The air seemed to thicken with tension, and not from the conversation they'd just had. If James was right, they were closing in on the killer.

James paused, checking his GPS, then found a rock and tugged her down beside him, facing the hillside they'd just climbed. "We need a break."

She smiled, unwilling to speak and show how winded she was. Winded and sore, and her head was pounding. She dug some Tylenol out of her pack and took them with a swig of water.

"We're a couple hundred yards out," he said. "I lost cell service about an hour ago. Down should be faster than up, though. If something happens, run until you get service and call 911."

"What? No. I'm not leaving you."

"You're staying in this spot"—he pointed to the ground at their feet—"right here. Hidden from above, not too far to find service. Not too close to the killer."

She turned to face him. "Forget it. I'm not letting you do this by yourself."

"I'm not putting you in danger."

"I didn't come up here—"

"You were shot yesterday. You have a huge lump on your head

and bruises all over your body." Gently, he traced the one on her shoulder, visible thanks to her tank top, the last of her clean clothes. "I love that you want to save Ella. I do too. But not if it means putting you in danger. I need somebody down here to listen, to be ready to contact the police."

"Forget it."

He shifted so his face was inches from hers, studying her through narrowed eyes.

"I'm not—"

But his lips covered hers, cut off her words.

He slipped his fingers onto her neck, sending tingles down her spine.

She laid her palms on his chest, enjoying the strength she felt there, the steady beat of his heart.

He ended the kiss suddenly and pulled her against him.

Neither of them spoke.

She wasn't going to be dissuaded by a kiss, but she'd enjoyed it nonetheless.

"I can't lose you again," he said.

"I didn't come all this way to hide. If I'd wanted to hide—"

"If I'm right about who..." He backed away, shook his head. "Scratch that. Whether I'm right or wrong is irrelevant. If the kidnapper is up there, then this is going to be dangerous. I have no intention of confronting him. My plan is simply to learn what I can. That's it. I'm going to go up the long way, get as close as I can, and listen. If I hear nothing, I'll get closer, hopefully go inside. If Ella's there, I'll get her out and we'll leave together. If I hear a man's voice, then I'll know."

"I can hel—"

"I don't need your help." James took her hands and rested his forehead against hers. "I need to know you're safe. If you're with me, you'll only distract me."

She backed away from him. "If you didn't want my help, why did you bring me?"

"If something happens to me, you need to run and call the police. You need to tell them what happened here."

"How can I do that if you won't let me get close enough to see who it is? And if you don't tell me your suspicions?"

He stood, looked over her head. Obviously, he hadn't thought this through.

"Look," she said, "I'll stay out of the way. But this is too far. Hundreds of yards? How will I hear if you call out to me? How will I know anything?"

"I want you far enough away that you're out of danger."

"I have a gun, too, James, and I know how to use it. If I stay here, I'll be far enough away to be of zero use to you. Every moment I hear nothing, I'll worry. There's no way I could just sit here and wait. Eventually, I'll get closer, just to be sure."

His growl of frustration was uttered so quietly that she almost missed it.

"How about this?" she said. "How about we get closer, within fifty yards. I'll hide, but from there, I'll be able to hear if you call me." And help if he needed her, though she didn't say that. "I'll be able to see who you're confronting up there, assuming anybody's even there."

He studied the slope ahead of them, then lowered his head and rubbed the back of his neck. He met her eyes, and before he spoke, she knew she'd convinced him. She worked hard to hide the triumphant smile that wanted to show itself.

"You'll stop where I tell you and stay hidden?"

Though she didn't relish the idea of James going up to the cave alone, she'd be lying if she said she wasn't a little relieved. Truth was, she was terrified to be back here. And having James working to protect her... It wasn't very women's-libby, but she liked it. She could definitely get used to it. "I promise."

"Anything happens to me, you run. You don't try to save me or rescue Ella. You just run."

"I'm not making that promise, James. If Ella's up there, I won't leave without her any more than you would."

When he blew out a long, defeated breath, she stood, knowing she'd won. "Lead the way."

He said nothing as he passed her.

They climbed in silence.

As they neared the rocks that formed the cave, the little hairs on her arms stood, and a ran slid down her spine despite the warm temperature.

Something evil lurked above. The feeling stole over her like a long-forgotten scent. He was here. He was close. One way or another, after ten long years, this was nearly over.

# CHAPTER THIRTY-ONE

James wasn't sure he'd made the right choice. Cassidy's logic was sound. From two hundred yards away, she'd have surely heard a gunshot, but if there were a confrontation, and if it came down to a fistfight or a battle between James's hunting knife and the kidnapper's weapons, it might not be very loud.

She wouldn't know. And the not knowing would send her on a quest to find out what was going on. And if James were bested, then Cassidy would be in even more danger.

James wanted her safe, so he needed to find a closer place for her to hide. A place where she could run down quickly and call for help. It would take hours for the police to get up there, though.

If he were injured or killed, would Cassidy get away? Would she try? Or would she go after Ella?

He should have thought this through better.

Thing was, if he was right, then there was a good chance the killer wouldn't be here. Cassidy had said he left her and Hallie tied up in the cave for hours at a time. Whoever the killer was, he likely had a job, a life off of this mountain. James was banking on the kidnapper being gone.

And if he was, James didn't need to confront him. He just

needed to get Ella to safety and call the police. The police could take it from there.

If the killer was here, then they'd call the police and wait and pray the killer didn't get wind of them.

James lifted prayers for help and guidance and protection. He'd been a fool to put his relationship with God away after Hallie's death. God was the Source of comfort, the Source of peace, two things he'd needed desperately in the last decade. Right now, he needed God the Protector to show up. And the God who Sees, who knew exactly where Ella and the killer were. The God who cared about His children.

James paused to check his map again. The trail they'd gone down the day before was thirty or so yards to the left, but he stayed his course, far from the path, blocked from sight from the giant boulders above.

At the foot of a particularly steep rise, he turned and extended a hand for Cassidy.

She took it and joined him on a small flat of land no more than three feet wide. "This is a good spot. Hidden from above." He looked at the tree, thick with vegetation, growing from the slope below. "Hidden all around. You can wait here."

She lifted her hand over her eyes and peered up. "That's it?"

He followed her gaze. They were a good hundred feet below the stone that made up the ceiling of the cave. From this vantage point, the lower stones weren't visible. "If my map is correct, that's it."

She gazed around. "Where was I standing when he shot at me?"

James pointed to a spot on the right of the boulders. "I think about there."

"So that's where the passageway comes out."

He looked down at her. "I want you to stay here where it's safe."

"Just trying to get my bearings." She looked off to her right.

"You think he was standing over there somewhere when he shot me?"

"Had to be."

From here, all they could see were trees and bushes and rocks and hillside. If he searched that direction, he'd likely find the shooter's position. Had the man watched them go up? Had he been watching the back and seen her climb from the passageway?

Too many questions with no answers.

"You'll stay here?"

She plopped down on a tree root jutting from the hillside. "Who is it?"

"I don't know for sure."

"Best guess."

He shook his head. "Let's just see what we find. Take out your phone, would you?"

She did, and he navigated to the map, then tipped it to face her. "If anything happens to me. If you hear gunshots or... or whatever. If you think there's any danger, I want you to run." He pointed to the map. "The road's here. Your car"—he pressed the screen and saved the location—"is about here." He scrolled out and indicated a spot halfway between where they were and the car. "You should have service around here. Call 911 as soon as you can, and keep going until you reach your car and get out of here."

Her lips were set in a grim line, and for a moment he thought she'd argue. But she only nodded and took the phone. "I don't like this."

"Me either." He kissed her forehead. "We're doing this to save Ella."

She wrapped her arms around his middle and looked up. "I want to save Ella, James. But I don't want to sacrifice you to do it. Promise me you'll be careful."

"I promise."

She tried to tug him down, seemed to want another kiss, but he backed away. He needed to focus, and not on her. "I'll probably be right back. Just sit tight."

And he started climbing.

~

THE GOING WAS SLOW. The closer James got to the boulders that formed the cave, the steeper the way. It wasn't as bad as the cliff he and Cassidy had climbed the other day, but it was bad enough. It was no wonder nobody else had found this rock formation before. It was as if it'd been intentionally tucked away. Thick vegetation all around mostly hid the cavern from view. Steep hills on three sides and only a very twisted, winding path on the fourth. This had been the perfect hiding space until Cassidy and James had exposed it.

He was banking on the fact that the kidnapper wouldn't have a backup plan. And that he was arrogant. And, probably, the biggest issue was that James had no other ideas. Maybe nothing but blind hope had brought him back here today.

He couldn't let himself worry about what would happen next. One step at a time. *Go with me, Lord. Protect Cassidy. Save Ella.*

He crept up the hill, though it would've been faster to take the trail, and paused on the back side of the rock that made up one wall of the cave.

He listened, heard nothing. Crept closer to the opening. Paused to listen again.

Heard... whimpering.

Ella? Was it her?

He inched closer to the entrance, pausing every few feet to listen. The sound of crying carried from inside.

He reached the edge of the giant boulder and peered around it toward the entrance. Nobody at the mouth, but he couldn't see inside from here.

Back against the stone, he strained to hear signs that there was somebody else in the cave. Heavy breathing, footsteps.

Nothing from the cave but Ella's cries.

He stayed unmoving, listening.

Coming from the far side, he heard something different. The sound of movement in the forest. He looked back to where he'd left Cassidy, but it wasn't coming from her. It was too loud to be almost any animal. Possible it was a black bear. More likely, it was a man. A man unafraid of giving himself away.

James peeked around the rock, and this time, focused on the path. Nothing.

He'd confirmed Ella was here. He needed to tell Cassidy to run and call the authorities. Would she leave as she'd promised? Or would she insist on staying to help him rescue Ella?

*What should I do, Lord? Guide me.*

He needed to see who he was up against. Then he'd tell Cassidy who it was and have her get help. He'd stay and, if he could rescue Ella, he would. Worst case scenario, assuming the killer didn't find him and take him out, he'd be here when the police arrived. Either way, he wasn't leaving this mountain without Ella.

He no longer heard footsteps. Had the killer stopped? Or had he seen James and simply quieted?

James headed to the back side of the stone outcropping, maneuvering around the smaller boulder that made up one of the rear walls of the cave. Dropping to his knees, he crept along the spot where Cassidy had been shot, peering at the gap in the stones that made up the passageway Cassy had come through. Hidden from here, he thought if he climbed up, he'd see the narrow opening. If only he were small enough to climb through.

Cassidy was.

No, he wouldn't put her in danger.

Staying low, he peered toward the front. Here, the narrow pathway was lined on one side with the giant rock, on the other with the cliff they'd climbed the day before. Nobody was in sight.

Where was the killer?

James backed up, returned to the mouth of the narrow passageway and, using those uneven rocks, climbed on top. Flattening himself to the cavern's granite roof, he army-crawled forward, studying the forest up ahead.

Saw nothing. Nobody.

Was he crazy?

He lowered his head to the rock and listened again.

Ella's soft cries. Nothing had changed there, which told him the kidnapper probably hadn't gone into the cave.

No other noises.

Had the killer seen him? Heard him?

He looked behind, just in case, but nobody was there.

What now?

He returned the way he'd come. The cliff was still empty of people. James again circled the cavern toward the hillside where he'd left Cassidy. No sign of her, but she'd be hidden from here.

Silently, staying low, he climbed down the steep hillside, then moved toward the path. He'd watch from below, see if anybody turned up.

He found a spot away from the nearly hidden path and, crouching behind a tree, waited.

The snap of a branch too close had his head whipping around.

Vince stood ten feet behind, finger over his mouth in the universal sign for silence.

He closed the distance and crouched near James. "We had the same idea."

James nodded once, heart thumping, and turned his attention back to the mouth of the cave. "She's in there."

"You saw her?"

"Heard her crying."

"Poor kid." Vince looked around the hillside. "No signs of the guy?"

"Just you and me."

"And Cassidy. Where is she?"

"She's not here."

When Vince said nothing, James glanced his way. Saw Vince's smirk.

"If you say so," Vince said. "Either way, this is no place for you. You and your girlfriend need to head down the mountain and call 911. I'll stay here."

"Not a chance."

"You're not trained for this." Vince's voice was low, but not low enough.

"I've got enough training in what it feels like to lose someone I love. I'm not leaving without Ella."

"You're committed to that girl," Vince said.

"Committed to her. Committed to Reid." He turned and met his friend's eyes. "Committed to seeing the person responsible for this pay."

Vince settled in beside him. "I would've expected nothing less. So, you got any ideas?"

# CHAPTER THIRTY-TWO

Fear wrapped around Cassidy's throat, threatened to close off her airways.

Fear birthed a scream deep in her belly.

Fear choked it off.

She pressed her hand over her mouth, just in case some of it escaped in a whimper. She knew better than to scream. Nobody would hear her.

No. Not true.

Focusing on the day around her, the time, the truth, she shook off the past. She wasn't a captive. She was free. This time, she would fight.

She pressed herself against the hillside not fifteen feet from where James and the other man crouched.

When she'd seen James settle, she'd decided to find out what he knew. Based on the way he'd been moving, though, she'd realized he feared someone was nearby. So she'd been smart. Stayed low. Stayed quiet. Which was the only reason the stranger crouching beside James didn't know she was there.

The kidnapper.

The killer.

It was the voice. The cadence of the words. The way he'd said, *You're committed to that girl.*

She could feel him on top of her. Feel his hand pressing against her neck. *You're committed to that girl, so don't fight me. Don't make me kill you.*

She should shoot him. Right now. She could do it. She had the weapon. But did she have the skills? What if she missed and the killer came after her?

What if she missed and hit James?

No, she didn't have the confidence, not from this range.

And she carried enough regret. How could she justify killing a man in cold blood? Even *this* man?

If she called out, could James get away? Except James trusted him, whoever he was. The kidnapper would have the upper hand. He was armed—Cassidy had seen a holstered gun.

The kidnapper could start shooting before Cassidy could do anything. He was probably more experienced with weapons than she was. No way would she match her skills against his. Shooting at targets in a range wasn't the same as shooting at humans in a forest, no matter what the stakes.

Slowly, slowly, she backed away on hands and knees. Keeping bushes and trees between them, keeping her eyes in their direction, praying the men would continue talking and cover the rustling of leaves. *A breeze, Lord. A strong wind. Hide me. Protect us.*

Maybe the breeze picked up. Maybe the trees rustled. Maybe an answer to prayer.

Moving backwards, heartbeat racing, panic telling her to run, Cassidy traversed the hillside, inching downward until she was out of sight of the men, who continued to study the cavern's entrance. Only then did she turn, still keeping low, and hurry to the base of the cliff.

There was no other option. Where the men hid, they'd see if someone came up the path or the way she and James had come. This was the only way.

As she climbed, she wondered why they didn't split up, one watching the cliff while the other watched the path. Thank God they hadn't thought to do that. But they might soon. She prayed, if they did think of it, it would be James who perched above her, not the killer.

*Please, Lord.*

She'd made this climb the other day. She could do it again. Up was easier than down.

The thought of trying to get back down it had her stopping, hands gripping the stony cliff, breathing through the terror.

She had to focus. One handhold, one foothold at a time, she climbed until she finally pulled herself over the top and scrambled to stand.

Nobody in sight.

They hadn't seen her.

Pressing her back against the stone, she inched her way to the hidden passage, no longer a secret but at least out of sight of the watching men.

The sound of soft crying carried through the narrow gap in the boulders.

Ella.

Cassidy tried to slow her heartbeat. She could rescue her. This time, she would do it right.

She took off her backpack, found her water, and took a swig of it. As she was returning it to the pack, she spied something else at the bottom.

A knife wrapped in a leather sheath. After their conversation about one's need to carry a hunting knife, James must've put it in there. She shoved it deep in her front pocket.

Checked her handgun. It would be a challenge to wear it through the passage, but she wasn't leaving it, and she'd need both her hands.

She found a bush, stashed the backpack behind it. Not well hidden, but it would do.

Her gaze traveled the hillside below, wondering where the killer had stood when he'd shot at her before. She turned her back on that phantom fear and looked up at the rock wall beside her.

It took two tries, but she managed to climb the boulder and into the cramped space. Stone on all sides, barely enough room to move, she wiggled her way, pressing hands and feet against the rough walls to keep moving upward, fighting the gravity that wanted to push her down and spit her out. She reached the curve and took her gun from its holster. Keeping it in her hand in front of her, she bent her body over and around the stone, feeling the scrape against her hips as she wiggled through. She made it to the slightly wider opening.

Ella's cries were louder here.

Could James and the killer hear? Would they notice if they suddenly stopped?

*Father, please. Help.*

After sliding the gun back into its holster, she reached the mouth of the passage and caught sight of the child.

Ella lay curled on a blanket, head on a pillow, back against the stone wall that had been Cassidy's prison for days. Thumb in her mouth. Her eyes were closed, her hands unbound.

Unbound? Cassidy's and Hallie's hands and feet had been tied.

And then she saw it. A thick, black... something. Looked like iron or steel. Was it an anvil? She'd never seen one in real life, but it looked like the images she'd seen.

Admittedly, most of those images had come from the old cartoons.

There was nothing amusing about this one. A hook connected a chain to a leather cuff wrapped around one of Ella's ankles.

Cassidy crept toward her. When she was within five feet, she whispered, "Shh."

The girl gasped.

"Shh." Cassidy pressed her finger to her lips and shot a look at the mouth of the cavern. "He's out there."

The girl's eyes widened.

Cassidy closed the distance between them and swept the child in her arms. The metal chain clanged, and she froze at the sound.

So did Ella.

A normal sound. The girl could move. The sound of chains would make sense.

"It's okay." Cassidy kept her voice so low that she wondered if Ella could hear it. "My name is Cassidy. I'm going to get you out of here."

The girl's gaze flicked to the cavern opening.

"Ella, right?"

The child nodded.

"There's another way out." Cassidy pointed to the back, though the opening was hidden from there. "It's how I got in. I'm going to get that off your foot, and we're going to crawl out. Okay?"

Again, Ella nodded.

Cassidy set her back on the blanket, realizing then that it wasn't just a blanket but that there was padding beneath it. It was actually soft. Better than the cold stone she and Hallie had suffered.

Well, mostly her. Hallie had stayed on her lap most of the time. Her sweet little body had been so warm. She'd been so trusting, looking at Cassidy just like Ella was now.

*Father, please, please.*

She couldn't lose another little girl.

Shaking off the fear, she focused on the cuff that kept the girl chained to the anvil. Made of thick leather, it was padded on the inside, but not well. Ella's skin was scraped raw. The metal clasp opened with a key. She looked around, hoping the key was nearby.

There was a cooler, but that was close enough for Ella to reach.

There was a bucket. Cassidy didn't look inside it, figuring it was where the strong scent of urine came from. At least Ella had had a place to relieve herself. Cassidy and Hallie'd just had to hold it until the kidnapper returned.

"Does he keep the key here?"

Ella shook her head.

"You're sure?"

She whispered, "In his pocket."

Figured.

She found the knife. James was a genius.

She prayed a quick, *Don't let me hurt her. Or accidentally slit my wrist.* Hoping to avoid cutting the girl's raw skin, she set to work trying to force open the lock.

Thirty seconds of that and she admitted she'd make a terrible thief.

Okay, plan B. She slid the knife between Ella's leg and the cuff and started sawing.

It was working, slowly.

Ella's eyes were scrunched up, her lips trembling.

"Am I hurting you?" Cassidy whispered.

"Get it off."

A minute, two, and she'd hardly made a slit.

*Lord, keep the men out there until we can escape. Then, help me figure out where to hide Ella. And how to warn James.*

# CHAPTER THIRTY-THREE

James resisted the urge to look for Cassidy. Was she where he'd left her? Was she safe?

He and Vince had been crouched, side-by-side, for ten minutes or more. How long did Vince plan to watch an empty trail? To wait for someone to emerge from a cavern free of everybody except a trapped little girl?

"It's obvious to me now that Cassidy isn't the kidnapper." Vince's voice seemed too loud in the silent woods. "If she's here, she doesn't have to be afraid of me."

"Cassidy took off after you came to my house yesterday."

Vince nodded slowly, kept his focus on the path. "If she were here, would you tell me?"

"You say you believe me, but have you convinced Detective Cote?"

At Vince's shrug, James added, "You still have a job to do, right? Finding Cassidy is part of that."

"I'm not on the job right now. Not officially, anyway."

"Take the day off?"

Vince shot a glare his way. "I wanna find Reid's daughter as much as you do."

"I'm sure that's true."

More long minutes of waiting followed. Finally, Vince said, "I don't think he's in there. Let's go get Ella." He nodded toward the mouth of the cavern, but James shook him off.

"You're the professional. I'll follow."

Vince gave him a long look through squinted eyes, then nodded and started up the steep hill. From behind, James caught sight of the handgun holstered on Vince's right hip, some kind of black contraption on his left. Looked like it could be official police gear, but he'd never seen it before.

And then he realized it was a satellite phone. Vince had told him he'd bought one to stay in touch while he searched for the cave.

Only when James was sure Vince wasn't looking did he turn toward where he'd left Cassidy. No sign of her, but that didn't mean anything. She could still be where he'd asked her to stay. She could have run to call 911, thinking he'd confirmed that Ella was here when he didn't come right back.

He highly doubted that second option.

She could be in the cavern. Vince could be on his way to her right now.

*We need help, Lord. Please, protect them.* He trudged behind his friend, unsure how to proceed but knowing he needed to do so very carefully.

At the top of the hill, Vince crouched to offer him a hand.

"I got it," he said and climbed the last few feet.

Vince waited until James was beside him, and they stalked nearer the mouth of the cavern.

Ella was no longer crying.

Vince glanced back at him. "I'll go first. Stay here, just in case he's in there."

"I'll stay behind you." Which wasn't the same as staying outside, but Vince didn't argue.

James followed, keeping his handgun pointed at the ground.

Out of the bright sunshine, he let his eyes adjust to the darkness. Sidestepped to see beyond Vince.

A blue cooler, a grocery bag, a bucket. Near them, an anvil, a chain.

A leather cuff, sliced open.

No Ella.

Vince bolted deeper into the cave, gun drawn. He got to the narrow escape passage and crouched, reached inside.

Yelled, "Stop. Police."

Then pulled his weapon.

James barreled into him, knocking him to the side.

Vince turned the weapon his direction.

James dove, lifted his own, pointed it at his friend.

Neither fired.

Neither moved.

James did his best not to focus on the gun aimed at his heart. Not to focus on the fact that, with a single squeeze of the trigger, he'd be dead.

Vince's gaze flicked to James's gun as well. That neither had fired proved the friendship was real. Even if it had been built on shifting sand.

"They're getting away," Vince said. "I don't want to shoot you."

James wasn't sure he could say the same.

"If Cassidy didn't do it," Vince continued, "she'll get a fair trial."

"This isn't about Cassidy."

Vince's eyes narrowed. His expression hardened, and he shouted toward the opening, "Bring her back around or your boyfriend dies."

"Don't do it!" James yelled. "Call 911."

From the other end of the passageway, only silence.

Vince smirked. "I guess she's not as devoted to you as you are to her. Of course, I could've told you that a long time ago, considering she killed your sister and disappeared."

James wouldn't rise to Vince's bait. Where was Cassidy? She

had to have been in the shaft when Vince pulled his weapon. Otherwise, why show his hand?

Had she made it through? Was Ella safe?

"What do you think is happening here?" Vince asked. "I'm trying to catch Ella's kidnapper, and you're letting them get away."

"You're trying to catch Ella and the one girl you let survive."

"What are you talking about?"

"I figured it out, Vince. It was you. It had to be you."

"You're insane."

"Here's what I know," James said. "I think *you* did it. Everyonw else thinks *Cassidy* did it. If you're innocent, then use that handy little contraption on your left hip and call your friends at the station. They can take you both into custody, and we'll let them sort it out from there."

Vince scoffed. "Reid's daughter is out there, and you're letting her get away."

"Escape. I'm letting her escape."

Vince yelled, "Cassidy, you still there?"

A moment later... "I'm here. Ella's hidden." Her voice echoed from the passageway. James wanted to glance that way, but he was afraid to take his eyes off Vince and his weapon for even an instant.

"Come on through where I can see you," Vince said.

"Stay where you are, Cassidy. I can shoot him as easily as he can shoot me."

"I'll stay where I am," she said.

"Seems we have some time." Vince leaned against the stone wall behind him. "Why are you so sure it's me? Your girlfriend tell you that?"

"She didn't know. I didn't either, not until just now. But I suspected."

Vince's lips curled at the corners. Not a smile as much as a sneer. "Why's that?"

"You were in charge of the search for this place ten years ago yet swore you couldn't find it. You told me a few nights ago you'd continued searching. For ten long years, you searched. It took

Cassidy and me less than twenty-four hours. Tells me you weren't trying that hard, or you were lying."

"It's not like it's easy to find."

"And you called it a cave. The other night at Teresa's, you were emphatic when you said it. 'There are no caves.'"

"So what?"

"Cassidy said she was careful never to call it a cave. She said she always called it a rock formation, which is what it is. But it feels like a cave." He didn't look around, kept his focus on the man, the gun. But Vince's gaze flicked to the stone walls surrounding them.

"That doesn't mean anything. She described it like a cave."

James shrugged. The gun was getting heavy in his hand, but he didn't shift it. "Not proof. I never had proof. Only suspicion. Like the fact that you were the first to show up when that family reported finding Hallie's body. The rest of the town cops were elsewhere, making calls, knocking on doors. But you were on this side of the lake, Johnny-on-the-spot. Because you knew where Cassidy and Hallie had last been seen. Not at the rest stop near Concord. Not in town. Nope. They'd still been on this mountain."

"The search took us all over."

"Yesterday, you showed up at my house alone. You said it was because you trusted me, but that's not why. You showed up alone because you wanted to catch Cassidy without cops nearby to witness it. You need her dead."

"You really think I'd have killed your girlfriend in cold blood?"

James's lack of response to the question was all the answer he planned to give. "Lorelei still out of town?" James asked, referring to Vince's girlfriend. "She was last month when Addison went missing too, wasn't she? Convenient."

Vince's expression gave away nothing.

James continued. "One of my biggest questions all along has been about the ten-year gap in kidnappings. Assuming they were related, nobody could explain why the killer would take ten years off. Something had to happen in the killer's life to get him started again. Something drastic. Like, say, for instance... his mother's death."

Now, Vince flinched as if James had wounded him.

"And then there's the fact that Eugene and Wilson reported having seen us on the mountain two nights ago, and the next day, the killer had emptied this place out. How would he know to do that? How would he know to be prepared for us?"

"Word gets around."

"After I was arrested, sure, the stories got out. But before that? When you were still theoretically trying to catch a killer? Surely the department keeps such things a little closer to the vest."

"Rumors." Vince shrugged. "Leaks. They're the bane of our existence."

"More circumstantial evidence. It's possible word got out that we'd been seen up here, the killer heard, ran up to the mountain, hid Ella and all this gear somewhere, and then waited to try to kill Cassidy, the only person who could recognize him. But it feels unlikely.

"And then there's the other question, the one that's been nagging us. Why didn't the killer shoot us both yesterday? Why let us go after Cassidy was shot?"

"He probably ran. Stayed with the kid."

"I think he wanted to kill Cassidy, but he didn't want to kill his friend."

Vince's gaze hardened. "He didn't want to, but he will."

"Problem is, Vince, I'm not the only one who knows. Before we started this morning, I left a message for Reid. I don't know if he's listened to it yet. Considering how ticked at me he was"—the reminder had James wanting to rub his jaw that still hurt—"I wouldn't be surprised if it took him a day or two. But if I turn up missing or dead, he'll listen. I laid out for him all the reasons why I think you might be the guy. It's circumstantial, like you say, but I'm sure his uncle, your boss, would take it seriously. Especially if I'm dead."

For the first time, Vince had no answer. No defense. No argument.

Which meant this conversation was over.

Vince's eyes didn't shift, but his lips flattened. His shoulder lifted the tiniest bit.

And he fired.

# CHAPTER THIRTY-FOUR

Ella sat in the sunshine, her back pressed against a skinny tree trunk. The pretty lady had freed her from the chain, and they'd crawled out a back hole Ella hadn't even known was there. But the lady knew. The lady said if Ella was really quiet, she'd get her out of there, and she had.

But then, the lady had wanted her to go closer to the cave's entrance, but she wasn't going back there. She couldn't. She grabbed the trunk and held on and cried and begged the lady not to take her back inside.

The lady had run her hand down Ella's hair, which was probably all matted and yucky, kissed her on the temple, told her to stay put, and crept to the entrance.

Ella couldn't look. She hid behind the tree and hoped the man wouldn't find her there.

He was inside. Ella wanted to run away, far away where the man wouldn't find her. But the lady promised to take her home to her daddy if she stayed where she was, and she was too scared to move, too scared to do anything.

She sucked her thumb and prayed to God to please keep the lady safe.

But then, a loud bang came from the cave, and Ella screamed.

# CHAPTER THIRTY-FIVE

James dove to the side just in time.

The bullet ricocheted off the wall behind him, sending stone fragments in every direction.

James rolled onto his knees, prepared to shoot.

But a shadow darkened the cave. Vince turned that direction, shifted his aim.

Had to be Cassidy. But James didn't look, just lined Vince up in his sights.

And squeezed the trigger.

Vince crashed back against the stone wall behind him. Lifted his gun. Aimed at James.

Cassidy fired, and Vince flinched, then raised his gun again, this time aimed at Cassidy.

James vaulted across the ground, lowered his shoulder, and tackled his friend. He tossed his own gun away, snatched the weapon from Vince's hand, and threw it across the cavern.

Vince struggled beneath him, still strong despite the bleeding wounds.

One bullet had hit just below Vince's collarbone on the right side.

Another had grazed the outside of his shoulder. Blood seeped there, but not nearly as much.

James pressed his weight onto his friend's biceps and turned toward the mouth of the cave, where Cassidy stood, gun still trembling in her hands.

"Come closer. Aim at his head." James turned to Vince. "You'd better stop struggling, or she'll have no choice but to shoot you again."

Vince glared past James at the woman standing behind him, but he let his muscles relax. Blood poured from his injury. Didn't look life threatening, assuming they could stop the bleeding. "You wouldn't let your girlfriend murder your old friend in cold blood, would you?"

James pressed his hand onto Vince's wound, eliciting a scream of pain, and punched him in the jaw with the opposite fist. "You killed my sister."

"I didn't kill her." He almost looked amused when his gaze shifted to Cassidy. "Hallie was still alive when they escaped. Cassidy killed her."

To silence him, to keep the doubt from creeping in, James punched him again.

Vince's head bounced off the hard floor. Tension leached from his body. Was he unconscious, or was he faking?

James flicked his gaze to Cassidy's. Her skin was pasty white. The hands holding the gun still aimed at Vince's head trembled. From having nearly been shot? Or from the truth Vince had just revealed?

If it was true.

James didn't know what to think. "We need to bind him," he said. The rest would have to wait. "Dig in my backpack. I have some rope."

She did, and James rolled Vince over—no exit wound—and tied his hands behind his back. Then he grabbed the satellite phone holstered to his hip and handed it to Cassidy. "Call 911."

She stepped out of the cave to make the call while James tied

Vince's feet together. He dragged the anvil—had to weigh a hundred pounds—nearer Vince and tied the rope to the hook. Just in case.

And for the sake of justice.

When he pressed the thin blanket Vince had left for Ella against the bullet wound, Vince screamed in pain. That bullet probably hurt like a hot poker on tender skin.

"Shut up," James said. "I'm trying to save your life."

"Why?" Vince's voice rasped.

"Because you're a human being, and vengeance is God's, not mine."

James needed to show mercy. No easy feat when fury coursed through his veins. Fury and fear.

Where was Cassidy? Where was Ella?

James dug in his backpack for his first-aid kit. Found antiseptic and poured some on the wound, eliciting another scream. This one made his stomach clench with sympathy. He unwrapped a handful of gauze and pressed it against the spot. Taped it in place. Blood was already seeping through, but that couldn't be helped.

He threw the filthy blanket over his former friend to help with the shivers and shock.

James was standing to search for Cassidy when she stepped inside. "They're on their way."

He tried not to let his relief show—that she'd called 911. That she was still there. That Vince's revelation hadn't sent her running again.

With the light behind her, he couldn't see her expression, didn't know what she read in his.

"Where's Ella?" he asked.

"She won't come back in here."

Made sense. "She okay?"

"Scared, mostly. I'm going to stay with her until they get here." She disappeared outside again.

James tested the weight of the anvil, the knots in the ropes. Vince wasn't going anywhere. Even if he could drag the anvil behind him—which James would surely hear—he wouldn't fit through the passageway at the back of the cavern. And James and Cassidy would be at the mouth.

He snatched both guns from the floor and looked down at Vince's weakened body—shivering, pale, bleeding. He tried to feel something besides anger.

His friend. But why? Why had Vince befriended him?

He resisted the urge to kick the wound, hated himself for considering it, and stalked outside.

Leaning against the stone wall, the little girl in her arms, Cassidy looked at him.

And then Ella did, too. "Uncle James!" She launched herself at him.

He took her in his arms and hugged her tight, hid his tears in her messy hair. "Sweet girl, I'm so glad we found you."

"I want my daddy."

"I know. I know." Over Ella's head, he asked, "You have that phone?"

Cassidy held it up, and he rattled off a number. She dialed, then handed it to him.

"Hello?" In the single word, James heard defeat in Reid's voice.

"It's James," he said. "I have Ella."

"Wait? Where? Is she okay?"

He handed the phone to Ella, who said, "Daddy?" The word cracked, and she buried her face in James's T-shirt, keeping the phone to her other ear.

With the girl so close, James could hear Reid's calming voice, his promises to see her soon. Not asking all the questions that had to be filling his mind. Just being the gentle father he'd always been to his little girl.

James turned to watch the man in the cave, but Vince hadn't moved.

They'd done it. He and Cassidy had saved Ella, together.

# CHAPTER THIRTY-SIX

Cassidy couldn't stop shaking.

She couldn't stop hearing the gunshots.

She couldn't stop seeing James on the ground. Those first few moments, she'd been sure he'd been shot.

Couldn't stop seeing the killer's gun pointed at his head.

Then pointed at her.

James had gotten off a shot before her.

Her bullet had grazed his shoulder. Not deadly, not where she'd aimed, but she should be thankful she hadn't hit him in the chest. She might not want to live with having killed a man, even that man.

The killer had attempted a shot, but it had gone wild. Thank God. *Thank God.*

She and James and Ella had survived. Somehow, they'd all three survived.

James transferred Ella into Cassidy's arms and returned to the cave to check on the man. His friend.

Ella wrapped her arms around Cassidy's neck, her legs around her waist, and hung on as if she'd never let go. The feeling was so familiar, terrifyingly familiar, she had the urge to push the child away for fear of failing her as she had Hallie. But she didn't. Ella needed her.

Finally, the faint whir of helicopter blades interrupted the forest's eerie silence, growing louder. It landed in a distant clearing and, a few minutes later, armed men climbed the path.

A blanket was thrown over Cassidy's shoulders. With James's help and gentle assurances, Ella allowed a paramedic to pry her from Cassidy's arms to examine her.

Vince was carried away on a stretcher, and one helicopter took off, allowing another to land.

Ella was taken to the second helicopter, and, after a quick kiss on Cassidy's cheek and a tossed "See you soon," James accompanied the little girl to the hospital.

Not until they were gone did a heavyset man with a gruff voice approach Cassidy.

"Detective Cote," he said.

Her fake name hovered on the end of her tongue. When had she last said her own name, her real name, to another soul?

Ten years past. Ten long years.

"Cassidy Leblanc," she said.

"Wanna tell me what happened?"

She watched as James and Ella were loaded on the helicopter. Ella was safe. James was safe. The killer was in custody.

She'd done what she'd come to do. Now she had to face the rest of it.

"Yes, I do."

# CHAPTER THIRTY-SEVEN

The hospital was cold and sterile. As James followed nurses onto the elevator from the helicopter pad to the ER, Ella in his arms, he spotted hospital personnel, patients, and visitors, all acting as if life were business-as-usual. As if James hadn't just shot a cop, shot his friend. As if he weren't holding a little girl who'd been missing for eight days.

She'd cried the entire flight, terrified.

The moment the helicopter had touched down, she'd screamed for James to hold her. The paramedic released her from the bed, and she'd scrambled into James's arms and held on tight.

James followed nurses down a corridor and around a corner and down another corridor to a double door.

The nurse in front of them pressed a button on the wall, and the doors opened.

And there was Reid.

"Daddy!" The single word was broken by a sob as Ella leapt from James's arms into her father's.

Reid snuggled his daughter, tears streaming down his face.

James had to wipe his own away. Not that anybody noticed. As Ella's grandparents crowded around, James backed up, gave the family space for their reunion.

So few words were spoken. Just gentle touches, praises to God.

James was stepping out the door when he felt a hand on his shoulder and turned.

Reid pulled him into a hug. "I can never... I'm sorry about—"

"We're good."

Reid backed up. "Where's Cassidy?"

"Cote told me he was going to take her back to the station."

"She in trouble? She didn't do it, right? Not Ella, not Hallie. Was it Vince all along?"

"Yeah. Not sure if Cassy's in trouble. I'm going to go find her now."

Reid squeezed his shoulder. "Thank you. Thank you for"—he glanced at Ella, who was in her grandmother's arms.

"I'm glad we found her. But the person you should be thanking is Cassidy. She made it happen."

"I will. I can never..." But his voice faded as if there were no words. Maybe there weren't.

After a quick kiss on Ella's cheek and a promise to stop by the following day, James stepped into the ER waiting room, trying to figure out who to call for a ride home.

He realized he needn't have worried when a uniformed Coventry police officer approached. "Mr. Sullivan?"

"What's wrong?"

"Nothing, sir. Just have orders to bring you in."

They stepped into the warm summer evening and walked to the waiting cruiser. "Am I in trouble?"

The man shot him a grin. "For saving a kid's life? Hardly."

It took nearly forty-five minutes to make the drive from Plymouth to Coventry, thanks to Friday night tourist traffic. Forty-five minutes during which James checked and rechecked his phone for a message, a phone call—something—from Cassidy.

Nothing.

Finally, they passed the front of the police station, where news vans and reporters had already congregated, and made their way around the building to the lot where official vehicles parked. The officer led him in through the rear door.

Inside, the room hummed with activity. Phones ringing, people moving about. When he'd come a few days ago, the mood had been solemn. The faces worried. Now, people seemed angry.

The killer was one of their own, and the good men and women on the police force were furious. James knew how they felt. Not only had he trusted Vince as a friend, he'd trusted him as a law enforcement officer. Vince had betrayed them all.

But Ella was with her father.

If only there'd been a happy reunion with Hallie and James and Mom and Dad. There'd been no reunion for them, not this side of heaven.

He let that thought settle. His parents and Hallie had celebrated their reunion, and it had been as beautiful, if not more so, than Reid and Ella's. Mom and Dad and Hallie were waiting for James now.

They'd already gone home.

James was the one who tarried on this side of the veil.

Where hard truths needed to be heard and dealt with. Where pain and mourning still existed.

A uniformed police officer got his attention from across the room and waved him over.

James weaved through the space and into the small interview room where he'd been a few days earlier.

Inside, Cote sat at the far side of the table, and James took the seat facing him. He didn't ask after Cassidy, though he wanted to. Cote would get to that.

"Tell me what happened." Cote pressed the button on a recorder on the table. "Starting from when you were released yesterday."

James recounted all the events, including Cassidy's part. Ella was safe, and the killer was in custody. There was no reason to hold back now.

Detective Cote made notes as James spoke but mostly kept his gaze on him. When he was finished, Cote set down his pen. "That tracks with what Miss Leblanc told us. Anything you want to add?"

"Cassidy didn't do anything wrong."

Cote's smile seemed indulgent. "That does seem to be the case. I've already spoken with her employer, who confirmed that she was in Seattle when both Addison and Ella were kidnapped, that she hadn't missed a day of work until last week when she flew out here. As to Hallie—"

"Vince admitted it was him. He told me Hallie and Cassidy escaped..."

"I know," Cote said. "I know what happened."

Judging by the look on his face, it seemed Cote knew more than James did at this point.

"Sit tight." The detective stepped out of the room.

James checked his phone yet again. Still no word from Cassidy. Was she in custody? Was she safe?

The door opened, and Cote held it open and backed up to allow another to enter.

Cassidy stepped inside. "Hey."

James stood and pulled her into a hug.

She fit so perfectly, right there in his arms, her head on his shoulder, her face nuzzled in his neck. He could hold this woman forever. Much as he hated to do it, he leaned away. "You all right?"

She nodded, but her wary expression concerned him. Especially the way it was aimed at him, not the detective.

She turned to Cote and said, "We'll let you know if we need you."

Cote glanced between them, then closed the door, leaving them alone.

"What's going on?" James asked.

"I need to tell you what happened."

James's heart thumped as he pulled the detective's chair around so Cassidy could sit beside him.

He took her hands. "I know you didn't kidnap my sister."

"I didn't. Everything happened just like I said. We ran into that... Vince person. Your friend?"

"I think he must have befriended me in hopes that I'd lead him to you." James had been thinking about it for days, ever since the thought first occurred to him that Vince could be the kidnapper. "That's my best guess, anyway. Those first few years, he used to ask about you a lot. Ask if I'd heard from you—always prefaced with, 'I'm asking as a friend, not as a cop.' Maybe he thought I'd give him a clue as to where you were."

"That makes sense," she said. "And then...?"

James shrugged. "At first, he was more of a mentor, since he's so much older, but by the time I graduated college, we were just... friends."

She nodded slowly. "I never saw his face back then. Today, I'd crept closer when I saw where you were. I was going to ask if you thought she was there. When he joined you, I hid. And then I heard his voice."

James couldn't imagine how that must have frightened her.

"He hadn't had all the supplies up there like now." Cassy's eyes looked beyond James, her voice lowered to a whisper. "The first time he left, he came back with blankets, but nothing like what we saw today.

"When he got back the second day in the cave, he untied us so we could use the bathroom. Like he had the day before, he let us move around in the cave when he was there." She faced James again, took a quick breath as if for courage. "I'd found the passageway the day before, but not in time to get us out. This time, the second he stepped out of the cave, I grabbed Hallie, and we crawled away."

Just like Vince had claimed. They were alive when they escaped.

"I was so scared he would see us. I was so scared." Tears dripped from Cassidy's eyes, but he couldn't comfort her, not until he knew the rest. He waited while she pulled a tissue from her jeans' pocket and wiped her eyes. The tissue looked as if it had already seen its share of tears.

"I thought he would see us if I went to the path. Today, when I looked at it... He might not have. We might've gotten away. But I didn't know. I just... I went down the first way I saw. The fastest way I could find."

His stomach dropped as he considered what she was saying. He leaned closer to her, tried to infuse her with courage, with confidence. "You were trying to save her."

"I was." Her voice cracked, and she wiped her eyes again. "I told her to hang on, and I started down the cliff. We were almost there, no more than ten feet from the bottom, when... She slipped off. She just... she fell. I rushed down behind her, but..."

Her voice broke, and Cassidy's sobs filled the room. "A million times, I've seen her there, her lifeless body on the rocks. She was gone. I knew it. But I just... I grabbed her and carried her. When we were safely away, I tried to revive her. But her head ..." She blinked, as if trying to rid herself of the sight. "And there was so much blood..."

When Cassidy's voice trailed, James tugged her close, and she rested her head on his shoulder. He couldn't speak for the emotion clogging his throat. His sweet sister, gone so tragically.

So suddenly.

"I'm sorry," Cassidy said. "I'm so sorry. I tried to save her. I did everything I could. It was my fault. I should have gone down a different way. I should have—"

"No." He leaned back in his chair so he could look into her eyes. "You did your best. You could have escaped with your own life and left her with Vince. You stayed to save her."

"I failed." She glanced at the door. "This was the part that bothered Cote the most. He said the coroner said she'd only been dead two hours when they found her body. She'd been dead longer than that, but..." She sniffed, blinked a few times. "I wrapped her in my jacket, and I held her close. I think my body heat messed up the coroner's...

calculations or whatever. I don't know how it works. I just... I couldn't leave her. I thought... It was irrational. I thought if I could just keep her warm... I'm sorry, James. I'm so sorry. To you, your parents..."

"Cassy, sweetheart."

Her gaze held somewhere around his chest, so he tipped her chin up with his finger. "Sweetheart, you tried to save her life. What happened was tragic, but it wasn't your fault. It was Vince's fault. All of it."

She looked at him with those mesmerizing eyes, red-rimmed, tear-filled. But hope shone there. Hope in him. Hope in love. Her voice was small when she said, "You forgive me?"

"There's nothing to forgive."

James had always known Cassidy was no killer. He stood and pulled her into his arms, needing to be closer to her. Needing her to feel his comfort, his love. "God numbers our days, Cassy." He paused, let the emotion roll away, tried to keep his voice strong and steady. "For whatever reason, God took Hallie home that day. I can't tell you the comfort it brings to know she wasn't beaten to death. That her death was sudden. That, at the end, she was with you, someone she loved dearly. And she had hope."

Cassidy collapsed against him and wept.

# CHAPTER THIRTY-EIGHT

Cassidy settled onto the couch beside James late that night. It had been a long day, the longest day since the worst day of her life. The one when she'd awakened in the cave, escaped a killer, seen Hallie's lifeless body, and then run, chased by guilt and grief and fear.

Today, those feelings were gone. She'd told the truth. She'd faced the demons, and she was forgiven. Exonerated of the crimes leveled against her for a decade.

If Detective Cote was right, there would be no charges related to her having used a false identity. Though she'd broken laws a few times when she'd signed her fake name on legal documents, she hadn't used that false identity to commit any crimes. She'd worked hard, paid her taxes. She'd been a law-abiding citizen. Apparently, no state authorities from Washington nor New Hampshire intended to prosecute. And the FBI didn't seem overly interested in prosecuting the woman who'd been falsely accused of kidnapping and murder for ten years.

Cassidy would deal with her employer when she returned to Seattle, but she believed her job was secure. If it wasn't, then she'd get another. The girls in Seattle would survive without her. It wasn't her job to save them, to save anybody. The runaways' lives,

Ella's life, Addison's life, and Hallie's life—they were all in God's hands.

She was really and truly free of it all. Free to be herself again.

"I should probably go," Cassidy said, though she'd abandoned the dingy rented cabin and had no desire to return.

James's arm tightened around her shoulders. "You can stay here."

Here, in the living room where she'd spent so many evenings with the Sullivan family, watching movies, eating popcorn, laughing. Hallie used to vie for her attention, squirming between her and James, chattering like a magpie. Cassidy could hear the echo of Mrs. Sullivan's *Give the girl some space* and Mr. Sullivan's low chuckle. Cassidy never minded Hallie's attention, nor James's parents' presence. She'd felt a part of their family. She'd felt more loved in this home than she'd ever felt, anywhere—before or since.

Right now, that love lingered. Or what she felt in the room came as much from the man beside her as the memories in the past.

The TV wasn't on, yet James and Cassidy stared in that direction as if riveted. She couldn't speak for James, but she felt too tired to move. Still... "You think there are any hotels with vacancies in town?"

He shifted to look at her. "You don't want to stay?"

"I don't want to put you out."

A smirk, a quick shake of the head, and he settled beside her again. "There are no vacancies, especially now with all the news media."

A good point. The reporters lined up at the end of the driveway had to have hotel rooms somewhere. Thanks to the police presence around the perimeter of James's property, none had gotten close. It was unsettling, knowing the house was being watched. Knowing everybody out there knew James and she were inside.

"You get used to it," he said, reading her mind. "This is nothing compared to last time. It was a circus."

She'd caught much of the footage on TVs at bus stations and

restaurants as she'd made her way west. Microphones, cameras shoved in the faces of the family she loved so dearly. Seeing their grief plastered across the TV screen—it had been more than she could handle.

"I'm sorry," Cassidy said. "For all of it. For ever leaving your house that day with Hallie. For not getting away with her sooner. For not protecting her. I'm sorry it all happened."

"Stop apologizing. You did everything you could." James kissed the top of her head. "Now that you've seen him, heard his voice again, any new memories you want to share?"

There were, but... "It's late."

"Yeah. Still..." When she lifted her head from his chest, he faced her. "It is late, and I understand if you don't want to talk. But I want to know, whatever you want to share, I want to know. Today, next month... whenever. Just know I want to hear everything."

She shouldn't get into it. Shouldn't let the memories out. But they were bubbling up. If she let them out, the pressure might release.

"He called me girl, just *girl*, the whole time. The way he said that is so clear in my mind."

She snuggled against James again. And kept talking. "Sometimes it's that single word that yanks me from sleep. He was angry I was there. And afraid. It was like... like he'd felt compelled to take Hallie. Like there was something he needed her for, though I never understood what."

"You said that he carried Hallie most of the way to the cave, right?"

"I carried her some, when she screamed for me. But after a while, she became accustomed to him. She was less afraid."

"I hate to think of her coming to trust him."

"It wasn't trust, I don't think. Just a belief that he wouldn't hurt her. Better than to be in constant terror."

"Yeah." He shifted again, and she sat up to face him. "If he had Hallie, then his hands would have been full. Why didn't you run?

On the mountain, with trees and rocks all around, you could've gotten away."

"You really think I'd have left Hallie to him? I'd have just saved myself?"

"You could've told someone where they were."

"I didn't know where he was taking us. I didn't know where I was. I didn't know how to get back down. There was no way I could possibly have directed anybody to him. Even if I'd found my way out, who knew what he'd have done to Hallie by the time someone found them. How could I take that chance?"

"You'd have been safe, though."

She scooted back and folded her leg between them.

"I'm sorry. I didn't mean to—"

"I imagined myself at your door, imagined seeing your parents, telling them what happened to their daughter." She closed her eyes as the old images surfaced, all she'd feared at that time. "I could see the horror on their faces. I couldn't do it." She opened her eyes again. "Your parents trusted me to protect her. That's what I tried to do. I failed"—her voice cracked—"but I tried. I did everything I could."

"I know." He wrapped his arm around her and cuddled her close. They were silent a few moments. Then he said, "Anything else?"

"I think that's enough for tonight."

"Anytime you want to talk about it, I'll be here to listen. You and I have a lot of catching up to do."

"But I have to go—"

"We'll figure it out," he said. "But not tonight. Tonight, let's just relax. Let's trust God with tomorrow."

Trust God with tomorrow. She could do that. They could do that together.

# CHAPTER THIRTY-NINE

E lla was afraid to open her eyes, afraid it was all a dream.

She slid her hand across soft sheets. Her fingers curled around a fuzzy thing that felt a lot like her favorite stuffed unicorn.

*Please, God. Please let it be real.*

She peeked one eye open and saw her own pale green walls, the white bookshelf with all her favorite books, the toy box filled with dolls and dress-up clothes.

It was true. She really was home.

Ella sat up. Even though it was morning, the sun shining outside, the birds singing, her daddy was fast asleep on the floor by her bed, curled up under a tiny blanket, his long legs sticking out.

Her eyes got all full of tears seeing him there, even though she was so, so happy to be home.

She climbed out of bed, yanked her comforter behind her, and laid it over him. Then, she crawled underneath and tucked herself right up next to him.

His strong arm came over her and pulled her close. He kissed the top of her head, and she smiled and closed her eyes. *Thank You, thank You, thank You, God, for bringing me home.*

# CHAPTER FORTY

J ames still had trouble wrapping his mind around the idea that his friend had kidnapped three little girls, kidnapped his own sister. The more information he got, the more surreal it felt.

Though Vince didn't repeat his confession when he was questioned by the police, Cassidy's and James's statements, combined with Ella's accounts of what happened, were enough to have him arrested and held under guard at the hospital in Manchester.

A judge denied bail Monday morning. Later that day, when Vince was recovered enough to be released from the hospital, he was taken straight to the county jail to await trial.

A search warrant of Vince's property uncovered damning evidence.

The backpacks James and Cassidy had left at the bottom of the cliff were discovered in his garage.

In the center console of Vince's SUV, authorities found a spent bullet, which they speculated he'd dug from the stone behind Cassidy after he tried to kill her. The bullet's caliber matched Vince's rifle. In time, authorities believed the blood on the bullet would be matched to Cassidy's.

They also found a flight itinerary in the vehicle—leaving from

Quebec City Saturday—and a printout of a beachside cabin. There were fake passports for himself and Ella.

When Cote called James that morning with the update, he'd told him another piece of evidence had been recovered, and James and Cassidy needed to go to the police station to identify it.

Late Monday afternoon, James picked Cassidy up at Reid's parents' house. Reid's mother had offered her a room until everything was settled. James had delivered her there Saturday morning. One night under the same roof with James was one thing—Cassidy had slept in Hallie's old bedroom—but any more than that and the kisses they'd shared might easily have become more. And, though James was eager for more, he wouldn't allow them to cross that line, not until they'd made it official.

Assuming they ever did.

They still hadn't discussed what would happen next. Would she return to Seattle? Would she consider moving back to Coventry?

Or would James be moving west? Either way, he wasn't going to lose Cassy again. For the first time in too long, he felt like he had a family again. Not the one he'd grown up with, but Cassy was the family of his future. He wasn't going to lose her. Not for anything.

He drove slowly past reporters in downtown Coventry, who shouted questions and aimed cameras their way, and into the gated lot of the police station. He held Cassidy's hand and hurried her inside.

Whatever Cote had called them in to do, it'd better be worth the trauma of dealing with the media. He glanced at Cassidy, expecting to see pale skin and frightened eyes, but she smiled at him. "That was interesting."

"They'll go away soon enough," James said, hoping it was true. "As soon as they have the whole story."

They sat across from Detective Cote in the interview room. Before the detective could speak, James said, "What's the holdup? Why haven't you issued a statement?"

"We will," Cote said. "We just have a few loose ends to deal with." The table between the detective on one side and James and Cassidy on the other held one thing—a cardboard box. From it, Cote pulled a clear plastic evidence bag. Inside, James saw a tiny stuffed bunny on the end of a plastic keychain.

James took the bag and closed it in his fist as memories of his little sister assailed him. Hallie had carried that silly little rabbit with her everywhere for weeks before she'd disappeared. She'd loved it, pretended to feed it, and even slept with it.

Vince had kept it.

Cassy slid her hand over his biceps and looked at the toy. "I thought she'd dropped it on the trail."

Based on the dirt smudges on the pink rabbit, it was likely she had. And Vince had picked it up.

His friend. All those years...

He squeezed the toy, then took a deep breath and set it in his lap.

Detective Cote reached in the box and came out with another plastic bag, which he handed to Cassy. She lifted it to see inside.

It was a small silver heart attached to a thin chain, a gift James had bought Cassidy for Christmas the winter before it all happened. She'd put it on the day he'd given it to her, and he'd never seen her without it again—not until she'd stumbled into his yard the week before.

Her fingers closed over the necklace, and she held it to her chest. "It got caught on the rocks when we were escaping."

"Is that what you had me looking for the other day?" James asked.

She nodded.

"Guess Vince found it," Cote said. "I'm sorry, but I need to keep them for now. After he's convicted, they'll be returned to you."

They handed the treasures back to Cote, who put them in the box and closed the lid.

"You have enough evidence to convict?"

"More than enough," Cote said. "We'll see what the DA's office does with it. Hopefully, they won't make a deal."

James didn't want to think about a deal. "Any idea...?" James's voice trailed off. He tried again. "I mean, we both knew him. What would prompt him to do something like this?"

Cote leaned back, eliciting a squeak from his chair. "He ever tell you about his mother?"

"Not much."

Cassidy leaned forward. "What about her?"

"I was on the force back when he was a kid. We always suspected abuse, but we could never confirm it. Vince never admitted to anything, and nobody witnessed her hurting him." Cote looked away, frowning. "Even as an adult, he would never talk about it, but she was a nightmare."

"So what? Lots of people have bad childhoods." He took Cassy's hand. "They don't turn out to be murderers. What does his mother have to do with him kidnapping my sister?"

"He had a sister. She wandered off one night and drowned when she was five."

"Did the mother—?"

"It was ruled an accident," Cote said. "Kid just wandered off and drowned. Vince was eight when it happened. Had to be traumatic for him. Add that to having an abusive mother..."

"His taking Hallie," Cassidy said, "it was a spur-of-the-moment decision. Aside from the ski mask, which he'd probably just rolled up and used as a skull cap before he saw her, he wasn't prepared. He hadn't planned it. And I think... he treated her like a sister. I think that's what he wanted—a sister."

Vince had spoken to James about his mother only once. They'd been at Teresa's, and Vince had had a couple of drinks. "He told me once his mother never wanted a boy. Didn't say anything about a sister, though."

"Far as I know," Cote said, "he never talked about her. It probably terrified him when you"—he nodded to Cassidy—"disappeared with Hallie, and then she died. It's possible that he was scared enough that he vowed never to do anything like that again."

"And then his mother died," James said. "And, for whatever reason, that pushed him over the edge."

"The idea tracks with what Ella told us," Cote said. "She said he kept calling her his little sister and promising that he was going to take her somewhere far away, and they were going to swim in the ocean and build sand castles. At his house, we discovered that he owns property in Honduras. The flight he bought would have taken them as far as Cancun. From there, we figured he would have driven over the border."

"And disappeared," Cassidy said. "Would they ever have been found?"

"I don't know." Cote shook his head. "Vince is smart. With his law enforcement background... He knew what he was doing."

"How could he be so smart and so... crazy?" James rubbed the back of his neck. "I don't understand how I could have missed it all these years."

"We all did, son."

Cassidy squeezed James's hand and spoke to the detective. "What happened with Addison? If Vince wanted a sister, how did she end up dead?"

"We don't know." Cote opened the shoebox again. "We know he had her because"—he lifted out another plastic bag for them to see—"we found a barrette that belonged to her. We think she made him mad and he killed her. We're hoping Ella will eventually give us more information about what happened when he held her. That should help us piece it together. The manner of death, though..." His glance bounced off James, landed on Cassidy. "It's possible she escaped and tried to climb down the same cliff. More likely, though, he dropped her down that cliff so the injuries would be consistent with Hallie's. He was trying to make it look like the same person."

How awful. Poor, sweet little girl. What must her last moments have been like?

They let the questions settle a moment, questions they'd never have answered. Then Cote glanced at his watch and pushed back in his chair. "Mayor's probably here. We ought to get out there."

James leaned away. "Out where, for what?"

"Oh." Cote ran his hand over his thinning hair. "I should've warned you. We're having a press conference. Want you two up there with us. You won't be expected to answer questions, but we want to make it official that Vince is our suspect and that Cassidy is off the hook."

Cassidy glanced at James, eyes wide. She looked terrified.

"You don't have to," Cote said, focusing on Cassidy. "But we'd sure like it if you'd stand up there with us. Mayor hopes it'll show there're no hard feelings and all that."

James's heart thumped, and he stood to face the older man. "No hard feelings? You accused her of kidnapping and murder and sent her on the run for a decade. I think she's entitled to hard feelings."

"We didn't force her to run. That was her choice." Cote turned his attention to Cassidy. "What do you think?"

James turned to her as well.

She looked from one to the other, then stood and slid her hand into James's. "They got the guy. That's all that matters."

"No, it's not," James said. "You matter. Your life matters."

She stood on her tiptoes and kissed his cheek. "Thank you for saying that. Right now, what matters more is that Ella is home with her father, the killer is in custody, and I'm free to be myself again."

She was free. That was what mattered. And if she could forgive, so could James.

# CHAPTER FORTY-ONE

assidy held James's hand as they stepped onto the front steps of City Hall. Beyond the microphones and reporters, a crowd of townspeople had gathered.

With her were Detective Cote and two men she recognized from recent news coverage as the mayor and the chief of police. They introduced themselves, but she forgot their names immediately, too focused on the other man nearby and the little girl in his arms.

Reid and Ella.

Somehow, though she'd been staying at Reid's folks' house for two nights, this was the first time she'd seen her old friend. She hadn't seen Ella since the girl had been taken from her arms Friday and loaded onto the helicopter.

As soon as the introductions were over, Reid pulled Cassidy into an embrace. "I can't thank you enough."

She backed away, tried to speak through the tears. She wanted to tell him he didn't owe her thanks. That she should have told the truth years before. That if she had, Vince Pollack might've been caught, Addison wouldn't have died, Ella wouldn't have been taken.

Or Vince might've killed her back then. Maybe nothing would

have changed. It seemed just as likely that it could all have been worse. She didn't know. She only knew she'd done the best she could.

Before she could figure out how to respond, little Ella leaned herself into Cassidy's arms and hugged her tight.

Cassidy couldn't help the tears that filled her eyes. Over the little girl's shoulder, she saw the crowd. Every eye on her. The noise had faded, though she hadn't realized it until just that moment. Cell phone cameras—and TV cameras—were aimed her way.

She buried her face in the little girl's hair. It was too much.

After James and Reid exchanged a hug, Ella went back into her father's arms, and Cassidy wondered if the child's feet had touched the ground since her father had gotten her back. If he'd ever let her out of his sight again.

The mayor stepped away from the mic, and Detective Cote approached and related the facts of the case. Cassidy hardly heard him as her gaze scanned the crowd. Some familiar people from high school smiled and waved as if they'd been friends back then. She hadn't had many friends, but it seemed, like James had said, everybody had grown up. Those old rivalries had passed away.

She recognized the old vice principal and the man who ran James's family's restaurant.

She saw Wilson Cage, who waved, looking uncomfortable. Eugene had followed them, stolen their food, and inadvertently, told the killer they were on the mountain. But he hadn't hurt them. He'd only done his best to do the right thing. She smiled at him, and his face lit up as if she'd given him a spectacular gift.

Lots of other faces were familiar, though the names were lost to her. They could be found again. She could move back here. She could try it. As James slipped his hand over hers, she realized the thought of staying in Coventry didn't bring anxiety. It brought peace.

When the prepared statements were over, reporters called out questions, most of which were directed to her. She'd been told she didn't have to speak, and she was thankful for that. Detective Cote spoke. Reid spoke, mostly thanking her and James.

Now, every question yelled was prefaced with her name.

*Cassidy, where've you been?*

*Cassidy, are you going to sue?*

*Cassidy, how does it feel to be exonerated?*

*Cassidy, are you angry?*

That last one felt so odd, so foreign.

It needed to be addressed.

All the questions needed to be addressed.

She dropped James's hand, tapped the mayor on the shoulder, and whispered, "I'd like to say something."

He nodded once and stepped out of the way.

She stepped to the podium, breathed a prayer for help, and spoke.

"I don't have much to say right now. I'm a bit overwhelmed by"—she gestured to the microphones—"but I wanted to say that I've had a lot of years to process this. I wouldn't wish what happened to me on anybody. But then, I wouldn't wish what happened to Hallie or Addison or Ella on anybody. Or what happened to their families. This was a terrible tragedy, and I was just one of the victims. At least I got to walk away."

She glanced at James to find his gaze on her. Filled with love.

"There's only one person to blame for what happened to all of us, and he's been arrested. He'll have to answer for his crimes. The rest of us"—she looked at the chief of police, the detective, the uniformed officers—"we all just did our best. We did what we could with what we knew. I'm not going to sue anybody." She smiled at the reporter who'd lobbed that question. "I'm not angry. I'm just..." She reached for James's hand and tugged him close. "I'm glad to be home."

# CHAPTER FORTY-TWO

"That was a lot of work to move into a temporary place."

Cassidy collapsed on the sofa beside James and surveyed her new apartment. New furniture, new... everything. Well, new to her, anyway. "I need a place to live."

James frowned, and she giggled. It was an argument they'd had since she'd gone home to Seattle a few months earlier, just a week after Ella had been found.

The summer tourists had packed up and left Coventry by the time Cassidy returned. It had taken a couple of months to find and train a replacement at her job—one of the girls who'd come through the program a few years earlier. Between that and selling everything she owned and saying good-bye to her friends, it was the week after Labor Day before she went back to New Hampshire.

James had found this apartment for her and signed a six-month lease on her behalf. She liked the place he'd chosen. It was right off Main Street in downtown Coventry, walking distance to the youth center where she'd start her new job on Monday, and just a mile or so from the church James had been attending. She'd only gone once, but she'd known the instant she walked through the door that it was just where God wanted her to worship.

"It's perfect."

His scowl wasn't so intimidating now that he'd shaved his beard and cut his hair. He looked like the clean-cut James from her past. "Perfect would be if you'd moved into my house, where you belong."

She slapped her hand on her chest and dropped her jaw in mock surprise. "I'm not that kind of girl!"

He barely cracked a smile. "You know what I mean." He pulled her left hand to his lips and kissed her palm, which raised goosebumps and had her second-guessing her choice. When he settled their joined hands on his lap, her engagement ring sparkled in the light. "We should've just gotten married and skipped all this." He gestured to the space.

She took in the one-bedroom apartment, the new-to-her furniture that James and his friends—soon to be her friends, she hoped— had collected for her. They'd not only furnished the space, but they'd decorated it, filled it with dishes, toaster, coffee maker, microwave, and the other things she'd need to live. They'd even stocked the cabinets. To make her feel welcome. To make her feel like she truly was coming home.

"You know it's not that I have doubts about us."

"So you say." But he didn't seem convinced.

She sat up to face him. "I need to establish my own life here. This town knows me as the foster kid who was accused of murder. The kid whose mother killed her sister. The woman who helped find Ella. I need to become... you know, just Cassidy. I need to make Coventry my home again."

"We could do that together."

"And we will. But..." She didn't know how to make him understand.

When she didn't finish her sentence, James tugged her back to his side. "I don't understand, but I don't have to understand what you need in order to support it. And I do. I support this. I support you. And I really support the fact that we've set a wedding date."

"February twenty-second." She shook her head. "It'll probably be snowing."

"A September wedding would have been nice," he said.

"But I don't want to wait a year."

The noise from low in his chest sounded like a growl, and she stifled her amusement. He'd wanted them to get married the second she'd landed in Manchester the day before. They'd negotiated and settled on the date in late winter. Hopefully, by then, she'd have some friends who could act as bridesmaids, maybe a few people to sit on her side of the church.

Her mother would be there, though. The thought of it still brought tears to Cassidy's eyes. She'd visited the prison to see Mom the day after Ella had been found, only to discover her mother had been paroled the previous summer. Cassidy got her contact information and met her at a coffee shop in Manchester, where Mom had been working since her release. She was living in a halfway house, learning how to take care of herself. She was clean and sober and attending church. When Cassidy had seen her, she'd hardly recognized the woman. Gone were the gray pallor, the dark smudges under her eyes, the angry sneer. The woman who greeted her looked healthy. With tears in her eyes, she'd begged Cassidy for her forgiveness, and Cassidy had given it. Because she'd been forgiven much, she'd never hold back forgiveness from another.

She and Mom had been forging a relationship across the miles. Now that Cassidy was back in New Hampshire, they could make that relationship even stronger.

It was weird, the idea of having a family again. A mother who loved her—probably for the first time—and soon, a husband.

Joining herself to James, being a part of his family, still felt foreign, like a language she struggled to translate. The idea that she would be part of a real family, that there could be children, beautiful little people who called her *Mom*...

She wasn't ready yet. But she would be. God willing, by February twenty-second, she'd be James's, and he'd be hers.

"Thank you for being patient with me."

His scowl faded, replaced by a tender smile. "Somehow, I survived ten long years without you. As long as you're back in

Coventry, I suppose six more months won't kill me. And then we'll be together forever."

Forever. She loved the sound of that.

## The End

I hope you enjoyed James and Cassidy's story. If you did, I know you'll love Tabby and Fitz's tale. Turn the page for more about book 2 in the Coventry Saga, Tides of Duplicity.

**A jewelry heist, a kidnapping, and a choice. When Fitz's sister disappears, he'll do anything to get her back, even if it means betraying the woman he's come to love.**

Private investigator Fitz McCaffrey went to Belize on a case, bringing his teenage sister Shelby along with him. They have no good reason to leave the resort and hurry back to the harsh New England winter. They lost their parents, he lost his job as a cop, and they both need time to heal. Besides, when Fitz meets and spends time with the beautiful and charming Tabitha Eaton, he falls hard.

But minutes after Tabby's flight leaves, Fitz is summoned by a mobster who believes Tabby broke into the hotel safe the night before and made off with half a million dollars' worth of jewels—and he has the video evidence to prove it. As Shelby's guardian, Fitz has to focus on caring for his sister, whether Tabby is innocent or guilty. He refuses to help the man—until he learns the mobster has taken his sister.

The clock is ticking as Fitz scrambles to recover the jewels. If he succeeds, it'll cost the woman he's come to care for. If he fails, it'll cost his sister's life.

Mystery, suspense, and a sprinkling of romance to keep it fun. Buy **TIDES OF DUPLICITY** today.

# ALSO BY ROBIN PATCHEN

The Coventry Saga

Glimmer in the Darkness

Tides of Duplicity

Betrayal of Genius

Traces of Virtue

The Nutfield Saga

Convenient Lies

Twisted Lies

Generous Lies

Innocent Lies

Beauty in Flight

Beauty in Hiding

Beauty in Battle

Legacy Rejected

Legacy Restored

Legacy Reclaimed

Legacy Redeemed

Amanda Series

Chasing Amanda

Finding Amanda

Standalone Novellas

A Package Deal

One Christmas Eve

Faith House

# ABOUT THE AUTHOR

Robin Patchen is a *USA Today* bestselling and award-winning author of Christian romantic suspense. She grew up in a small town in New Hampshire, the setting of her Nutfield Saga books, and then headed to Boston to earn a journalism degree. After college, working in marketing and public relations, she discovered how much she loathed the nine-to-five ball and chain. After relocating to the Southwest, she started writing her first novel while she homeschooled her three children. The novel was dreadful, but her passion for storytelling didn't wane. Thankfully, as her children grew, so did her writing ability. Now that her kids are adults, she has more time to play with the lives of fictional heroes and heroines, wreaking havoc and working magic to give her characters happy endings. When she's not writing, she's editing or reading, proving that most of her life revolves around the twenty-six letters of the alphabet. Visit robinpatchen.com/subscribe to receive a free book and stay informed about Robin's latest projects.

Made in the USA
Coppell, TX
03 January 2023